RAVES FOR HUNGRY EYES!

"... on ... *Eyes* ... most ... in contemporary writing. This novel's clear, unsparing gaze puts it leagues ahead of almost anything these days passing as horror or suspense fiction."

—Peter Straub, author of *The Hellfire Club*

"Absolutely fabulous! A taut, arresting, offbeat thriller, rich in psychological insight. Hoffman's narrative is riveting and dynamic; he compels you to keep turning the pages, and pulls off the impossible feat of actually garnering sympathy for a serial killer."

—William F. Nolan, author of *Night Shapes*

"A masterful portrait in psychopathology. [The killer] inspires pathos as well as terror, for Hoffman's characterization transcends the simpleminded killing-machines who populate the genre."

—*Publishers Weekly*

"*Hungry Eyes* is a fast-reading, complex, fascinating debut. Barry Hoffman's characters come to life on the page and resonate long after the story is done."

—Poppy Z. Brite, author of *Lost Souls*

"A new voice—and a telling one—in the horror genre."

—Richard Matheson, author of *I Am Legend*

"A fast-paced, thrilling reading experience, played out to a logical and exciting conclusion."

—Rick Hautala, author of *Impulse*

MORE PRAISE FOR BARRY HOFFMAN!

"Barry Hoffman's debut novel is a solid, tense thriller featuring one of the most unusual and vividly drawn serial killers in years. I was in Hoffman's grip from the end of the prologue to the last page, and the characters stayed with me even after I put the book down. Take the phone off the hook and curl up by the fire with *Hungry Eyes*. If you're like me you'll be left wanting more from this talented new writer."

—Ray Garton, author of *Live Girls*

"A well-written, thoughtful, and unsettling novel."

—*Booklist*

"Hoffman has succeeded in crafting a novel populated by believable human beings. Even minor characters are interesting and realistic, unique in their occupations, behavior, mannerisms and speech. While treating a serial killer as a character study is a difficult task and one fraught with potential dangers, Hoffman pulls it off. An impressive and assured debut by a talented writer."

—*Hell Notes*

Hoffman takes us that one uneasy and often perilous step into the mind of the mentally disturbed. And, like the true master he is, he's made that mind worryingly understandable. A wonderful book!"

—*Interzone*

"An admirable first novel that raises legitimate questions regarding the cycle of abuse, and where the next generation of 'victims' is headed."

—Nancy A. Collins, author of *Sunglasses After Dark*

"A powerful piece of work. Barry Hoffman brings you just as close to a serial killer as you'd ever dare to be. *Hungry Eyes* puts a new face on terror."

—Robert Bloch, author of *Psycho*

HUNGRY EYES

BARRY HOFFMAN

LEISURE BOOKS NEW YORK CITY

As always, for my children—
Dara, David, and Cheryl

A LEISURE BOOK®

November 1998

Published by

Dorchester Publishing Co., Inc.
276 Fifth Avenue
New York, NY 10001

ISBN 0-8439-4449-8

HUNGRY
EYES

Introduction

Throwing Down
The Gauntlet

William F. Nolan

First, I want to tell you about this novel. Then I'll tell
you about the man who wrote it. They are, of course,
inseparable; we *are* what we write.

Hungry Eyes is a taut, arresting, offbeat thriller rich
in psychological insight. The theme is mind control and
the manipulation of what is human in us, as opposed to
what is animal. While partaking of mystery, it is *not* a
whodunit; by the second chapter we know that the killer
is a mentally disturbed young woman. The author is not
out to trick us, and there are no cheap shots in this
artfully-textured book.

Style, character and plot are marked by careful discipline. Hoffman maintains a level of strict control
throughout, resisting any temptation to join the "splat-
terpunk" school, to gross out his readers, to substitute

gore for good taste. All this is quite surprising, given the author's strong anti-censorship background (which I'll be getting into later). I had expected explicit violence and raw shock. Not so. Admittedly, there *is* one explicitly violent scene (having to do with hungry eyes), but it is integral to the plot and wholly in keeping with the carefully developed personality of the killer. Barry Hoffman also pulls off the impossible feat of actually garnering sympathy for a serial killer whose victims are themselves victimizers. Hoffman deserves much credit for his sensitive approach to potentially sensationalistic material. It would have been easy to go for the jugular, and I kept waiting for him to cross the line. He never did.

Which is not to say that his novel is at all tepid. On the contrary, Hoffman's narrative is riveting and dynamic; he *compels* you to keep turning his pages.

Confession: I set out to read *Hungry Eyes* as a matter of duty (because Barry had published some of my work and because he *asked* me to introduce his book). Almost instantly, however, I found myself caught up in his vivid characters and emotionally involving storyline. Once you begin, I guarantee you'll read to the finish.

Who, then, is Barry Hoffman? How did he reach the point of writing *Hungry Eyes*? What elements of his life and personality did he bring to this, his first published novel?

Far too many Introductions examine the creation and not the creator. The reader ends up lacking a personal insight into the unique human being who shaped the words. I determined that this would not be the case with *Hungry Eyes*.

In preparing for this assignment, I hit Barry with a ton of questions and he patiently responded to each of them, allowing me to access his background, his philosophy, and his working life. I'm going to share this newfound knowledge with you.

Barry Hoffman was born on January 30, 1947, in New York City. His mother was a homemaker; his father worked in creative services for Westinghouse Broadcasting. Barry spent his early childhood (until he was 12) in Forest Hills, establishing a very close relationship with his father, an "avid tennis player." The elder Hoffman taught his son to handle a tennis racquet and also took him to numerous baseball games. (Barry later became a devoted basketball fan and still passionately follows the fortunes of the New York Knicks.)

"From my father," says Hoffman, "I got my philosophy of doing a thing right if you're going to do it at all, of giving everything the best that's in you to give. I remain grateful to him for this."

Barry's parents were, as he puts it, "nominally Jewish." His younger sister, Steffi, died of leukemia at the age of nine—a major family tragedy. "Her death soured my father on religion," says Hoffman. "I now classify myself as an atheist. I have no problem with people who are religious so long as they don't try to convert me. My ex-wife was Catholic, and we battled often." (Hoffman married in 1968, had three children, and was divorced in 1980.)

Barry recalls an early childhood fear of horror movies. One in particular, *Village of the Damned*, was so frightening that he's never been able to watch it again. "What I remember most," he says, "are the glowing eyes of the children. [Hungry eyes?] Scared the absolute hell out of me!"

His brother, Andy, was born nine years after Barry and "I was elected to be his baby-sitter. We're very close now, as adults, but in those early days Andy was a real pain. To get him out of my hair, when I had to baby-sit him, I'd cook pizza. He couldn't stand it, and my cooking would drive him back to his room. To this day, I still love pizza."

After Steffi Hoffman's death the family moved to a

house in Westbury, Long Island. Barry was never really happy there. "I missed my friends and found it hard to adjust. Went to Westbury High, played some basketball, and graduated in '64."

"Played some basketball" is an understatement. Barry was (and remains) obsessed with this sport, eventually coaching first a boys' team, and then a girls' team, for a total of 12 years. The girls' team, he reports, "won two championships."

Writing came along fairly late in his life. "For many years I thought I'd end up in a courtroom. When I was in the 8th grade we staged a mock trial, with me playing a lawyer. From that day on, that's what I wanted to be."

He was a pre-law major at the University of Wisconsin, and later attended law school in the evenings, "but my logical arguments didn't mesh with what my law professors wanted, so I gave it up. Being a lawyer, I found, had little to do with trial work."

It was while he was attending the university that Barry got "heavily into reading." He discovered Ray Bradbury and Stephen King, among others, and developed a lifelong taste for offbeat fiction. "My interests centered around horror and suspense. I never cared much for science fiction or outright fantasy."

After graduation Barry faced the prospect of serving in Vietnam. "I was solidly against the war," he says, "and so I decided to become a teacher in order to avoid going to Vietnam. I joined the Teacher Corps, a federally funded program designed to prepare you to teach in the inner city. At Temple University I received my Masters certificate in 1970, and I began teaching right away."

Four years later, in 1974, Barry became a 6th grade teacher at an inner-city Philadelphia public school, where he got into what he terms "media work."

Hoffman relates: "When I first came to the school, I was the Media Specialist. My students and I produced a schoolwide daily news program which was videotaped. And I also produced a videotaped investigative report series with my students. These shows were aired on a local station. I taught myself how to videotape, edit, and put a script together. Then the funds dried up and I returned to the classroom.''

While teaching at the school in the 1980s, Hoffman wrote and produced several plays. ''They dealt with real-life issues, which were important to these young people. One play, for example, examined the reasons why kids run away from home. All were musicals. For each, I had a composer create original music while my students provided the lyrics. It was a big job. I wrote, directed, promoted, and raised the money to pay for everything. Put in literally hundreds of after-class hours. My play on runaways ran afoul of our local PTA (the Home and School Association). They censored the lyrics in two of the songs, and had some other objections. The final result: I didn't get to write any more plays, although my last was an award winner. That was my first brush with censorship.''

Hoffman experienced more censorship problems with regard to his student reading program. One of the parents lodged a complaint about a story he'd assigned. ''It was approved reading, but that didn't seem to matter. I was directed to stop my program, temporarily—which was when I became aware of how special interest groups operate. In this case, a single parent among dozens was able to override the wishes of the majority. All this led to my decision to publish an anti-censorship magazine.''

Barry asked his father to suggest a title, and the elder Hoffman came up with *Gauntlet*—as in ''throwing down the gauntlet.'' ''Which was perfect,'' says Barry, ''because that's exactly what the magazine does, it throws down the gauntlet. It challenges the status quo.''

To finance his first issue (released in March of 1990), Hoffman invested five thousand dollars in savings.

"That was all I had at the time," he declares. "Luckily, it was enough to launch *Gauntlet*. I can honestly say that I don't think that *Gauntlet* would exist were it not for Ray Bradbury. His giving me permission to reprint the Afterword to *Fahrenheit 451* was the deciding factor. Being able to say that Bradbury was appearing in *Gauntlet* sold a number of other authors on the concept." Hoffman has done 12 issues so far, staying with his teaching job and handling the magazine in his off hours." *Gauntlet* was never meant to make money, and doesn't, but I've always managed to pay my bills. At first, I brought it out annually, but with the fourth issue I began publishing it twice a year. Time consuming, sure, but worth the effort. With *Gauntlet* I'm able to tackle a wide variety of topics related to censorship."

These topics (themed to one per issue) have included media manipulation, prostitution, sexual harassment, cultism, pornography, racism, and political correctness. Hoffman pulls no punches in his tough and unrelenting stand against any form of censorship, and his controversial publication has aroused heated criticism as well as enthusiastic support among a multitude of readers.

"When *Gauntlet* tackled Scientology my friends thought I was crazy, and that I'd be sued. But that didn't happen. We had some trouble in Canada, but upon appeal two early issues got in, and since then all the others have crossed the border without a hitch. I now have a number of investigative journalists who write for us, and our reputation has spread with each issue."

Hoffman has demonstrated that anti-censorship begins at home. "I've always shared the magazine with my children. Dara is now 22, just married. David, 19, is an acting major at Boston University. Cheryl, 16, has a strong interest in engineering. They're all proud of *Gauntlet*."

Hoffman completed his first novel in the late 1980s. "It was a supernatural thriller," he says, "and in writing it I learned a lot about what *not* to do. The sentences ran on for paragraphs, and my paragraphs for pages! It was poorly written, to say the least.''

After this aborted venture, Hoffman turned to the short form, placing several stories and articles with *Castle Rock*, the Stephen King newsletter, and with *Cemetery Dance*.

''My first stories were pure horror with lots of grue and gore,'' he recalls. ''Soon, though, I moved into psychological horror, dealing with rape, suicide, arson, and serial crimes. And out of all these shorter works I found the confidence to begin another novel.''

This was *Hungry Eyes*. He finished writing it in November of 1993; he's done two more novels since, and is now into a fifth.

In *Hungry Eyes* the two main characters are women, rendered with depth and reality. Hoffman points out that ''females have always played a more pivotal role in my novels than males. Most of my protagonists and antagonists are women. This I attribute to the fact that I teach 5th and 6th grades where the personalities of the girls have evolved far more than the boys. My current novel, for example, is about a female police detective stalked by her past.''

Hoffman recently expanded his creative energies to include publishing his own line of ''rediscovered classics'' in limited, signed, special editions. The idea is to publish books that totally please the author. Special editions of their work the way *they* want it to appear. So far, starting with Robert Bloch's *Psycho*, the line has been successful. These books have helped pay the bills on *Gauntlet*.'' Hoffman admits that he is ''stretched out pretty thin, what with the classics line and turning out two issues of *Gauntlet* each year, plus parenting my three kids, plus writing my novels and stories, plus holding down my full-time teaching job, but I somehow manage to handle the lot. Hard work has its own reward.''

As to his future, after 26 years of teaching, he's looking forward to stepping away from the blackboard in four more years (''the earliest I can retire and get my pension''). Then he plans to spend the extra time on his fiction, with the goal of turning out two books per year.

''And I'll keep on publishing my line of classics,'' he declares. ''It's my way of paying homage to those masters who have given me so much joy and who helped me understand, through their works, what quality writing is all about.''

Who *are* his favorites, the major talents who influenced him and helped shape Barry into the writer he is today?

''First and foremost, Stephen King and Ray Bradbury,'' says Hoffman. ''Then, in no particular order, Richard Matheson, Robert Bloch, Charles Beaumont, George Orwell, Dick Francis, Dean Koontz, F. Paul Wilson, Robert R. McCammon, David Morrell, Donald Westlake, Andrew Vachss, Ross Thomas, and Stuart Woods. Each of them taught me important things about the creative process. It's a real tragedy that Beaumont died so young, in his 30s, when he had so many more tales to write.''

Surely, Barry Hoffman has ''many more tales to write.'' I, for one, look forward with great anticipation to his next published novel.

For now, though, we are very fortunate to have *Hungry Eyes*, a book to remember by a writer to remember.

Ladies and gentlemen . . . here's Hoffman!

—W. F. N.
West Hills, California

Prologue

"Why don't you climb back into Mama's womb where you belong," Bobby said, with a sneer.

Renee didn't know what her fourteen-year-old brother was talking about, but from his tone she knew it was a putdown, and probably something nasty.

"Mom!" Renee yelled across the room, "Bobby's calling me names *again*."

Her mother laughed. "Don't be fussing so, Renee. Bobby's just funnin'. They're teaching him about how you make babies in school, and he's just showing off."

"But, Mom . . ." eight-year-old Renee whined.

"That's enough, child," she said with an edge to her voice. "It's family time. You know the rules. No fussing during family time." She turned to Bobby, who tried to hide the smirk on his face. "Leave your sister be, now."

"Yes, m'am," Bobby said. As soon as his mother turned back to her book, he gave Renee the finger.

Renee wondered why *she* always got scolded when Bobby teased her. Her mother seldom raised her voice to Bobby, especially when Renee was his target. It gnawed at her young mind, but she knew better than to voice her concern during family time.

Renee hated family time. Every night, just after dinner, she had to wait at least an interminable fifteen minutes before she'd be allowed to go to her room.

Family time was a ritual her mother insisted upon; a time for the Barrows family to bond. In reality, each inhabited his or her own space in the cramped living room of the South Philadelphia rowhouse, each doing their own thing, ignoring the others.

Renee watched her mother settle into a frayed, oversized easy chair and open one of her romance novels. She was settled in for the evening unless she had to pee; *really* had to pee. For Loretta Barrows was fat; not chubby or portly or pleasantly plump. Plain old fat. Renee had once heard a neighbor whispering something about 300 pounds. All Renee knew was her mother only sat when she didn't plan on getting up for a long time. The effort it took to rise was just too great. Nevertheless, her mother sat an awful lot.

Renee noticed that everything her mother did was in slow motion. If she was standing and the phone rang, she sauntered over without any sense of urgency. If it was someone who knew her, they'd let it ring a dozen times, knowing Loretta might be seated and need the extra time. If it rang just three or four times, it was probably one of those nuisance solicitation calls and Loretta had no use for those anyway.

Her mother even read slowly, Renee thought to herself. She'd watched the clock once, and it took her mother a good ten minutes before she turned the page. She had been reading the same book she now opened for over a month and hadn't reached its midpoint.

Renee's stepfather was cleaning his gun. This too he'd gotten into the habit of doing every night since he purchased it a few months before. He drove a cab and had been robbed on three occasions. He vowed it wouldn't happen again. He kept his gun wrapped in the *Daily News* on the seat beside him in the cab. And each night he cleaned it. He was short and plump, though nowhere near the size of her mother. Standing, he came up to Loretta's "love pillows" as he called them. He was as fidgety as Loretta was sedate, never quite finding a comfortable spot in the twin of Loretta's chair that all but swallowed him up.

Her half-brother, Bobby, sat silently now, at a desk in the far corner of the room working on his homework. He wasn't terribly bright, Renee knew, and it took him hours to do homework she'd already completed. Granted he was six years older than she, and the homework was more demanding, but he worked at a pace akin to their mother, and came home with report cards with C as the highest grade.

Renee, for her part, sat on the floor trying to occupy herself until she'd be allowed to go to her room. Sometimes she would read a book she got at the school library or work on a Word Search puzzle purchased at the corner store. Tonight she bounced a hollowed-out pink rubber ball against the wall. Like a turkey awaiting slaughter, she knew, pretty soon the ball would be sliced in half to be used in the daily halfball games she was so fond of.

Renee was all tomboy and proud that kids two and three years older than her not only allowed her to play, but eagerly sought her for their team. She was wiry, all skin and bones. Her friends teased her that after her mother got done eating, all she got were table scraps. Actually, though she didn't admit it to them, it wasn't too far from the truth.

She wore faded jeans with holes in the knees, and an Eagles t-shirt, a hand-me-down that no longer fit her half-brother. One might have mistaken her for a boy from afar if it were not for her flowing brown hair that wended its way down to her backside. She would tie it in a ponytail when she played with the boys, to keep it out of her face. At night, after her bath, her mother brushed out all the snarls, almost as if she were a doll. Her mother would sometimes talk to herself, while brushing, as if Renee weren't there. Still, for Renee it was about the only time, other than when she'd misbehaved or was told to do her chores, that her mother acknowledged her existence.

Now Renee tossed her ball against the wall. Bounce, hit the wall, bounce back and catch. Bounce, hit the wall, bounce . . .

Without warning the front door imploded.

"Police! Everyone down on the floor! Now!" a voice commanded, as three uniformed men with rifles burst through the doorway.

The scene unfolded before Renee in slow motion. The first man in stared at her stepfather seated with a gun in his hand. Without hesitation the policeman lifted his weapon and fired.

Once. Twice. Three times.

Renee watched as her stepfather looked down at the red spot spreading on his white t-shirt, his mouth wide open in surprise. A second bullet hit him in the forehead. He didn't seem surprised anymore, as the force knocked him and the chair over backward.

Three more men entered, and the one who had fired his gun demanded Renee, her mother and half-brother get on the floor. Loretta tried to rise, but plopped back in her chair. It took two of the men, each grabbing one of her arms, to lift her out. Face down on the floor, one of the men attempted to handcuff her arms behind her back.

"Lieutenant, they won't fit," one of the men said in exasperation.

The man named lieutenant glanced around the room quickly, saw the blinds and yanked the cord until it came free. He threw it to the man with the handcuffs.

"Here, use your imagination," he said, shaking his head in annoyance.

Renee lay on the floor as the lieutenant's eyes fell on her. Her hand touched the ball she'd thrown against the wall. It was bleeding. It's been shot, Renee thought to herself, and she held it protectively.

Three hours later Anne Spinetti, their neighbor, held Renee by the hand as an ambulance took Loretta Barrows to the hospital. Renee was all but ignored, as an angry mob of over twenty neighbors confronted the man called Lieutenant, who tried in vain to calm them. Renee couldn't see much with all the adults around, but could clearly follow their conversation.

"What the fuck are you doing, storming into decent peoples' homes?" yelled Mr. Giordano, who owned the corner store at the end of the block.

"We had reliable information we'd find a substantial amount of drugs . . . ," he tried to explain.

"Find any drugs?" Renee recognized the voice as Anne's husband, Al.

"I can't comment on that, right now."

"Bullshit," another voice, which Renee couldn't identify, boomed. "The Barrows ain't got no drugs. You fucked up. Admit it."

"We're continuing our investigation . . . ," he tried again, but was shouted down.

"Was killing Steven Barrows part of your investigation?" Renee recognized the voice as that of Joseph Pagano.

"He had a gun." Now the lieutenant was angry. "Innocent people don't point guns at the police."

"He was cleaning his gun," Renee said not much above a whisper, hardly aware she was speaking. "He does it every night."

This only seemed to fuel the crowd's anger.

The policeman was clearly nonplussed. His ace in the

hole, it seemed, was Steven Barrows pointing a gun at his officers. With the gun no more dangerous than a water pistol, there would be no reasoning with the crowd. The officer stepped back toward the house, seeking comfort in the men on either side, both with rifles pointed in the air.

"You're going to have to disperse . . ."

"Or what?" a voice interrupted. "You'll shoot us, too?"

"You'll have to disperse," he said, his voice shaky and unsure, "or we're going to have to start making arrests."

At that moment several police cars screeched to a halt at the end of the block, their sirens wailing, and the crowd grew silent.

More in control with reinforcements on hand, the Lieutenant spoke with a bit more compassion. "Please folks, let us sort this out. We'll have a statement tomorrow. I promise."

"What about Loretta Barrows? Did you shoot her, too?" someone yelled.

The policeman shook his head no. "Mrs. Barrows was in shock and was taken to the hospital as a precaution."

Their anger finally spent, and with more police cars filling the street, the crowd sullenly began to disperse.

Anne Spinetti bent down to Renee. "We've called your Gramma. She's on her way over. Come on inside and I'll fix you and your brother some hot chocolate."

Renee went with the Spinettis, the rubber ball still clutched in her hand, sticky with the drying blood of her stepfather.

Chapter One

Lamar Briggs was waiting when the driver left Deidre off in front of the townhouse on Tryon Street. He was chewing on a Milky Way candy bar, milking it, so to speak, as if it would be his last.

"You've come up in the world, Ms. Caffrey," he said, not hiding his antagonism.

"And you must be on a diet," she retorted, looking at his ample gut. "You used to polish off those candy bars in two bites."

That Deidre and Briggs had never hit it off was no surprise. When she had been a reporter she'd taken the police to task often, and had once almost cost Briggs his job. Five years before, two cops had chased what they thought was a burglar six blocks, finally cornering him and beating him to a pulp. The black youth turned out to be a track star at Ben Franklin High; an honor student with a scholarship all lined up, no less. A cop's worst nightmare. They'd planted a vial of crack and a throwaway .38 on him before calling for an ambulance.

One of the cops, Calvin Barfield, had been Briggs'

childhood friend, and the detective did all in his power to run interference so his friend wouldn't take a fall. He'd fed the media misinformation, buttressed with just enough truth to send them scurrying in circles, looking for drug dealers who might have supplied the youth.

Deidre hadn't bit. She'd honed in on the boy and his family, finally getting an exclusive interview with the youth and his doctor. TRACK STAR WILL NEVER RUN AGAIN, the page one headline in the *Daily News* bannered the next day. "Honor student had kicked the habit, and was right on track," was the lead of the story about an inner-city family that had clawed its way out of the gutter.

Jeremy Townes' father had been a crack addict who'd hooked his son. Both had been literally saved by the track coach at Ben Franklin, who had seen a rare talent within the boy. With his intervention, both father and son had been clean for two years.

The day after the story ran, Deidre received two calls: one from the burglar who told her where he'd fenced the jewelry; another from a witness who'd seen the cops pummel the kid and plant the gun and drugs.

Both cops were summarily suspended. Tried and convicted, both did time in prison. Briggs' integrity had been called into question. There were innuendos that Barfield had confided in him, and that Briggs had purposely led everyone astray.

While Deidre never crucified Briggs in print, she knew he blamed her. She had made a powerful enemy. In the end, though, he'd rebounded. He had, after all, come to the aid of a fellow officer, and while the brass pilloried him in public they backed him in private. After two years of keeping a low profile, he was back, and heading up the Vigilante investigation.

Their paths hadn't crossed since, but she now saw the simmering hostility in his eyes. Taking a big bite out of the candy bar, he smiled. "You in bed with the Mayor, girl, but you been to bed with him yet?"

"Look, Detective . . ."

"Briggs to my friends . . . my friends in high places."

"We both have a job to do, detective," she said ignoring him, "and you will cooperate with me."

"Or what? You'll get my ass kicked off the case?"

"I'll recommend that Chievous or McCauley head the Task Force the Mayor is going to announce tomorrow. You can work under them."

He mulled her threat over for a moment.

"You got balls, lady. I still have no use for you, don't get me wrong. But if it takes cooperation to head the Task Force, you've got it."

"I knew we'd come to an understanding," she said, without a smile. "Now will you fill me in before I have to meet the press?"

Briggs finished off his candy bar and ushered Deidre into a small but expensively decorated living room. Briggs seemed to fill the room. A six-foot-four former linebacker at Temple University, he towered over her by a good nine inches. He was a good deal heavier than the last time she'd seen him five years ago. He seemed to have given up the battle of the bulge.

He was a dark-skinned black. She could imagine him becoming one with the dark on a moonless night. When she'd first seen him standing on the stoop, she'd thought he was balding. But up close she noted he'd shaved his head. It made him look even more formidable, if that was possible. She guessed his new "do" was intentional.

"Are you sure it's the Vigilante?" she asked.

"No doubt about it." He took out a pad and read from it. "Walter Grimes, 35 years old. Owned a print shop on Chestnut Street. Copped a plea to one count of rape four years ago. Served seven months." He closed the pad.

"The killer left two polaroids. Two girls, one definitely a minor. Raped, beaten, either unconscious or dead, left in an alley. Our Mr. Grimes clearly hadn't been rehabilitated."

"The killer had to have been stalking him for a while," Deidre said.

"Just like the others. Freaks who slid through the system, either freed on a technicality or given a ridiculously light sentence. If form holds, the photos are recent; just a few weeks separating each attack. Grimes was probably on the prowl again when he was taken out."

"Any signs of forced entry?"

"No, and that's a puzzle. *All* the Vigilante's victims seemed to have let him in willingly."

"Any connection with the other four?"

"Look, lady . . ."

"Call me Dee, seeing as we'll be working together. And, as one of your friends in high places," she said with sarcasm, "do I call you Briggs, or do you want me to be formal?"

"Briggs will do," he said with the barest trace of a smile. "We'll have to check out any connection," he went on as if he hadn't been interrupted, "but if form holds, no connection."

"Tell me how he was killed."

"Just like the others. Sprawled naked on his bed, arms and legs tied to bedposts. For now the ME figures, like the others, his mouth was covered with duct tape so he wouldn't scream. He was blinded with acid. The killer pinched his nose, and he asphyxiated."

"Any struggle?"

"No. He was very cooperative."

"Why would they all let the killer in, and willingly allow themselves to be immobilized?"

"You're thinking a rogue cop, right?" He shook his head in disgust. "Still the reporter, huh."

"Cop. Parole officer. Or someone masquerading as

one," Deidre said, ignoring his attempt to goad her, "to get a foot in the door. With a gun pointed at them, there'd be no struggle."

"It's a theory," Briggs said noncommittally.

"It's got to be someone with a police background," Dee continued pressing the issue. "Aside from getting in without the use of force, the killer had to be trained in surveillance. He followed his victims around for weeks or longer."

"Or a Vietnam vet, Persian Gulf vet, security officer . . ."

"Don't want it to be a cop gone bad, do you?" she said.

"To be honest, no. But more importantly, I've got to keep an open mind. What you say is all true. Our killer probably had training in surveillance, and very possibly used a uniform or badge to gain entry. But there are a lot of people besides cops trained in surveillance. Go to Macy's and try to pick out who's in security. They get damned good at becoming part of the woodwork. Hell, it could have been a reporter; someone trained to ferret out information on these freaks, with the experience to trail them without being spotted. Maybe even a former reporter working for the Mayor."

"Oh, am I a suspect?" Deidre asked, not certain if he was being serious or yanking her chain. Just how far would Briggs go, she wondered, to satisfy his hostility toward her?

He shook his head no. "My point is, with what we've got we shouldn't narrow our search to just cops. That doesn't mean I'll eliminate the possibility, either."

"I stand corrected," she said, still not willing to offer an apology. "Any way to target his next victim?"

"No. The first victim had just gotten out of prison; raped an eleven-year-old within two days of his release, though we didn't know that at the time. Number two was acquitted when the girl he attacked cracked under cross-examination. Reasonable doubt bullshit. That was three years before he was killed. The third went after old ladies. Plea bargained and served a year-and-a-half. He'd been free for five years. And number four was *never* charged. According to his wife, molested his own daughter and she kicked him out. Went to live with two other relatives and each of them gave him the boot. He picked up his daughter after school one day, raped her and left her comatose.''

"Still is, isn't she?" Deidre interrupted.

"Yeah, no telling when or *if* she'll awake. At the time, though, all we could do was question the bastard. The family wouldn't press charges. If it weren't for the way he died, we'd have concentrated on the family. If the Vigilante hadn't gotten to him first, I'd bet my pension they would have taken care of him, if you get my meaning.''

Deidre shook her head, understanding completely. "No patterns, then?"

"Our killer's too smart. He's methodical in who he picks, so we can't get a bead on him.'' He paused. "Now I've got a question for you. Why is the Mayor's Media Liaison so interested?''

"The Vigilante's becoming a folk hero; a darling of the media.''

Briggs smiled at that, but Deidre ignored the gibe.

"The Mayor fears a wave of vigilantism that could easily get out of hand. This bastard's going after scum, but there's all kinds of scum. Next thing, some citizen decides to blow away some crack dealer. Maybe he misses his target and kills a child. I've got to convince the media the Vigilante is as bad as those he kills.''

"I don't envy you your job," Briggs said with a sly grin. "The media's got a bug up their ass that this guy is a hero, and it's near impossible to change their minds, if you get my drift. The Vigilante's becoming bigger than life. He sells papers, leads the evening news, and is the hot topic on talk shows. You got your job cut out for you. But having been one of them, I'm sure you'll figure a way to handle them.'' He laughed a deep rich baritone that resonated in the tiny living room.

At that moment two officers came down the narrow winding stairway carrying a body bag.

''Any chance I can see where he was killed?'' Deidre asked.

''Nothing much to see.'' Briggs looked uncomfortable.

''Then no reason not to let me see it. Look, Briggs, I work for the Mayor now, not a newspaper. I'm not going to be anyone's anonymous source.''

He seemed to consider what she'd said, and nodded.

''All right. C'mon.''

He trudged up the stairs, and narrow as they were Deidre feared he might get stuck. At the bedroom she looked briefly at the bed, noting the ropes that had held Walter Grimes defenseless, then swung her gaze to a mirror. Scrawled in lipstick were the words NO MORE HUNGRY EYES.

Deidre felt lightheaded and her knees turned to jelly as she fainted.

Chapter Two

She paced the room like a caged animal. Naked, she was oblivious to the sweat streaming from her body from the exercise routine of pushups, situps and aerobics.

The room itself resembled an oversized jail cell; spartan to the extreme. No bed or mattress; only a pea green blanket she'd purchased from an Army Navy store spread under the room's only window indicated this was where she slept. Unbreakable mirrors covered three walls and the ceiling, watching her every move. She instinctively touched the three-inch scar on her left breast, now covered by a tattoo, recalling the glass mirrors she'd had to replace. In one of her rages against the eyes peering at her, she had broken one; shards, like razors, piercing her body. A dozen stitches, and a hard-earned lesson.

To the left of the one bare wall was a wide-screen TV she kept on day and night, muting the sound only when she played her music.

She'd felt exhausted after her work of the night before, and had called in sick. Though she knew otherwise, she'd hoped Walt Grimes' death might end the attacks, but the hungry eyes had ravaged her as she'd tried to sleep.

In the beginning she'd gotten a reprieve after her kills; two weeks after the first was the longest. But the eyes always returned, as she knew they would, mocking her. Last time they'd returned after only three days. This time they'd never left. She'd had a fitful sleep and felt drained.

She now scoured the newspaper's TV listings and planned her day. *Good Morning AM* on Channel 6, *Donahue* on 3, *Montel Williams* on 3, *Joan Rivers* also on 3, flip back and forth between 6 and 10 for the noon news, then Channel 10's soaps for today—*One Life to Live* and *Guiding Light*. Then *Oprah!* on 6. Always *Oprah!* Infuriating, but oh so satisfying. She'd channel surf with her everpresent remote from five to seven o'clock. Snatches of *Action News* mixed with *Inside Edition* on Channel 3. *Current Affair* on 3 at 5:30 looked interesting, though an occasional flip to *Action News* was necessary. At 6:00 she'd surf from one local newscast to another; at 6:30 one national news broadcast to the next. Cartoons on TNT filled her evening until 8:00, then an HBO film till 10:00 and *Dateline* until the news at 11:00, topped off by *Nightline*, though she might take a sneak at *Letterman*. She'd fall asleep to music: MTV, BET or VH1.

Pacing back and forth she'd interact with the tube. On *GMA* a 200-pound anti-porn feminist, with enough hair on her upper lip to resemble an adolescent's first attempt at a mustache, was plugging a book on pedophiles, referring to a Sunday School teacher who videotaped young boys playing with one another's genitals. "He had been exposed to pornography at an early age," she lectured. "But the vicarious thrill wasn't enough . . ."

"Bullshit," Shara yelled at the blimp who kept on talking.

". . . desensitized . . ."

"Right on sister," Shara's voice dripped with hostility. "Like without porn he would have been a model citizen. Give me a fucking break."

". . . been at a religious retreat for six months . . . embraced Jesus . . . well on his way to recovery . . ."

"Well on his way to recovery my ass," Shara barked at the woman. "Put him back on the streets and see how long he embraces the Lord." She threw a nerf ball at the screen, as an act of final dismissal.

Nerf balls of every sort littered the floor. They'd become a necessity after she'd broken her third TV in as many months; the result of heaving whatever came to hand when some dweeb on the tube was particularly infuriating. The widescreen she had recently bought was a real indulgence, and she wasn't about to let some fool anger her to the point where she would react hastily and destroy it. Nerf balls were another thing, though. She could vent her spleen without a second thought.

The ball bounced off the screen harmlessly and landed on her desk, falling onto a straight-backed chair to the right of her window. These were the only furnishings in the room, although it contained thousands of dollars of state-of-the-art electronics: a computer, six cameras—still and video for surveillance work—a microcassette recorder, boom mic and more. Above the desk on a corkboard were newsclips and charts. On the back of the chair her uniform and gun. On either side of the desk small piles of clothes randomly tossed. On the left there were those that were clean; on the right those that needed to be washed. When the pile on the right exceeded that on the left, Shara grudgingly wasted an afternoon at a nearby laundromat.

She was awash in anticipation as *Oprah!* came to a close. The news at noon reported a mid-afternoon press conference on the latest victim of the Vigilante. A break in the case? she wondered. No, she'd be the *first* to know.

On *Action News* the killing of Walt Grimes was the day's "big story" as the anchor was fond of saying. After a brief intro by the station's crack City Hall reporter, a lumbering black man at a podium announced the formation of a special Task Force to coordinate the investigation. The FBI's Behavioral Sciences Unit was sending a special agent to assist. The man looked uncomfortable, Shara thought. In one of those deals with the devil, he'd been given command of the Task Force in exchange for genuflecting before the assembled press. Poor bastard, she thought.

The camera cut to their reporter who explained a coordinated effort was necessitated by overlapping jurisdictions; two of the victims had been killed at their homes in the suburbs. He then said the Mayor was quite concerned and would be in daily contact with the Task Force leader Lamar Briggs. The camera pulled back exposing a thirysomething woman to the reporter's left. "We have with us the Mayor's Media Liaison Deidre Caffrey—"

Shara, who'd been watching intently, stepped back involuntarily as if she'd been struck.

"—who says the Mayor is upset with the media's coverage. Miss Caffrey, what is the Mayor's concern?" A closeup of Deidre as she began to speak. "Dan—"

Deidre was working for the Mayor! Shara recalled reading something about it, but she hadn't been this close to Deidre since . . . since just before her death.

"—the Mayor fears the media is turning a vicious killer into a folk hero. The whole idea of anyone acting as judge, jury and executioner is totally repugnant to a civilized society."

"But isn't the Vigilante sending a message to the police and judicial system that pedophiles and rapists must be dealt with more severely?"

Shara had recovered and pressed the record button on her VCR, and gazed intently at the screen. "Let him have it Dee," she cheered her on.

"The means don't justify the ends, you should know that Dan," Deidre said with just a hint of condescension.

"Way to go, Dee!" Shara threw a nerf football at the reporter's head.

"This Vigilante of yours doesn't dispatch justice," Deidre continued, and now looked directly into the camera, speaking to the viewers, not the reporter. "He tortures his victims, not for their alleged crimes, but because he gets off on it. This Vigilante is demented. If someone barged in while he was torturing a rapist, he wouldn't think twice about killing that person, too." She snapped her fingers to underscore her point. "Think about that before you put him on a pedestal."

"No Deidre!" Shara shouted at the woman looking at *her*, talking to *her*, and *only* her, even as she continued to speak. "I'd never hurt an innocent!"

But Deidre was gone, the reporter summing up the day's events.

Shara turned to *Eyewitness News*. ". . . That was Deidre Caffrey, the Mayor's . . ." Then to Channel 10. "In other news . . ."

"Damn," she shouted at the TV. She rewound the tape and replayed it.

". . . means don't justify the ends . . ."

". . . tortures his victims . . ."

". . . gets off on it . . ."

". . . put him on a pedestal . . ."

And again.

". . . tortures his victims . . ."

". . . gets off on it . . ."

And again, and again, and again.

". . . gets off on it . . ."

". . . gets off on it . . ."

". . . gets off on it . . ."

"You don't understand, Deidre," she said to the freeze-frame image of the woman on the television. "You *must* understand. I don't get off on it." She smiled. "You *will* understand."

She turned off the VCR. Ignoring the Acu-Weather forecast, she went to the mirrors, looking at herself.

She was oblivious to the gaunt diminutive figure that stared back at her; just over five feet. The short cropped brown hair held no fascination. Neither did her angular face or the smooth tawny skin that had yet to see a trace of makeup. Some thought she was Hispanic; others that one of her parents must have been black. Truth be told they could all have been right. Her mother had been a tramp. Any of a half-a-dozen men could have been her father.

It was her breasts that grabbed her attention, though. Not the fact they were large and firm, so out of proportion to the rest of her. Her eyes, rather, were drawn to the tattoos that adorned them; eyes that stared at her. Dead eyes, eyes that couldn't peer into her soul. Eyes that had been hungry, but were no longer. Eight eyes stared at her. She caressed them, and groaned at the touch. Tomorrow, after work, she'd add two more: Walt Grimes'. She pinched the two that cupped the bottom of her nipples until she cried out in pain.

Tomorrow she would begin to stalk her final victim.

She raked the eyes on her breasts with her long nails until they bled.

She should wait, savor the moment, but somehow she knew she would get little satisfaction in replaying Grimes' death. And she would be haunted by the hungry eyes until she'd fully played out her hand.

Watching the unseeing eyes bleeding at her in the mirror, something about Deidre's interview bothered her. She played the tape a half-dozen more times until she was sure. *"The eyes,"* she whispered. *"You clever little bitch!"* she yelled at a freeze-frame picture of Deidre.

35

"You know! You don't believe a fucking word you're saying. The eyes, the mirror to your soul, you once told me. You couldn't read mine, and it drove you to distraction; really disturbed you. See, Dee, it's the eyes that betray you. Erect a curtain behind them and no one will ever know your innermost thoughts. But *you*, you're transparent. You *know* it's me. Trying to get under my skin, anger me so I'll make a mistake. How did you find out, Dee?'' She paused in thought.

"My messages!'' she said finally.

She smacked her forehead with her palm. "Of course, my 'hungry eyes,' messages'' she said to the still visage. "Have you known all along or did it just dawn on you? Have you told the police?''

She began to pace the floor, blood dripping from the scratches she had inflicted on her unseeing eyes. Two thoughts crowded her mind, finally crystallizing. She wanted a confidante; someone who'd understand what drove her to kill. *Needed* someone to know the need to silence the eyes. Maybe even someone to tell her side of the story if she was caught. And she needed someone to feed disinformation to the police, so she could complete her mission, and free herself from the eyes once and for all.

She met Deidre's eyes. "You can't deceive me, Dee. You're an open book. I've got your number; always have. Catch me if you can,'' she taunted. "I'll even give you some help.'' She threw a nerf ball and hit Deidre between the eyes. Then another and another and . . .

Chapter Three

Deidre didn't know how she had gotten through the day, much less the countless interviews. She hadn't fallen asleep until four in the morning, and then only with the help of sleeping pills. No matter how she had tried to immerse herself in her work, the message scrawled on Walt Grimes' mirror intruded into her consciousness opening a floodgate of memories.

She remembered the day before, following Briggs into Grimes' room; the bed with the disembodied ropes; the message NO MORE HUNGRY EYES. She'd awakened on a couch back down in the living room, a concerned Briggs holding a glass of water in his hand. She drank it, hands trembling, spilling half on her blouse.

"Shouldn't have let you go up there," Briggs said, trying to sound irritated, but not succeeding. "Kind of queasy for a reporter, though. I know you've seen worse."

Deidre had to get a grip on herself. She had to get away from Briggs' probing eyes. She had to be alone to sort things out.

"Not in the last two years, though," she answered. "I . . . I just felt so, well, so claustrophobic. The bed took up half the room and I imagined Grimes tied up, trying to scream but unable, and it was a bit too much." She sat up, still woozy, and reached for the phone to call her driver. Briggs stopped her, his huge hand dwarfing hers, not letting her pick up the receiver.

"Let me drive you home."

She shook her head no, willing words to accompany her actions, but she still had a lump in her throat.

"Please, Dee." He sounded so unsure of himself, none of the arrogance or hostility of earlier. "Look, I imagine tomorrow I'll be tied up all day with briefings on the Task Force. To tell the truth I'm worried about the press conference. I can deal with reporters a couple at a time. Hell, I can chew them up and spit them out. Microphones stuck in my face gets my juices going. But a press conference is like a . . . a speech, and well, I was wondering if you could give me some hints." He turned away, as if he had somehow betrayed some deep inner secret.

Deidre stifled a laugh. This was no time to antagonize him. Make him feel the fool, and a wall would forever separate them. Help him and he would owe her, though he'd never admit it. And he was justified. A reporter all her adult life, she'd always been on the other side of the microphone. When she'd accepted the new Mayor's offer of Media Liaison, she didn't know if she could handle being queried by her colleagues.

It was the same with Briggs. He had to come across as competent and firmly in control or he'd lose the press, and more important, the public. So she let him drive her home, temporarily locking the words on the mirror in the attic of her mind.

Her advice was simple. "Say as little as possible when you're introduced. Pick out somebody you've got a good rapport with and address him . . . or her, and ignore the rest. Tell them there'll be periodic briefings with the Mayor's Media Liaison. Take three or four questions—no more, and keep the answers short. You may want to write out the questions yourself and pass them along to any friends you have in the media. That is, if you have any.''

He looked at her, saw she was smiling, and laughed. "You sound like a damned politician.''

"Well, unfortunately, that comes with my new job.''

"Don't like it much, do you?''

"I had a tough couple of years, Briggs, and I was in no shape to be the reporter I'd been. I don't know if I even liked the reporter I'd become. Anyway, the pay's good, there are a lot of perks, and until the Vigilante showed up it's been pretty cushy.''

"Don't like it much, though, do you?''

She laughed. "Don't miss much, do you, Detective? Yeah, I miss being on the front lines; the rush when you get a tip and can scoop the competition. Basking in the limelight when you hit the motherlode.'' She sat back, feeling comfortable in his presence. "I'd love to be investigating this case. I'd make your life miserable.'' She laughed, unable to control herself.

"It's a game to you,'' he snapped, his anger seeming to get the best of him.

"Look, Briggs, reporters and cops are a lot alike. Take a story, any story. We're both out to find out the who, when, why and where. The difference is as a reporter I don't care how I get my information. I've got fewer rules to follow. I'm more interested in the why than the who. As a cop you have less latitude. And as a cop you could care less about the why. You want to know who did the deed and back it up with enough evidence to convict. So, no Briggs, it's not a game. I take my job as seriously as you do yours. Your job tomorrow is to give as little information as possible; to keep us at bay. My job is to make that difficult.''

"You're talking like a reporter."

"Yeah, well a zebra doesn't lose his stripes. I meant, if I were a reporter my job would be to make it difficult for you. But, I'm not a reporter. I'm one of the good guys now, as far as you're concerned."

She saw him looking at her, sizing her up, deciding whether he could trust her. Then his eyes were back on the road. She didn't think he'd made a decision yet.

"Anyway, you'll do fine tomorrow," she continued. "The reporters you plant questions with will owe you. They'll impress their assignment editors, so pick them wisely. Cultivate them, but don't neglect the others. You don't want to antagonize anyone, if you don't have to. As head of the Task Force, you'll need to be a politician as much as a cop. You know better than I the pressures you'll face. This case can make your career or break you. Use the press properly, and they can be an important ally. Ignore them or jerk them around too much, and you've got one more enemy."

She paused a moment. "Remember, though, I'll be there to help." Another pause. "Then you'll owe me when I'm back on the street again. Do we understand one another?"

"Sure. You scratch my back, I scratch yours. Look, I'm sorry I snapped at you. You're right, this can make or break my career. I want it, don't get me wrong, but I wonder if we'll ever snare the perp." He looked at her, and they locked eyes for a few seconds.

"I appreciate your help," he confided, "and I'll need a lot more of it before this is over. And I don't forget my friends. You more than anyone should know that."

They drove the rest of the way in silence. Briggs undoubtedly was thinking about the case; and Deidre had Hungry Eyes to contend with.

Chapter Four

Hungry Eyes. The phrase resonated in Deidre's mind as she nursed a diet coke. Her apartment on the sixteenth floor of a high rise off Rittenhouse Square had few furnishings. It lacked those little touches that gave it a character of its own; that told something about its inhabitant.

When she'd sold her home on the Main Line, shortly after her husband and son's death a year-and-a-half before, she'd purposely taken little with her. She'd grudgingly acquiesced to her father-in-law and put only the most cherished items in storage, then sold the rest with the house. She never regretted the decision. She had to start fresh, she told herself, and that meant both disposing of much of the past and weaning herself off the buzz of alcohol.

She hadn't quite drowned her sorrows in booze; hadn't succumbed to alcoholism. No, she drank just enough to keep her in a mellow funk. One day her husband, who as a reporter had survived assignments in the Persian Gulf, Somalia and Bosnia, and her eight-year-old son were playing touch football in the backyard; the next she was burying them after their car had been rammed into by a drunken driver.

A six-month leave of absence from the paper had passed quickly. Too quickly. She wasn't quite ready to leave the womb of her memories. Another month passed, then a second.

"No," she'd told her editor, "not yet. Give me a few more days, a week or two at the most. It wouldn't do you any good my coming back too early, have me go through the motions and basically fuck up, would it, Jack?"

Another month flew by and this time he hadn't called. Just as well, she told herself. I'm still not ready. Soon though. A few days, maybe a week or two . . .

Her father-in-law had slapped her out of her lethargy. A reporter himself, he'd grudgingly been dragged off the streets at fifty-five, and for the past five years had been on the editorial board of the *Inquirer*; allowed to vent his spleen twice a week with a column. Physically he resembled his son; tall—six-foot-six—gaunt, with a full head of straight hair he literally combed with his fingers. Where her husband's hair had been jet black, Jonas Caffrey Senior's was snow white; had prematurely grayed, he'd proudly proclaimed, in his twenties. "Distinguished. Helped gain their confidence. Better than bald anytime."

She'd noticed some liver spots on his cheeks, forehead and hands in the last few years, deep lines like streams cascading down his face, with others forming, branching off a main tributary. He now walked somewhat stooped, where once he'd stood proud, and there was a slight tremor in his right hand. Stubborn to the core, he'd taught himself to write with his left hand rather than admit to the ravages of age.

But his mind remained razor sharp. Often gruff and irascible, she'd learned that beneath the rough exterior was a man of uncommon insight and compassion.

His signature, however, was his clipped, almost staccato manner of speaking. He didn't speak in sentences, but in fragments, as if extra words were a waste of time, if he could make his point without them.

Six weeks after her editor's last call he'd come by unannounced. That, too, she'd come to expect. "Call ahead, a waste of time," he said on more than one occasion. "No one home, only my time I've wasted. Call first and you make a fuss. Then, I feel like a pain in the ass."

This time he'd used his son's key, when she ignored his persistent knock.

"Listen. Don't interrupt. I'll say my piece and leave." He hesitated, the look on his face showing he was not about to take no for an answer.

"I lost a son and grandson. I grieve for them. Eight years ago I lost my wife. Wanted to bury my head in the sand. My Angela would have slapped me silly. You've mourned your loss and then some. Draw strength from their love. Time to get on with life. Tomorrow you'll get a call. A new beginning." He bent down and held her chin firmly in his right hand. She felt a slight tremor. "You're the daughter I never had. My son, if he knew you'd caved in, would be heartbroken. Disappointed, too. My son didn't marry a quitter. You want to honor his memory, you tell the man yes." He kissed her on the forehead and left.

The next day John Cabot called. His mayoral campaign was in disarray; a twenty-point lead shrunk to five percent. As all politicians he had to find scapegoats. It couldn't be his fault, after all. He'd fired his Chief of Staff and Press Secretary.

Then he offered the job of Press Secretary to her, and she'd accepted. Took a drink as she hung up the phone, and decided she owed it to him to give it her best, which meant no more booze to dull the senses.

The campaign rallied, and she was appointed Media Liaison. A new beginning.

But tonight an even older memory tugged at her. A memory of a ten-year-old fearful of Hungry Eyes that assaulted her dreams. A girl who had committed suicide, but hadn't. A girl, no, now a woman, still apparently stalked by those eyes. In her heart, Deidre knew Renee Barrows had killed at least five, and would kill again. She had to find Renee and stop her, yet she couldn't go to Briggs. She could imagine his response.

"A girl who killed herself thirteen years ago is the killer. Your proof? The message on the mirror. Gimme a break."

She wouldn't have blamed him. She had proof all right; proof Renee hadn't died, hadn't jumped into the Schuylkill River after leaving a letter for her foster parents. She went to her desk. In the bottom drawer she took out a thick file. At the very end, yellowing at the edges, was a postcard. "Thanks for caring." Postmarked *three* days after the child had plunged off the bridge. The police then, and Briggs now, would say the Post Office screwed up. A postcard falls on the floor and someone finds it four or five days later, and it's mailed. Renee had written and mailed it *before* she took the plunge, so they'd say. End of theory.

But Deidre knew better. Renee loved playing with Deidre's mind. She'd cared for Deidre, but used her just the same. In the end, she couldn't resist one last taunt. And it *had* bugged her for many a night. But she knew if Renee set her mind to vanishing, she wouldn't be found, so Deidre had finally put it to rest.

But Renee was back, and Deidre *would* find her. Deidre for once had the advantage. She knew Renee was the killer, yet Renee wouldn't know she was on her trail.

One of the perks of her job was it left her with a lot of down time. She had no set hours; she was at the

Mayor's disposal when needed. And he'd told her to stay on top of the Vigilante case.

Could she somehow make Renee come to her? Yes, she thought to herself. A retrospective series on Renee Barrows and the kidnapping that had made national headlines—and propelled her own career. It would grant her the opportunity to dig into the past. And maybe with some slight revisionist history, she'd anger Renee enough so she'd contact her.

She could feel the juices pumping. The past nine months hadn't been the new beginning she'd sought. She'd wrapped herself in a cocoon of comfort and lay dormant; functioning on automatic pilot. But dammit, she was a reporter, and here was a life and death story only she could tell. And maybe she could do something for Renee. Maybe she could atone for abandoning her thirteen years ago.

Chapter Five

Much as she wanted to get on with her own investigation immediately, Deidre didn't have much time the next day. Briggs called her at seven, and told her to meet him at the old 9th Precinct Station on 19th and Tasker Streets.

In a move to reorganize, a euphemism for cost-cutting, two districts had been consolidated into one, the building at 19th Street abandoned two months before.

It looked like it had been vacant for years. The graffiti had been covered with graffiti, more than a few suggesting that the police have sex with themselves. Every window had been broken, and as Deidre approached, the smell of urine and human feces assaulted her nose.

Briggs met her at the booking desk and took her to what would be his office. The heavy smell of industrial disinfectant greeted her, and she was glad she'd had only a bagel and coffee for breakfast. The cleaning crew certainly had its work cut out. In the ultimate of ironies, it looked like the station had become a crack house. Briggs must have sensed her unease.

"They were supposed to tear it down weeks ago, but

you know how the bureaucracy runs. Seems the cops were so pissed at leaving, they purposely let it go to hell. I hear Superfresh bought the property. Few months, it will go down; next year the area will have a much needed supermarket.'' He saw Deidre staring at him. ''Rambling, am I?''

''You look like shit. You haven't been up all night, have you?''

''Course not. Caught a cat nap at six. They woke me up to call you at seven.'' He pointed to a cot in the corner. ''All the creature comforts of home.''

''You haven't solved the case yet, behind my back, have you Detective?'' she said with a smile.

''Cute, Dee. Spent the night setting up the Task Force, least a good portion of it. Truth is, we never should have announced the damn thing yesterday. I should have had three or four days to organize, *then* announce it to the press. But your boss got antsy and mine's got no balls.''

''Why here?'' Dee asked, noting the room contained a desk, two chairs, a filing cabinet, the cot Briggs mentioned and little else.

''The ambiance.'' He laughed, and despite the bags under his eyes, he seemed to be getting a second wind. ''Seriously, we can't afford leaks, and while the Roundhouse is the logical place for the Task Force, you'd need a dam to plug the leaks.''

The Roundhouse, Deidre knew, was a modern, state-of-the-art, relatively speaking, central police headquarters. Problem was, every beat reporter had several sources within the building. If Briggs took a piss, someone would be on the phone about it.

''By the end of the day,'' Briggs continued, ''except for some additional personnel, we'll have everything we need: communications, computers, maybe even electricity.''

''So what were you up to last night?''

''All the minutiae. The Task Force will consist of

eleven officers, not including me. I knew four men I wanted right off the bat. After a short meeting we'd added three more; including one woman, in case your friends in the media are interested. We'll be adding two from the suburbs today. The Chief will send over the last two. Hopefully, they'll be able to do more than just answer the phones.''

"Don't have much faith in your boss."

"Nah, just don't like the politics. Whoever they are, regardless of what I'm told, they'll report directly to the Chief. They're not exactly the enemy, but let's say they won't have my best interests at heart."

Two uniforms knocked on the door. It was more a formality. The glass was broken. They didn't have much privacy.

"Where do you want these files, sir?" a light-skinned black asked. He was young, probably barely out of the Academy, Deidre thought. She noted the starch in his uniform and boots like mirrors.

"In the corner, for now, with the rest of them."

When they'd left, he sighed. "Where was I? Let's see. We spent part of the night assembling the team. I had files on the cases, and we went over those. What you see in the corner is the raw data; you know, all the interviews of witnesses and shit like that."

She could sense he was becoming more comfortable around her, as he didn't apologize for his profanity. She wondered if she'd become one of the guys. Or maybe it was he was too exhausted to care.

"At about three, the dude from the FBI shows up. He's only going to be with us for the day. We'd already sent him most of what we've got. He's going to brief us at . . . ," he looked at his watch, "nine-thirty, then tell the press not to expect any overnight miracles, and return to Washington. We'll update him, of course, and he'll provide feedback, but after he's given us his profile on the guy he's not much use to us."

"Then you got some sleep?"

"Almost," he said with a weary smile. "Had to fill out a few dozen forms so we'd be functional; from plumbers so the johns work to staff to man the phones and computers. Besides the detectives, we'll have another dozen assorted personnel on the premises by noon."

"What's my role in all this?"

"Mainly to keep the press off my ass, so I can do my job. You'll be at the briefing at 9:30. Then you'll brief the media at four; in time for the TV people to get on the early evening news, not enough time to ask too many questions." He smiled.

"You're getting the hang of working the press."

"I've spent my whole life working with one kind of vulture or another, no offense. I've *always* known how to work the press. Just not too good at making speeches. That's where you come in. You'll be *my* liaison, as well as the Mayor's. The question is just where do your loyalties lie? I mean, just how much of what you hear goes back to the Mayor?"

Deidre shrugged. "What can I say. I work for the Mayor, but I'm not here to spy on you. As you said, he'll have two members of the Task Force as his eyes and ears. I was never all that close to the Mayor. I wasn't with his campaign from the get-go. He has his inner circle, and I'm certainly not part of it, nor do I wish to be. My future plans do not include politics. I'm to act as liaison between you and the Mayor's office, not spy on you. Take it for what it's worth."

It was Briggs' turn to shrug. "I can handle that. I basically need you for damage control. If anyone asks, I'm ass deep in pursuing leads the FBI provided. You might want to work up a press kit, giving background on the victims, where each was found, etcetera. You know the routine. I figure that after today things will quiet as we plod along. You tell your friends that we'll

49

advise them when we have something newsworthy. No regular briefings. You present our FBI agent, and he tells them we've got days, maybe weeks of legwork before we develop any leads. Basically, tell them to fuck off and let us do our jobs."

He stood up and stretched, a piece of glass crunching under his foot. He handed Deidre a thick manila folder labeled "Confidential."

"You might want to familiarize yourself with all the victims before the briefing. Don't take this wrong, but the 'Confidential' on the file is not ornamental. We tell the media as little as possible," he said with a wry smile. "Before anything goes out it gets cleared by me.

"Now c'mon, let me take you to your office. Use the phone at the main desk for now, if you need to. It's the only one functional for the next few hours. Order whatever you need." He pointed to the left as he walked. "We'll meet in the squadroom at 9:30. Any questions?"

"Like you're in the mood for any?" she said.

He stopped, and put his hand on her arm. "Dee, you're part of my team now. You got questions, ask. We've had our disagreements in the past, but I'm going to need you to run interference for me. No, more than that, I'm going to need your advice and expertise so we can get the media on our side for a change. If I wanted you out of the way, believe me, I could do it. I could have you giving individual briefings to each paper and every station. I *could* keep you out of my hair. So when I say you're part of my team, I'm not bullshitting you. Okay?"

"Thanks. Really, I mean it." She was about to broach the subject of their earlier alienation, but she decided against it. For now she'd take him at his word. If necessary, she'd confront him if all he was spouting was so much hot air. At the moment, she'd go with the program.

"At the moment, no questions. After the briefing, we'll see. Just point me to my new digs and you get back to work. Better yet, rest. You need it.''

"Yes, mother," he said with a smile and showed her to her office. The "office," painted institutional green, was all of four walls, a desk and chair. A legal pad and assorted pens adorned the grey metal desk. The heavy smell of disinfectant told her Briggs had earmarked it for cleaning before she arrived. She could picture it a few hours before, and it made her skin crawl.

She opened a window to rid herself of the stench, but it was already oppressively hot outside and wasn't likely to do much good. She hoped one of the forms Briggs had filled out was for fans.

With forty-five minutes to kill, she opened the folder he'd given her. Before she had a chance to immerse herself, there was a knock on her door.

A blond woman in baggy overalls was precariously holding an armful of supplies.

"Sorry to disturb you," she said with a heavy South Philadelphia accent, kind of like a female Sylvester Stallone in *Rocky*, "but where do you want these?" The woman looked around the room, then laughed. "Pretty stupid question. There's the desk or," she paused and smiled, "the desk."

Deidre laughed. "I guess it's the desk, then."

The woman was short, and her overalls completely obscured her figure. She seemed to swim in them. Your basic one-size-fits-all overalls some companies ordered in mass quantities. Her face was thin, pretty, but with two distinguishing marks that screamed for attention. She had a mole on the left side of her chin which sprouted hairs as if it had a life of its own. It looked like a bug, Deidre thought. A parasite, not caring at all how it marred the looks of its host.

Then there was a prominent scar which ran from her left eye to the corner of her mouth. It was rough and fibrous, as if stitched by an inebriated intern or not stitched at all, but left to heal. From the way the woman carried herself Deidre thought she must have got it in a fight as a teenager. A cat fight over a boy in high school, in all probability.

The woman was talking, but Deidre was so engrossed in her fantasy she missed the words. She had a bad habit of creating elaborate personas, of sorts, for strangers she met, and often found more than a kernel of truth in them when she learned more about the person. She noticed the woman had put the supplies on her desk. "Excuse me, I'm sorry."

"I was just saying, I like what you done to the place, you know. Understated, but conducive to work. Nothing to distract you."

Deidre laughed again. "I just moved in," she said defensively. "I mean *literally* just moved in."

"Well, I wish I could stay and chat, but you've got work to do," she said, gesturing to the file in Deidre's hand. "Be seeing you around. Have a good day, now."

"You too," Deidre said to the woman's back. A quirky sense of humor, Deidre thought. While born, bred and indoctrinated with middle-class values, unlike some of her fellow reporters Deidre did not look down on the working class. Cleaning ladies and janitors would stop by her desk to chat, and as Deidre was never condescending, she seemed to get better service simply because she didn't consider them invisible nonentities. While she couldn't envision becoming friends with the woman who was now leaving, she liked her instantly.

Enough, already, she chastised herself, time to focus on business at hand. She glanced quickly at the supplies: rubber bands, legal pads, a box of pens and pencils, a stapler and staples and a single file folder. Curious, she thought, but it reminded her of the folder in her hand.

Shara walked two blocks to where she'd parked her car and drove back to work. On the way, she slipped out of the overalls, removed the blond wig and peeled off the mole and scar.

Her bowels had turned to jello when she had knocked on Deidre's door, but the woman had shown no recognition. Not that she should have, but she'd taken a risk. She had thoroughly enjoyed the charade. What she'd give to be a fly on the wall when Deidre saw what was in the single folder she had left.

The idea had come to her around four in the morning. She slept in fits and starts, as usual. Always a light sleeper, it had become exacerbated when she'd been kidnapped. Literally caged, she was entirely at his mercy. Afraid he'd sneak up on her while she slept, she dozed, a part of her alert to every sound. Worse were his eyes, mentally raping her. She'd unconsciously claw at her genitals to rid herself of them, until she was raw, and even going to the bathroom was painful. She felt his eyes on her when he wasn't in the room; knew deep down within her being he could see her through the mirrors that covered the room. When she let her guard down, that was when he'd enter.

Set free, she was still his prisoner. A prisoner of his eyes. Her body had adapted to her psychological needs. She got no more than four hours of sleep a night, supplemented by a short nap after work. Even this was unnecessary when she stalked her prey. She'd go days on just catnaps, then sack out for as many as eighteen hours on a Sunday. Even the eyes cooperated with her at those times, assaulting her while awake, but allowing her to regenerate.

The night before she'd seethed at the thought Deidre had tried to bait her; had almost succeeded. Such arrogance demanded payback. A face-to-face meeting; a little chat.

Instantly awake, she tapped into her computer and found where the Task Force would be working. She noted work orders and requisition forms.

Computers. Wonderful tools in the right hands. So many businesses, the police among them, so dependent, they weren't even aware how vulnerable they were to interlopers like herself. There was so much information that could be easily obtained by anyone with the knowledge of how to look.

Deidre would be at the Task Force headquarters that morning. Yes, a visit was in the cards.

Shara had gone to work; the 6 a.m. to 2 p.m. shift that gave her the freedom she needed for her other work. At eight-thirty, complaining of cramps, she'd gotten a fellow worker to cover for her while she supposedly went to the drugstore for a prescription and took a short nap.

Instead, she'd donned her disguise. She was especially proud of the mole and scar. She'd learned from her many talks with uniforms how witnesses had a terribly difficult time describing anyone with any sort of deformity. Scars, burns, anything unnatural and hideous either attracted the eye from the rest of the face, or so revolted the looker that nothing else registered. The mole and scar would occupy Deidre. Just in case, though, she'd taken the precaution of adding hazel contacts. It wouldn't do for Deidre to see her eyes. They were as identifiable to Deidre as fingerprints to the police.

There was that one moment when she'd thought she'd lose it. Her natural nervousness, the adrenalin flowing, mixed with her first face-to-face encounter in thirteen years.

Deidre hadn't changed a bit. Aged to be sure, *her* eyes showing a haunted quality, but recalling what had happened to her family it was understandable. She remembered how Deidre, to gain her trust years before, had confided in her about how hard she worked to make herself look attractive. Looking at her now, Shara had to agree that Deidre was rather plain, with no one distinguishing feature. But the sum was definitely better than the individual parts. She'd also exuded an aura of self-confidence in her manner which surely caught others' attention. With her deft use of makeup to accentuate her better features, she'd turned herself into a good-looking lady.

Shara smiled inwardly as Deidre scrutinized her without an ounce of recognition. Drawn, she was sure, to the mole and the scar. The heavy accent hadn't been planned. Dressed as she was, with the gaudy blond wig, and particularly the mole indicating a lack of self-esteem, the accent came naturally.

It was a shame she had to go back to work. But it was part of the facade she had carefully constructed; patterns that must remain unbroken. Besides, she didn't know when Deidre would notice the single folder, open it and realize she'd been face to face with the woman she talked *to* via the TV the night before. Shara planned on calling her at home anyway. Meanwhile, today she'd start stalking her final victim. That would keep her occupied; her mind off Deidre for the time being.

Deidre opened Briggs' file and began to read. As always, when she did research, she skimmed first to familiarize herself with the big picture, putting checkmarks next to particularly relevant items, jotting down a question or notation or two as she went along. Then she'd go through the entire file a second time, noting similarities and differences in each of the killings, trying to look at each victim through the eyes of the killer. In this case, since she knew it was Renee, it gave her a perspective she was sure none of the others possessed.

The first killing was the sloppiest. Evan Grant had clearly put up a struggle, but had been quickly subdued. He had an abrasion on the left side of his head and swelling on his forehead. The report surmised he'd been knocked out, then tied up. Whatever resistance he'd put up had been feeble; there was no skin under his nails.

Deidre also noted he had only been out of prison six months. He wouldn't have felt complacent. Grant was guarded, not yet cocky. And he was clearly dangerous. Deidre wondered if Renee picked him out to start with on purpose or found she'd erred, and chose the others more carefully.

She'd scarcely finished getting filled in on the Grant killing when Briggs knocked at her door. He pointed to his watch. "You'll be late," he chided. "No way to impress the boss," but he was smiling.

Deidre returned the smile. "I got so immersed in the file you gave me I lost all track of time. Thanks for fetching me. Get any rest?" she asked as she rose.

"Tried to. Sat down and cleared my mind of everything. Only problem, some corner of my mind wouldn't shut down; the part that dealt with minutiae. Kept thinking of little things that had to be done. Requisition to repair windows on the doors; another for the clocks. I can see where that'll come in handy. Just things you need when you move into a new office. Only, in this case I don't have days or weeks to complete the job, and I'm moving an entire squad, not just one person." He abruptly shifted gears. "So, tell me, the report give you any insights? Raise any red flags?"

"In forty-five minutes? Give me a break." She put her hand on his arm and stopped him. "Briggs, can I be an active participant at the briefing, or do you want me to take notes and keep my mouth shut?"

He didn't answer immediately, but seemed to ponder the question. "Look, I made a mistake before. I said the Task Force consisted of eleven. Actually, it's twelve. You're not a cop, and won't take part in the actual investigation. As far as I'm concerned, though, you're every bit the investigator they are, though you come at your work from a different perspective. I want your input. Don't feel intimidated in there. You'll feel out of your element, but go with your instincts.

"C'mon now, they'll start without us."

The squadroom was as bare as the rest of the station; the pungent odor of disinfectant the telltale sign it had been cleaned during the early morning. Three large fans recirculated hot air. Without being told, Deidre knew which members of the team Briggs had chosen, which were from the suburbs, and those who were the Chief's eyes and ears. Her assumptions were confirmed as Briggs introduced the group.

Briggs' seven were comfortably dressed. They'd been at the station most of the night, had gone home for a shower, some rest and a decent breakfast. They had returned prepared for the adverse working conditions, obviously with Briggs' blessing.

Five were black, two white, one female; a light-skinned black. They sat together, like a clique in a high-school class. Six ranged in age from thirty to thirty-five; Briggs' contemporaries. The seventh stood out from the others. Skin as dark as Briggs, his body was lean and chiseled from daily workouts. She guessed he was forty-five. She couldn't tell by his face as it was surrounded by a thick wiry beard; now more gray than black. His short-cropped hair was gray as well. He looked like a drill sergeant and she guessed he was Briggs' mentor; his rabbi, she'd heard cops call those who'd taken officers under their wings. While Briggs spoke, Lucius Calvin, as he was introduced, like a bird of prey, searched the faces of the others.

The two men from the suburbs sat next to one another; the two outcasts of the class. Both white, both in their early forties, both wearing light-colored cotton suits that were already stained with perspiration.

The final two also sat apart from the others, but they had a haughty air about them. They were the Chief's men; one black, the other white, both in their mid-to late-forties, both dressed in dark suits in silent defiance to Briggs' handpicked crew. They both looked at Briggs with disregard, even contempt. Deidre knew them, and was certain they'd wanted to lead the Task Force. Deidre had kiddingly mentioned them to Briggs the day before; Chievous and McCauley. They'd be hoping Briggs would fail, and each would be first in line to take his place.

Deidre branded them worthless, and wondered how Briggs would handle them.

The only other person in the room, sitting alone in the front row, had to be the FBI agent, though he looked more like a college professor. He was fortysomething, medium height, but about twenty pounds overweight. He wore a navy sports jacket and faded bluejeans. His horn-rimmed glasses constantly slid down his nose. He dabbed his forehead with a handkerchief while readjusting his glasses.

After introductions, most of Briggs' comments were directed to the men from the 'burbs and the Chief's henchmen. He'd already brainstormed with his chosen seven. He clearly considered Chievous and McCauley irritants, and he would gauge the competency of the other two later. Deidre wondered if it were wise to antagonize Chievous and McCauley. She doubted, though, if there was any way to mollify them. They already had their knives ready to plunge into Briggs' back.

"I apologize for our working conditions," he said, his eyes darting back and forth between the four interlopers. "With the exception of the air conditioning, which may or may not be possible to repair, we should be fully operational by the end of the day. After lunch we'll review the files you've each been given, and I'll hand out assignments. First, however, I have the privilege to turn over the meeting to Special Agent Harold Logan, from the Behavioral Sciences Center at Quantico. The FBI has worked up a profile on our killer."

He nodded to the man in the front row. ''Agent Logan.''

There was a smattering of applause, and Logan looked self-conscious as he got up to address the group. Before talking he dabbed his forehead with his handkerchief, readjusted his glasses, removed them and then put them on again. Then like a professor he gave them a little background about profiling methods that had been developed, explained how they'd helped break two recent cases most of his listeners were familiar with, and then got down to the business at hand.

He'd clearly won over his audience with his description of how FBI profiles had solved two seemingly hopeless cases. Deidre could tell it was all cleverly calculated. There'd been a lot of squirming, some daydreaming, and a few with heavy eyelids, ready to close at the outset. But with stark grisly details of cases that had made national headlines he'd brought them back to attention. They waited on his every word now. He'd tell them who the killer was and how to track him down. A quick capture would mean promotions for all of them.

Logan opened up a manila folder, and only occasionally glancing at his notes gave them what they wanted.

''Now to get down to cases. We believe our killer is a white male, 25 to 34 years of age. He was probably physically and/or sexually abused as a child. It's possible someone close to him has been molested recently. That could have been what triggered him; the straw that broke the camel's back, so to speak.''

He paused, and took a sip of water, again wiping his forehead and adjusting his glasses.

''Our man is methodical. The pictures he's left indicate he must validate his suspicions before he passes final judgment. Also of significance, he seems to derive less satisfaction with each killing. It's a classic scenario. At first he savors each killing, relives them and can lead an otherwise normal life. However, with each subsequent killing there is less gratification. The need to kill gnaws at him like a cancer.

"In this case, between the first and second killing there was a three-month delay; two months with the next, then seven weeks and five weeks with the last. We can assume, then, he'll strike within three to four weeks."

As he was talking he took a picture of each victim, cut out in the form of pieces to a jigsaw puzzle, and pinned it to the board next to him. The last piece contained a large question mark.

Throughout his discourse Deidre felt a certain detachment. She already knew the killer. Nonetheless, she was fascinated by the speaker's technique, and the rapt attention of those he lectured.

"Our friend gets his thrills by stalking; accumulating proof the scum he's selected has gone on committing heinous crimes after thwarting justice. We believe he's a veteran of the armed forces with training in surveillance, as well as computer technology. Or he may have learned about computers before or after leaving the service.

"This guy's egotistical. To the extreme. He gets off, to use Ms. Caffrey's words, on being a hero; an avenging angel." He looked at Deidre as he said this, letting all know he was totally on top of the case.

"The kill itself has little meaning to him. It's the hunt, the discovery, followed by intense media scrutiny that makes it all meaningful for him. We can use this, hopefully, to make him come to us *before* he dispatches his next victim." He slapped the paper with the question mark with the palm of his hand to accentuate his last point.

"We want to entice him to contact the media. Detective Briggs and I have agreed that we'll approach a reporter, and suggest a series of negative articles; questioning the manhood of the Vigilante, his motivation, etc. It's possible he'll become so incensed he'll contact the reporter directly. His perception by the public is critical to him. An attempt to get the public to turn against him might bring him to us.

"We've also discussed setting up an elaborate trap, hoping he'll bite. We'll feed the media the names of three rapists and child molesters who have evaded punishment or received a slap on the wrist. Two will be real, one a plant. Our man's no fool, and this is a real longshot, but if *we* can choose his target, we've got him."

McCauley tentatively raised his hand, like a child in school not sure if he was going to make a fool of himself. "Isn't that unethical, Agent Logan? We're putting two citizens at risk without their permission."

Logan answered like a teacher lecturing a wayward child. "Unethical? We're after a killer here. We're not on a level playing field. Right now we're playing his hand. We have to try to get a look at his cards. To assuage your guilt, we have evidence the two we've selected are repeat offenders." He raised his hand to cut off McCauley who was about to interrupt.

"We don't have enough evidence to bring charges, but these are not law-abiding citizens we've chosen. Hopefully, we'll make our plant the most attractive, but it's impossible to determine just how he selects his victims."

He paused now, taking off his glasses, as if to punctuate his next point. He slowly surveyed his audience, then settled on McCauley.

"I want you to understand the problem I believe we're facing. This man is fast becoming a folk hero. In a free society, we can't muzzle the press. Unfortunately, the picture the media is painting is one of an avenging angel. It's just a matter of time before copycats crawl out of the woodwork. Just a matter of time before someone gets sick of seeing a dealer pushing crack on kids while the police seemingly do nothing. Even if it means putting someone at risk, we must take the chance for the greater good. Do the ends justify the means, you're asking? In this case, you're damn right. Now any questions?''

He fielded a number of questions before Deidre felt confident to broach what was foremost on her mind.

''You keep referring to the killer as 'he'. Is it possible we should be looking for a woman?''

''Anything's possible,'' he said without hesitation. ''Women are committing an increasingly higher number of violent crimes. Women are seeking empowerment and crime empowers. The talk shows are abuzz with women coming out of the closet admitting they were victims of incest and other sexual and physical abuse as children. Oprah and others of her ilk are telling them they can no longer turn the other cheek. Women who have been repeatedly beaten by their husbands are striking back, killing their spouses, and the juries are setting them free. I personally believe we'll see women serial killers ten or twenty years down the line. But for now the statistics tell us women are killing close to home: their children, their spouses.

''And looking at the facts of this case, two of the men were physically strong, and not to be sexist, I believe even taken by surprise they could easily have overpowered a woman.''

Deidre could feel the gaze of the others on her, at this last statement, but kept her attention focused on Logan.

''Lastly, we have to use a process of elimination, of sorts, or we'd be investigating the entire population. The profile I've provided comes from hundreds of interviews with serial killers. It narrows the search to reasonable proportions, which is why we were called in. That profile, Ms. Caffrey, excludes women, in this particular case.''

Deidre nodded. She'd already known, but needed confirmation, that her suspicions would be dismissed out of hand. She'd have to look for Renee on her own; and to be perfectly honest with herself that's the way she wanted it. She'd made the effort, at least, and assuaged her conscience.

There were a few more questions, which Deidre only vaguely heard, and then Logan sat down.

Briggs told everyone to take a break to digest what they'd heard. They'd reassemble in an hour to brainstorm. Then assignments would be made.

Deidre would meet with Logan and plan the afternoon press conference. She felt a bit like a fifth wheel. Logan certainly didn't need her expertise. He'd told the Task Force who the killer was, and how to smoke him out. Until they came up dry, they'd follow his lead without question.

She'd sensed a palpable fear among members of the Task Force, including Chievous and McCauley. Even Briggs wasn't immune. The enormity of their quest was just dawning on them. And there was the fear of failure; of careers put irretrievably on hold if they didn't succeed. They were drowning, grasping for a life preserver, and Logan was offering the best hope for success. No one was about to question his assumptions, conclusions and suggestions . . . and he knew it.

Logan would tell her how to handle the media. She, too, would do as she was told, though not for the same reasons. Only she knew he was wrong.

For her own investigation, she'd enlist her own troops; the equal to any on the Task Force, whose loyalty to her was beyond question.

Back at her office, Deidre saw that more supplies had been delivered in her absence; the most welcome a fan, telephone and radio. She began putting the supplies in her desk when she came to the single manila folder on top of several legal pads.

Absently, she opened the folder and some papers fell out. She picked up a yellowing newspaper article and immediately recognized the photo of 10-year-old Renee Barrows next to Deidre's page-three story in the *Daily News:* "SUICIDE CLAIMS ABUSED YOUTH." It was more a human interest story than a straight news report.

"Renee Barrows committed suicide today, apparently jumping from the Falls Bridge into the murky depths of the Schuylkill River."

Despite her unease, the writer in Deidre cringed at the overly melodramatic opening. A great writer she hadn't been thirteen years before.

"What could drive a ten-year-old to so abhor life as to throw it away? Of all the members of the media, this reporter knew Renee Barrows best. That she would commit suicide is incomprehensible, for this feisty youth was a survivor; a child who had been to hell and back more than once, yet seemingly had never succumbed to despair. Placed in a foster home that for the first time gave her structure, and, most importantly, love, she appeared to be on the mend."

The story went on to describe the many horrors that had been visited upon Renee Barrows; from her stepfather's death during an aborted police drug bust, to her becoming the family maid, at age eight—if not a slave in her own home—to her kidnapping at age ten. Now, six months later, her life apparently taking a turn for the better, something had driven her to suicide.

In the article, Deidre had attributed the cause to constant harassment by the media, the innate cruelty of peers who at best shunned her, at worst teased and goaded her into numerous confrontations, and a mother who refused to give up her quest to get her child back. Lastly, she placed blame on herself.

"I had long since abandoned the impartiality of a reporter. I had become her friend. More than that, her confidante. Yet, like so many before, I'd abandoned her, though not by choice. It was necessary to protect her from further prying by the media. As long as I maintained any type of association with Renee, I was perceived by some of my peers as privy to inside information; able to scoop the competition. To protect her, I had to distance myself from her, and though she said she understood, I obviously misread her. I was like all the rest. I used her and now abused her. For this I can never forgive myself. Renee Barrows committed suicide today, and I could have prevented it.''

Deidre stared at the photo of the child; a school picture of a gaunt youth with flowing brown hair. As always, she was drawn to the eyes. Even in the black and white rendition, they hid the hurt that marked her existence. Renee had long ago pulled down shades behind her eyes and wouldn't open them for anyone.

Glancing down at the floor, Deidre saw a second piece of paper jutting from under her desk. In block letters, cut from a newspaper: CATCH ME IF YOU CAN.

Deidre felt the walls close in on her; the oppressive heat a blanket that threatened to smother her. *Renee* had delivered the supplies, and this folder.

Anger and self-recrimination welled within her, throwing off the nausea. She'd been face to face with her that morning, and all she'd seen was a mole and a scar.

She tried to form a mental picture of the woman and drew a blank. ''Dammit to hell,'' she said aloud, knowing she'd been set up. Renee had walked right into the lion's den, offered herself up, and Deidre had been done in by a mole and a scar.

As a reporter Deidre had taken pride in not only quickly measuring those she met, but photographing in her minds' eye their appearance; able to commit the description to words to bolster a story. It was unlike her to draw such a total blank. Maybe she'd been out of practice, what with a job that demanded so little. Maybe she'd been preoccupied, ironically, with the knowledge Renee was at the center of the storm that was the basis for the Task Force. Maybe it was the oppressive heat mixed with the sickening disinfectant.

Regardless, the eyes should have been a dead give-away. Deidre picked up the picture with the photo of Renee at ten. No mole, no scar, *nothing* could keep her from recognizing those eyes. They'd haunted her from the first day she'd met Renee at the hospital until they stared at her from the newspaper detailing her suicide.

She'd barely noticed the eyes of the woman who'd visited that morning. Could it have been someone else? Someone Renee had sent to deliver the folder with its challenge? No, the Renee she knew, even at ten, would not have involved another. And she was certain Renee wanted the face-to-face meeting; the danger inherent in being recognized, the challenge of duping an adversary. It had been Renee, if only a facade, for Deidre was sure it was all a clever disguise: a wig, surely, the baggy overalls to mask her shape, and the damned mole and scar. The mole, she knew was fake; the scar she couldn't be sure.

More importantly, how did Renee know she was onto her? It must have been the press conference the day before, she reasoned. Maybe the barbs she had tossed out the previous day had succeeded beyond her wildest expectations. Somehow she'd communicated with the woman, and Renee wanted her to know.

And, oddly enough, Logan had been right. Renee wanted to be understood, wanted to communicate with the media. Wanted to communicate with *her*. Whether she wanted to go public or not, was something she was sure she would learn in due time.

Deidre pondered whether she should show Briggs the article and message, but quickly dismissed the thought. Renee didn't fit the profile, and neither the article nor the challenge proved she was alive. No, this was between her and Renee. She promised herself, though, that from that moment on she'd be on her guard. Fool me once, shame on you, fool me twice, shame on me, she recalled the admonition she'd heard more than once in her career. She had to be at her best or Renee would continually outmaneuver her.

Though thoroughly distracted, Deidre put Renee out of her mind to concentrate on finishing the folder Briggs had given her. She had to look at each of the killings through the eyes of Renee to gain an edge.

Chapter Six

For Shara, the day seemed interminable. The excitement of meeting her old friend . . . her *only* friend other than the first Shara, tickled at her memory as she tried to concentrate. Fortunately, her idea of an interpersonal relationship at work consisted mainly of communicating with her computer. She had been stuck at the same job for three years, though she could easily have risen if she'd wished. With all the excess baggage she carried, however, a low profile was at first necessary. Later desired. Now essential.

Once home at 2:30, naked, she went through her daily aerobic routine, sweat pouring from her body as she finished. She wouldn't shower. Not yet. The rancid smell of her body was cleansing in a perverse sense. The filth of the city, the mingling of bodies in the elevator, and the eyes that pursued her night and day poisoned her to the core. The mindless exercise released the demons from within; the pungent odor a reminder of the dry rot that could only be expunged by destroying the prying eyes.

68

A daily ritual, she flipped on her CD player and Tina Turner's "Private Dancer," the only recording she owned, filled the room.

With the music, she was ten again, with memories of Shara flooding back, bringing fresh tears. Her faked suicide. Running off to Philadelphia, living in the streets that horribly liberating summer thirteen years before. Free from the daily scrutiny, the thinly veiled looks, teasing and taunting of her peers, whispered conversations of neighbors and strangers. . . .

"That's the girl who . . ."

"What a terrible shame . . ."

"She must have brought it on herself . . ."

". . . nice enough, but I don't know if I want her around my . . ."

She'd wandered the streets, steered clear of shelters and their probing questions. Never laid claim to a corner, alley or park bench for fear of some cop becoming overly inquisitive. Fearing the night for both the hungry eyes she couldn't evade and the real-life dangers a ten-year-old, going on eleven, could attract. Meeting Shara, a runaway herself, now sixteen, who'd somehow managed to scrimp and save to rent a place of her own.

Shara, who'd taken her in without question. Shara, who'd become a mother and eventually her lover, her *only* lover. Shara, who worked at a topless bar, so they'd have a roof over their head.

Shara who had introduced Renee to the wonderful world of computers and computer hacking. It was the one luxury they enjoyed, and no matter how desperate they might be for money, they never entertained the thought of pawning their computer. Hard times to be sure, but Renee had never been happier.

Shara, who had known all along who she was, but hadn't broached the subject until Renee was ready to confide in her.

Six years of bliss shattered when Shara was savagely

beaten by a customer who wanted to do more than look, and wouldn't take no for an answer.

Caring for Shara, who refused to go to the hospital: the money she couldn't afford, the questions she wouldn't answer, the fear they'd find out she was a runaway, and call her parents. No, a fatalist to the end, she had put herself in Renee's hands whatever the outcome. Three days later she'd died in Renee's arms.

From that day on she had become Shara. Renee no longer existed. Though underage, the club owner, feeling responsible for what had happened, gave her work; first in the kitchen, later as one of the dancers.

The song played over and over again, with Shara preening before the mirrors that surrounded her. The eight eyes that adorned her breasts holding no fear, for they were dead eyes.

She was snapped out of her reverie by her alarm. Three-thirty. She'd had to set the alarm for when it was time to begin her surveillance. Otherwise, she could literally lose herself for hours in the music and the dancing.

As she showered she planned the rest of her day. Like her room, each wall of the shower was a mirror. Whenever she turned she could peer at the eyes that caressed her breasts; assure herself they were indeed dead. She turned on only the cold water and allowed her mind to wander.

A cat nap, no more than half-hour was all she would need to recharge her batteries. The tattoo; Walt Grimes' eyes would be next. Then follow Robert Chattaway from work. His activities would determine her evening. And finally, a chat with Deidre. Maybe at one in the morning, possibly as late as three or four; whenever she got home. By now Deidre must surely have found the folder. At the thought her nipples hardened, water cascading over her body. She could imagine the shock. Deidre had been at arm's length with her quarry.

—she massaged the tattoos on her breasts.

What had she done? Gone to the cop, whatshisname, who was in charge of the case?

—her hand roved down her body, past her stomach to her pubic hair. She gently massaged her genitals.

No, this was to be a cat and mouse game played without interlopers. Deidre wasn't the impulsive sort. She was angry to be sure.

—she inserted a finger ever so gently into her vagina.

Humiliated at being duped.

—she probed deeper, a sigh escaping from deep within.

But she'd bet her life—actually had already done so—that Deidre would play fair. That had always been her shortcoming. Deidre had *integrity*, a deep sense of morality and compassion that did not allow for duplicity. It was why she'd ultimately fail in her quest to trap the child who had now become a woman; and the woman a killer.

—she climaxed, her body shuddering. Her fingers still probing her genitals, she slid down in the shower until she was seated, watching the dead eyes watching her. Laughter welled within and burst out like molten lava, as she thought of the men whose eyes had sought out women and children to rape and sodomize. Eyes that now would have to be content with watching her play with herself.

With Robert Chattaway, she would finally rid herself of the hungry eyes that tormented her dreams.

Chapter Seven

Deidre showered when she got home, needing to rid herself of the smell of disinfectant that clung to her like cheap perfume. She rewound the videotape of the evening news and watched herself at Agent Logan's press conference. While she'd been peppered with questions, this evening they hadn't used any footage of her. In the world of TV news, there was just so much you could fit into a two-minute report, and Logan was the "big" story of the day.

She did see herself next to him, and noted the strain and fatigue on her face. She felt every bit of it, and still had so much to do before she could even think of going to sleep. Renee's brazen foray that morning made her determined to prepare her plan of action. If Logan was right, Renee would strike no later than three weeks. From now on there would no time for procrastinating.

Showering, she recalled the first time she'd met Renee thirteen years before. The ten-year-old had been missing for six days when neighbor Edward Costanzo, under intense police scrutiny, cracked and led them to a remote cabin forty miles north of the South Philadelphia neighborhood from which Renee had been abducted. It was Deidre's first day on the story; the beat reporter having called in with the flu.

It was a summer day, oppressively hot, much like today, and dozens of reporters—local and national—were at the crime scene, hoping to get a photo of the child. Deidre had seen an ambulance parked a block away and decided waiting for the little girl to be brought out was a waste of time. She'd sauntered over to the ambulance, made small talk with a paramedic, and found out the hospital Renee would be taken to for an examination.

She'd left immediately, a plan formulating in her mind. At the hospital, she had found a nurse uniform and waited for the child's arrival. When Renee had arrived the hospital wasn't yet prepared for the onslaught of the media, and confusion reigned. After an examination, Renee was put in a private room and left alone, with one guard outside her door. Deidre carrying a soft drink was admitted, no questions asked.

Deidre had seen pictures of Renee Barrows; knew of her troubled past, but was still shocked at the gaunt figure all but swallowed up in the hospital bed. She looked like a child brought up by wolves in the forest; her long brown hair was a tangle of snarls, surrounding a face all bones and angles. Her eyes were skittish, following Deidre's every movement. She couldn't read anything in her eyes at all. No curiosity. No anger. Just watching her, as she observed the child. Deidre offered her the soda, which Renee accepted without a word and greedily wolfed down.

When she was finished, a tight smile tugged at her mouth.

"You're not a nurse, are you?"

Instinctively, Deidre knew she shouldn't lie to the child. To do so would be to lose her for good.

"Why do you say that?"

"No name tag. All the doctors and nurses had a name tag. And your shoes. The nurses I saw wore those ugly white shoes. You're in heels."

Observant, Deidre thought, further confirmation she'd have to be straight with her.

"I'm a reporter. For the *Daily News*. Do you want me to leave?"

"No . . . I don't want to be alone."

"Can I ask you some questions?"

"No. How about I ask you questions? I'll interview you."

"Tell you what," Deidre said, sitting on the bed next to the youth. "You ask me a question and I'll ask you one. Fair enough?"

The girl shrugged. "Okay. When was the first time you had sex?"

Deidre was thrown for a loop momentarily, but quickly recovered. Again, she was reminded of her initial impression of the child. This was no ordinary ten-year-old. She'd had to fend for herself most of her life, and was streetwise beyond her years. This first question was a test. If Deidre failed to answer, Renee would dismiss her. So, she told the girl how she'd held out until her high-school prom, though most of her friends had considerably more experience.

"Have you had sex?" Deidre asked.

"I've played around a bit, but I haven't gone all the way, yet."

Deidre didn't know whether to believe the first part of her answer, but decided not to press the point. Next Renee asked for details of the prom, which Deidre grudgingly gave. Then it was her turn.

"Edward Costanzo didn't have sex with you?"

"No."

"Did he touch you?"

"No, he looked, but he didn't touch."

"Not here," Deidre said pointing to her own breasts.

74

"No."

"Not here," she said, putting her hands in her lap, resting on her genitals.

"He looked, but never touched."

"You weren't wearing any clothes?"

"He made me take them off. I only had a blanket. He'd tell me to put the blanket down, and he'd look at me."

"Did he ever take his clothes off?"

"No. He touched himself, though, his hands in his pants when he looked at me." She stopped. "It's my turn now. Will you print everything I tell you?"

Without thinking Deidre countered with a question of her own. "Would you if you were me?"

"Yes. Everything."

"Why?"

"I should know when I'm talking to you that everything is fair game. Only fools tell reporters things they don't want repeated."

"Is it all so black and white?" Deidre asked, genuinely interested in Renee's response. It was like talking to an equal. "Maybe you'll tell me something that will hurt you or embarrass you. Shouldn't I take your feelings into consideration?"

"Pleeease," she dragged out the word, dripping with sarcasm. Her hands clasped tightly in her lap until then suddenly became animated; gestures punctuating every sentence. "Life is tough. If I'm a reporter I tell you if you don't want to see it in the papers, don't say it. I'm looking out for number one. I don't care about *your* feelings. I care only about the story."

"Your life has been that bad."

"I haven't met a hell of a lot of people who've been nice to me. I don't tell anyone my secrets. *Anyone.*" Her hands were balled up, pent up rage allowed to escape. "Tell someone a secret and it's not a secret anymore. I'd use it if I needed to. In school, if someone confides

75

in me, fine. But it's not *their* secret anymore. As for me, I won't say something if I don't want it repeated.''

Deidre decided not to press the point. She knew Renee had just given her permission to print whatever they discussed.

The give and take continued, and Deidre had her exclusive. Edward Costanzo had asked Renee to help her load groceries into his station wagon. She'd driven with him to the cabin. He was a neighbor, not a stranger to be shunned. And he'd always been friendly to kids. He had a pool table, ping pong table, and a VCR, which were not common in her neighborhood. Kids were always around watching a film or TV, playing games and eating candy and junk food that never seemed depleted.

When he told Renee he had new games at the cabin, she took him at his word. Once in the cabin, though, he'd enticed her into the basement and before she knew it he'd picked her up and thrown her into a cramped cell, six feet long and four feet high. There was no bed, only a blanket. There was a TV, and a camera so he could see her when he was upstairs. There was an intercom, so he could communicate with her. And there was a pot in case she had to pee or take a crap.

Throughout Renee's recital Deidre hadn't taken any notes. She'd been blessed with a remarkable memory and learned in college that people were more comfortable when they just talk to you without your scribbling notes or using a tape recorder. Just as important, Deidre was not as interested in the words themselves, but what lay behind the words. With her full concentration on her subject, she caught little nuances those with pads or recorders missed.

Abruptly Renee decided the interview was over.

''I'm tired. I think I'll take a nap,'' she said, leaving Deidre still full of questions.

''Do you want me to sit with you?''

''So you can ask me more questions when I get up?''

Deidre smiled. "Got me."

Renee smiled, too. "You have enough for now. Write your story. Then maybe we'll talk again."

"I'm not going to press you, Renee, but I don't think the police will let me in again after reading my story. We both know I'm not supposed to be here."

"You let me worry about them," and with that she closed her eyes and feigned sleep.

Instinctively, Deidre kissed her on the forehead before leaving. Renee's eyes jerked open, and for a second the veil that had covered them almost lifted. Eyes that had been expressionless almost spoke to her. Just as quickly, the curtain descended again. Renee closed her eyes, but there was a smile on her face.

Deidre was brought back to the present by the ringing of her telephone. Naked, dripping water across the carpet, she reached it just before her answering machine kicked in.

"You looked tired today." It was her father-in-law. As usual, no wasted greeting. She refused to play his game, though. "Hi Jonas, and how are you?" He'd, of course, ignore the question.

"Come over for dinner. We'll talk."

Deidre was shaking her head no into the phone. She had too much to do. But before she could utter the words, she thought better of it. Jonas had been her mentor before and during her marriage. She had no secrets from him, and whether he believed her or not, she knew she needed his insight.

"How could I turn down such an invitation?" She didn't wait for a reply. "Do me a favor, though. I know you've got a file on Renee Barrows. Take a look at it before I arrive. Okay?"

"Bring a dessert." A slight pause. "I'll have it read."

They ate dinner in silence, as was their custom. No small talk. No shop talk. No fancy meal. Burgers rare, corn on the cob, and the seven-layer cake Deidre had brought.

Deidre had come from a typical white middle-class home; her parents springing the full bill for college at the University of Pennsylvania. A journalism major, she first met Jonas Caffrey when he'd conducted a series of guest workshops at school. Most of the other students had been awed and intimidated by the Pulitzer Prize winner. Their questions were timid and insipid, they groveled and kissed ass.

Even then, Deidre saw the man beneath the tough exterior. As preparation she read dozens of his articles between classes until she knew what made the reporter in him tick. By the third session, she'd captured his attention, and that summer she became his intern at the *Inquirer*. His first and only intern.

Upon graduation, he'd helped her land a job at the *Daily News*. He didn't want her at the *Inquirer* where it would be perceived she'd get preferential treatment because of his sponsorship. He'd help her with advice, but she'd have to sink or swim on her own.

After six months of mindless features, she'd caught a break with the Barrows case and had made the most of it. Now, over coffee, she asked if he had read the file.

"Some good writing. A lot of dreck, too; mostly the pieces about the child. Problem with you, girl, you always get too close to the victim. Protected them. Edited out the dirt. A lot of bullshit."

Renee had told her the same thing thirteen years earlier. After the interview at the hospital, Deidre had filed a story that had the populace setting up trust funds, sending her toys, and lining up to be foster parents, if her mother was denied custody. She'd told Renee's story . . . with certain omissions. The public wouldn't understand, she thought, the child's bitterness and "shit on you" philosophy. She felt Renee needed to know others cared, that the world wasn't filled solely with scum. So she softened the edges and painted a sympathetic picture.

That afternoon a Lieutenant Collins had called. "I should lock you up for obstruction of justice with the stunt you pulled at the hospital," he began.

"Flattery will get you nowhere," she responded, knowing she'd raise the ire of the police department and the admonishment was inevitable. But she wasn't about to apologize for doing her job.

"We've got a problem," he went on, ignoring her comment. "Seems Renee Barrows won't speak to us without you present. And . . . ," he hesitated, and she could feel his anger. "She *demands*, doesn't ask, but demands, mind you, that you have full access to her. Only then will she cooperate."

Deidre had to hand it to Renee. She had thought with today's story she'd be near the top of the police department's shit list, just below Edward Costanzo. No way, she had thought, she'd get a second interview, but Renee would not be denied. She decided to be conciliatory to win the officer's trust, if possible.

"Lieutenant, Renee needs a friend, someone she can trust. For whatever reason I've won her trust. I'll be up front with you. She's a tough kid, and she won't be intimidated by the police. I suggest you do as she asks. For my part, I promise I won't print anything that will compromise your case. Within reason, if you tell me something is off limits you won't read about it in the paper the next day."

He'd agreed and half an hour later, she was back in Renee's hospital room. Deidre had trouble negotiating her way through the room. Flowers elbowed one another for space. Toys, mostly dolls of every sort, lay in piles in their boxes. Renee was sitting on the bed, a stuffed teddy bear by her side, her hair washed and combed, a pink nightshirt replacing the hospital gown she'd worn the day before.

"Quite a haul," Deidre said eyeing the clutter.

"All due to your story." She sounded less than thrilled, Deidre noted to herself.

"You saw it?"

Renee put her finger in her mouth and made a gagging sound. "You laid it on kinda thick. The girl I read about *wasn't* me. You made me out to be weak and vulnerable. Someone to be pitied. I should be pissed."

"Then why do you insist on my presence before you'll talk to the police?"

"I'm a star," she said, her hands sweeping the room with all its gifts. "Or a freak. I'm not the naive child you make me out to be . . . and you know it. Sooner or later, I'll have to tell my story. This morning already three reporters tried to sneak in. I'm not going to be part of some circus. I trust you . . . sorta," she said with a smile. "We've got an understanding. Way I figure it, if I give you, what do you call it . . . uh, an exclusive," she snapped her fingers as she found the right word, "I keep them off my ass."

"I can live with that," Deidre said.

"Bet you can," Renee snapped. "I'll make you famous."

"I don't know about that."

Renee shrugged. "Just do me a favor. Don't make me out to be some wuss. If people want to give me money and clothes and toys and candy, who am I to say no? But, I don't want their pity. All my life those who've messed with me have gotten more than they bargained for."

"I won't make you into a wuss, but I don't think the public is quite ready for the real Renee. I'll give you to them in small doses."

"So they'll sympathize," she dragged out the last word derisively, then stuck out her tongue at Deidre.

"What's wrong with that? You've been screwed all your life. Now it's payback."

"Know what your problem is?" She didn't wait for

an answer. "You can't go for the jugular."

Deidre shook her head in astonishment. "Where does a ten-year-old learn about going for the jugular?"

"Not from school. I hang around with a lot of street people. Hookers, number runners—people like that. *They're* my real teachers. They teach me about life, about going for the jugular. It's like this, if I get into a fight at school with a boy bigger than me, I kick him in the balls and scratch at his eyes. He may hurt me, but he won't mess with me again, and others gets the message, too. It's too much trouble. There are so many others to pick on who won't put up a fight.

"You're like those soft kids in your reporting. I bet you've had an easy life." She lay back on her pillow, her hands behind her head, a smile on her face. Deidre could tell she was enjoying making her feel uncomfortable.

Deidre was about to protest, but Renee ignored her.

"You don't go for the balls in your story. You write what you want others to think of me, and to hell with the truth. It's all bullshit."

". . . bullshit," Renee had told her.

". . . bullshit," Jonas told her now, placing one of the articles on the table.

As usual he had picked up nuances others missed. *Edited out the dirt.* She began to defend herself to Jonas, but he dismissed her with a wave of his hand.

"We both know your strengths *and* your failings," he said. "I'm not into that saccharin crap, but I've never condemned you. You got the exclusive. You told her story. Leastwise some of it. Enough of that. Why am I reading ancient history?"

Deidre told him her theory. He asked no questions, and his face betrayed nothing as she spoke. She saved Renee's morning visit for last, showing him the article of her suicide, and the CATCH ME IF YOU CAN challenge.

"Never bought the suicide myself," he said as she finished. "Not the type."

While Renee's philosophy of life had remained hidden from the public, Deidre had shared it with Jonas. She'd used him as a sounding board, though she had for the most part ignored his admonitions about making Renee into a martyr. Until now, though, they'd never discussed the suicide.

"The question is what do I do?" she asked. "I'm not comfortable going to the police, even with this," she said holding up the paper she'd received that morning. "It'll be dismissed out of hand. It doesn't fit their profile. And even if they do believe me, I'm out of the loop."

"Still the reporter," he said, smiling for the first time. "Thought you'd gone soft on me. The mouthpiece of the Mayor." He spat out the last. He didn't have anything against the Mayor, just a disdain for politicians in general. It was ironic, since he had gotten her the job with the mayoral candidate when she had been in her funk. Now he just shrugged. "Flush her out."

"How?"

"Make her come to you. Come to you pissed. She'll slip up. Give herself away, if properly goaded."

"And how do I do that?"

He held up the file he'd read with clippings of the kidnapping. "It's all here. Do a retrospective. Talk to the mother; the half-brother, the kidnapper's family. But twist the stories. Sympathize with them. She won't . . . *can't* let it lay. Open up lines of communication, then go for the kill."

"I like it." Then she shook her head in exasperation. "She still is in control, though. It's all fine and good to make her come to me, but I've also got to go on the offensive.

"I've been thinking of two lines of attack to try to

locate her, in conjunction with the retrospective. Tell me what you think.''

Her first suggestion was a real longshot. Trying to find out Renee's new identity by locating someone who may have taken her in when she ran away.

"Let's assume, since she's here now, she never left the area after her faked suicide. She had no friends, no contacts. She's on the street in Philly, an eleven-year-old. No way she can live off the streets for long. Cops would have picked her up at some point. There must have been a shelter where she stayed or someone who took her in.''

Jonas looked doubtful. "Waste of time, if you ask me." Then he shrugged. "Worth a shot, though. You can't do it. Too recognizable.''

"I was thinking of Royce Timmerman. He's discreet, and could charm a farmer out of his prized bull.''

Jonas nodded approvingly. "Good choice. Your other idea?''

"I want to use the FBI profile, but apply it to Renee.'' She told him of Logan's view that the killer had to have access to police records not available to the public; that he thought to narrow the search to those with a military background, possibly a cop, and someone with a knowledge of computers.

"I think she's a cop or a secretary at the Roundhouse. It was just too convenient that she knew where to find me today *before* the location became public. I need someone to look for a woman who graduated from the Police Academy sometime within the past five years. Also those who enrolled but dropped out, and other women employed at the Roundhouse in that same period of time. Someone claiming to be twenty-three years old. Once we locate them, we eliminate those who couldn't fit her description. At that point, I'll have to identify her. What do you think?''

"That one I like. I know who can do the legwork.''

"Who?"

"You're looking at him."

"Are you sure?"

"I'm chained to a desk at the paper. Two think pieces a week. Could write them in my sleep. I'm not dead and I'm not senile. I've got the time. Got some contacts. Or are you putting me out to pasture, too?"

"I was hoping you'd volunteer," she smiled. She yawned, looked at her watch and started. "Jesus, twelve-thirty already. I best be off. If I'm going to interview Renee's family, I've got a lot of raw data at home I have to review."

"Whatever. Get some sleep, though. Can't think if your mind's in a fog."

As Deidre left she could feel the adrenalin flowing. She hadn't felt so alive since . . . since her husband and son had been killed. She'd find Renee Barrows. What she refused to consider, at least for now, was what she'd do when she found her.

Chapter Eight

To those he worked with at Duvall's Sunoco, Robert Chattaway was a free spirit. It was Friday. Payday, and all eyes were on him as he drove the Ford Taurus into the bay for an oil change. At four-thirty every Friday afternoon, Chattaway scheduled an oil change. He raised the Taurus on the lift, put a pan on the floor to catch the oil, and loosened the bolt that would send the oil cascading. As he did so he stood directly under the flow, and let out a whoop as it poured over his head, onto his uniform and all over his body.

The others cheered; two mechanics, and a gas jockey who'd come out to witness the weekly ritual. Two months earlier it had occurred accidentally for the first time; Chattaway's eyes glued to a teenager at the self-serve pump, her breasts all but out of her halter top as she bent to pick up the gas cap that had fallen to the ground.

Now it was his way of ushering in the weekend. He wouldn't be working until noon Sunday. Two days to *party down*.

After finishing the oil job, Chattaway collected his paycheck from Guy Duvall. Initially, Duvall had viewed with disapproval the young man's Friday antics. He had even confronted him with an ultimatum to cease and desist or find a new job. But it was an idle threat. For all his playfulness, Chattaway was a natural around cars, and astute customers refused to leave their cars until assured that no one other than the gangly young man would touch their vehicles. Duvall knew the kid could find another job within an hour at greater pay, so he'd swallowed his pride.

For his part, Robert—"Don't call me Bobby, I'm not a kid anymore"—made sure to clean up the area of the spill before clocking out. Looking at the paltry stub, he knew he could demand a higher salary, but it wasn't in his nature to be greedy. The tips he made more than compensated for his relatively meager wages, and they weren't taxed. Regardless of how much he earned, by the end of the week he spent all his disposable income, after making sure all his bills were paid.

Chattaway's mother had opened a savings account for him in grade school, but after depleting it upon graduation, it had sat dormant. He had no insurance of any sort. With no family to support, he had only himself to care for. A fatalist, he'd long ago decided if he got sick or seriously injured the State would have to bail him out.

He walked the three blocks to his apartment on Oregon Avenue, his greasy hair tied back in a ponytail. Those who didn't know him mistook him for a gawky teenager, though in point of fact he was twenty-nine. For no reason he could pinpoint, he'd stopped aging at sixteen. He'd never had to shave, and had long ago given up trying to grow a mustache. His face was baby smooth, with the exception of the few zits that erupted here and there, much as they had when he was a teen. Hence, his decision, when he turned eighteen, that all would address him by his given name Robert or feel his wrath.

At six-foot-four and 155 pounds those complimenting would refer to him as willowy; to most he was a string-bean. His colleagues—for he had no friends—knew better than to tease him, however. While his body appeared that of one of those nerds who muscle-bound beach brutes kicked sand on in commercials, his hand and arm strength were a match for those who worked out daily at gyms.

He'd won $100 when he'd first been hired a year earlier, beating each of the mechanics arm wrestling. He'd broken Luis Palmero's wrist, to Duvall's displeasure, and volunteered to do double duty without extra pay while it healed to avoid being fired right on the spot.

He had only two vices: cameras and women—*young* women. He'd built his own darkroom adjacent to the bathroom, and owned an assortment of cameras. The only magazine he subscribed to was *Popular Photography*, and when he saw the latest innovation in 35-mm technology, he could never pass on it. With no steady girl, nor other obligations, the tips he brought in usually made their purchase well within his means.

His wardrobe was fashionable, though not extensive. A television was his main entertainment except when he went clubbing. The rest of the furnishings in the one-room efficiency were second hand.

Showering with Lava to rid himself of the oil that clung to his body, he planned his evening. A new teen club had opened up near the Granite Run Mall, a twenty-minute drive since the completion of the Blue Route, which made the surrounding suburbs more accessible to city-dwellers. Pennsylvania's 21-year-old drinking age made these clubs popular hangouts, and when it was his wish he seldom returned alone. Admiring himself in the mirror, as he dressed, he knew that while his peers might tease him behind his back, he was a good looking *boy*; one teenage girls would fight to possess.

GYRATIONS was your typical teen dance club. Large, loud and impersonal. He arrived at ten, the din of the music, audible from the parking lot, assaulting him as he paid the five-dollar cover. With his predilection for young girls, he felt blessed with his youthful appearance. He received no more than a cursory glance when he entered and no suspicious glances from those serving soft drinks. To those in the dimly lit club he was just another teen out for some pussy, which suited him just fine.

For an hour he scoured the crowd, dancing only occasionally when a girl brazen enough asked him. Not wanting to attract attention, a few spins on the dance floor allowed him to blend in. The non-stop music, records, which on weekends were spun by a local deejay, discouraged conversation.

He was looking for a certain type, but a good many of the young girls appealed to him. Even those he'd bet had had sex exuded an aura of innocence. It was one thing to get laid, another to be on your own, fend for yourself, and come up against a hostile work world. A good many were virgins of the mind, if not the body.

He searched for someone who'd come in alone. As much as some girls might want to be picked up, those who arrived in groups invariably left together. While no bigot, he ignored the black chicks. He couldn't see bringing one to his lily white neighborhood. Didn't make sense to arouse suspicions.

Then he saw her at the door. Alone. Self-confident, she pretended to scour the room for friends who weren't there, or didn't exist. No more than fourteen, he'd have to find out how she got there; if she had a ride home or expected to meet someone to provide the necessary transportation. She was average height, with long brown hair and bangs she was forever moving from her eyes.

Tight jeans molded her body; a skin-tight body top accentuated small breasts. Too young to compete with those more endowed, she wasn't the least bit self-conscious about showing off what she possessed.

Robert watched for perhaps twenty minutes as she danced with several boys, none for more than one dance. Twice she shook her head no, probably, he thought, at an offer of a soda.

Robert had learned not to make his move too soon. Girls like this one never committed to the first guy they danced with, no matter how good-looking. She wanted to get the lay of the land, have a good time. If she met the right guy, so be it, but she wasn't about to accept sloppy seconds.

She bought a drink for herself, catching her breath. When the drink was almost empty, Robert made his way over, and asked her to dance. As the song wore down, and another took its place, he thanked her and moved on.

As he danced with another girl, he saw his mark giving him the once over. He noted her indecision and smiled to himself. This mating ritual had rules and the quickest way to score, oddly enough, was to break those rules. He hadn't allowed her to turn him down for a second dance or a drink. He'd suddenly piqued her interest. A new song, and he asked her to dance again. Her self-confidence was restored, but would she dare say no if he made his move now? Often the answer was yes. At one club Robert had been rebuffed by four girls before he connected. Tonight, though, luck was with him. He asked her if she wanted a drink, and she shook her head yes.

He led her to a spot where he wouldn't have to yell to be heard. A bit of small talk. Her name was Nicole—Nikki to her friends. He found out she went to school in the area. She said she was sixteen, a sophomore, but he doubted it. He asked if she'd driven to the club. There was a moment of hesitation; sixteen-year-olds could drive in Pennsylvania, and saying no might confirm she was younger than she'd said. She finally told him her girlfriend and her date had dropped her off and gone to a movie. They wanted to be someplace where they could talk, she said with a wink.

"Are they going to pick you up?" he asked.

"Only if I can't get a ride," she said, a smile telling him she hoped it wouldn't be necessary.

He knew he'd won her over when she added she wasn't going home; she told her parents she was spending the night with her girlfriend.

At eleven-thirty, he asked her if she wanted to go for a drive. They were both swathed in sweat from dancing, and he could tell she was a bit giddy, even though the drinks were non-alcoholic.

She acted surprised when he actually started the car. She assumed, he was certain, he'd asked her to the car to make out. She sat close to him, an arm around his waist, what there was of her left breast pressing against his side.

"Where we going?" she asked. "Gloria's expecting me back at one."

He ignored the last. "I thought we'd try my place." He'd told her earlier he'd dropped out of high school, found a job and a place of his own. Now, he felt her pull back a bit. He was enjoying this. She wanted to make out with him, not necessarily make it with him. Agreeing to go to his place was tantamount to giving the green light. He tried to put her at ease.

"I like you Nikki. Like you a lot." He put up a hand to stop her from interrupting. "I'm just not cut out to make out in cars. Hell, this is the first time I've been to one of these clubs." He paused a moment, as if in thought.

"Tell you what. You can call your friend as soon as we get to my place. Tell her exactly where you are, and that I'll drive you to her house by one. Or, I can drive you back to the club now. It's your call.''

Robert had used the same line on any number of girls. Two times girls had asked to return to the club. He'd brought them back. He wasn't about to force a girl against her will. There would be no yelling or struggling in his car. It was far too risky, and there were far too many fish in the sea for him to act foolhardy. Now he slowed the car, awaiting Nikki's decision.

''Long as I can call Gloria from your place, I don't see the harm.'' She snuggled up to him again.

When they entered his apartment, she went straight to the phone.

''I don't think so, Nikki.'' There was a hard edge to his voice.

She turned, her eyes widening at the straight-edged razor in his hand.

He liked this part. Liked it a lot.

''I don't want to hurt you, Nikki,'' he said without raising his voice, ''but I will if I have to. Scream and I'll cut you. Your face will look like railroad tracks, and you'll need a bag over your head before you get another date. Do exactly as I say, and you'll leave without a scratch.''

She looked at the knife in his hand, and began to whimper. ''I lied. I'm not sixteen. I'm fourteen. Look in my purse.''

He ignored her. ''Take off your clothes and lay on the bed.''

She was sobbing now, paralyzed like a cornered rabbit knowing she was doomed.

He crossed the room and put the knife within an inch of her face.

''Take off your clothes and lay on the bed. Now!'' he said, with controlled fury.

Fumbling, she undressed and did as he said. Once on the bed, he put leather straps from the bedpost to each of her arms, spread-eagled, then did the same with her legs.

He went into the bathroom and got his camera, a Nikon F1. She was crying, begging him not to rape her, as he began taking pictures. He spoke to her nonstop to heighten her fear, for the camera to document.

"It's your own fault, Nikki."

Snap.

"Going off to a stranger's apartment. What did you expect?"

Snap.

"At the very least, I'm going to screw you."

Snap. Snap.

"I wonder, are you still a virgin?"

Snap.

"Don't mind someone touching your little titties."

Snap.

"Maybe don't mind a hand in your pants."

Snap.

"But have you gone all the way?"

Snap.

"Would you do it for me?"

Snap.

"Will you beg me to screw you to save your life?"

Snap. Snap.

"How important is your life?"

Snap.

"Give me a blow job?"

Snap.

"Would you do that?" Here he pulled down the zipper of his jeans. Her eyes widened even more.

Snap. Snap. Snap.

"If I brought friends in, would you do us all?"

Snap.

She was shivering now, eyes closed, as if she didn't look, she wouldn't hear.

Snap. Snap.

He bent down and stroked her cheek. She opened her eyes, a new dimension of terror seemed to grip her at his touch.

Snap. Snap.

He told her to close her eyes, and she instantly obeyed. He put a piece of duct tape over her mouth and went into his darkroom. Forty minutes later he came out, a dripping stack of 8 × 10 black and white prints in his hand. Her eyes were still closed and he laughed cruelly at her blind obedience. Told her to open her eyes, so he could show her something.

He showed her the pictures. She looked bewildered as he slowly flipped through the headshots. He had captured her torment with shots of only her face, as if her body didn't exist.

He untied the straps. Told her to get dressed. Said he was taking her to Gloria's just as he had promised.

Once in the car, she screwed up her courage. "You won't get away with this. I'll tell. I know where you live. I'll have the cops on your ass like white on rice . . ."

With one hand on the wheel, he flipped open the knife. "Haven't you learned anything, you dumb bitch? I could have raped and killed you. Still can, and you go mouthing off to me about going to the police. Even if you were to go to the police, don't tell me. I'm a crazy son of a bitch, or haven't you figured that out? Do you think you're out of the woods yet?"

This shut her up.

"Let me tell you something, you little shit. What are you going to tell the police? I didn't rape you. An exam would prove that. And I'll burn the photos and negatives when I get home." A lie, but there was no way she'd know.

"The police come, and I tell them we met at the club. You told me you were sixteen, and I thought we'd have some fun. I found out you were fourteen, and didn't want to get involved with no minor. So I drove you back to your friend's house. You were pissed off. You invested a whole evening with me, and I wouldn't even feel you up. Now, are the police going to have much sympathy for you, dressed like a tramp, or are they going to look at the evidence and see nothing?

"So, go screaming to the police, little girl. They won't believe you. Worse, your name will be mud. Word will get around, you know. What will your parents think? You lied to them. And the boys. Think of the boys whispering behind your back at school. A slut, or worse, a cock-teaser. Think about everything I said, and everything I didn't do. Then do what you gotta do."

They drove in silence for a while. Finally, he asked her for directions to Gloria's house, dropped her off and made his way home. He knew she wouldn't call the police. Everything he'd told her was true. Actually, he'd done her a service. She wouldn't be driving off with any strangers soon. He might have even saved her life.

At home, he took out the pictures which were still damp. Looking at her tortured expressions, he jerked off.

Chapter Nine

Shara watched, the headlights of her car off, as Robert Chattaway dropped the teenager off. She had seen enough to confirm her worst fears. Bobby had come back into her life, as dangerous as ever.

He had enlisted in the army two months after her suicide.

She had totally lost track of him until two years earlier, when, with her hacking skills honed, she'd been able to access certain military files. Curious, she had checked to see if he was still serving his country. He was. Based in Germany for eight months, he had just returned to the States. He was posted at Fort Bragg his last five months in the service.

She found it somewhat odd that he'd never risen in rank. And while she knew soldiers were routinely transferred from base to base, she noted he never remained in one place more than two years; usually far less. He'd separated from the service, of his own volition, a year ago, but there was a flag on his record used to alert civil authorities of misconduct that should be made available under special circumstance; those dealing with sex crimes.

There'd been a number of complaints in his records of his penchant for underage girls. The word rape was never mentioned, but apparently wherever stationed, he'd soon worn out his welcome and been transferred. The complaint at Fort Bragg had been filed by a Major, and Bobby's behavior apparently could no longer be swept under the carpet with another posting.

Shara found he'd been given a choice of a court-martial or resignation. He'd chosen the latter then moved back to Philly. Shara had been haunted by his presence ever since. Only now would he have her full attention.

Shara had followed him to the night club, remaining in her car until he'd come out with the teenager. She parked outside his apartment until he brought the shaken girl downstairs, and followed him to see what he planned to do with her.

While curiosity burned, she fought the urge to question the youth when he let her out. She had to maintain a low profile. Anyone associated with Robert Chattaway would soon be questioned, and she couldn't chance any encounter with one of his victims. And she knew the girl surely was a victim, from the way she stumbled to the front door of the house.

A part of Shara wanted to instantly know what had occurred at the apartment. Was the girl forced to perform oral or anal sex? Had he videotaped their sexual escapades with threats of blackmail? Shara didn't need instant gratification, though.

The mystery actually intensified her curiosity. As before, Bobby Chattaway's secret would unfold in time. Learning his secrets would be infinitely more satisfying than their final confrontation; though in this particular case, she longed for the confrontation itself more than any of the others.

She'd follow Chattaway for the next week. Learn his

patterns. At the appropriate time, when he was off hunting, she would break into his apartment for a thorough search, bug his place so she could document what he did, then retrieve the device, if he stuck to his habit of taking the girl home when he finished with her.

She was more than satisfied as she got home and freed herself from the confines of her clothes. More often than not, her initial surveillance was uneventful. Days, even weeks had passed before the offender would make the move that confirmed her research. Bobby had gone hunting the very first night she'd sat in wait for him. He must be a busy man, she thought. What aroused her curiosity, now, was what he had done to this girl, and undoubtedly others since his return, that dissuaded them from going to the police.

She paced her room, marveling at the new tattoo that adorned her breasts, while mulling over the possibilities. He must have learned something from his indiscretions in the army, for there hadn't been one complaint filed since his return. It was a puzzle, but far from being frustrated, when she found no answers it only excited her more.

Now, just after two, there was something more she had to do. She carried the phone from her desk to the opposite corner of the room, where two mirrors converged. While on the phone, she would watch the silent eyes watching her, as she watched them. If she kicked back and lay down, she could stare at herself from the mirror on the ceiling.

Surrounded by herself, she dialed Deidre's number.

Deidre picked up the phone on the first ring, and Shara was surprised there was no sign of sleep in her voice.

"Did you get my package this morning?"

There was a gasp on the other end of the line. Shara lay back, looking at herself in the mirror, her back resting against the cold concrete floor. She was enjoying this. *C'mon, Dee*, she thought. *Get a grip on yourself.*

"Renee . . ." a tentative question?

"Not any longer, but I guess it will do for now. How's my favorite reporter, or should I say, *Mayor's Media Liaison*. You've come a long way since I made you."

"What are you talking about?"

"Without me, you'd still be covering the opening of the new Convention Center or a baby born in an elevator during a power outage."

"Bullshit," Deidre snapped at her.

"Whatever," Shara said nonchalantly.

"Don't patronize me, you son-of-a-bitch!" Deidre fumed.

Shara kicked her feet in the air with glee. She'd hit a raw nerve, and could feel the anger reaching out from the other end of the line. She could picture Deidre trying to regain control, and remained silent.

"Why contact me now? This morning, I mean?" Deidre asked. "I knew you were the Vigilante, you know," she said smugly, "*before* your little message."

She's bounced back, Shara thought, and, oddly enough, she was glad. She relished the challenge Deidre presented. She had so little human contact; no close friends at all since the first Shara. She'd secretly hoped this confrontation would be one between equals.

"Of course you knew, but honey, I *knew* you knew. That's why my little visit. It was in your eyes during your press conference. Trying to get to me by saying how I 'get off' by killing. Please, it was a little too transparent. Just blowing hot air. Your eyes told the story. When did you figure it out?"

"You tell me, since you know it all."

"C'mon, Dee, if you're going to be hostile, I'll just hang up. I didn't call for abuse." A ruse, but a necessary risk. How much did Deidre want to keep the dialogue going? As much as she? Maybe more?

"Don't hang up," Deidre said hurriedly.

More, Shara thought, and had to stifle a laugh.

"I . . . I didn't know till that day. I hadn't been involved until then. It was the message on the mirror."

Shara was silent for a moment, thinking how Deidre could have linked her to the missive on the mirror. It was true she had mentioned Hungry Eyes to her often enough after the kidnapping. She saw the connection, but marveled how quickly Deidre had noticed it.

"You're good, Dee, I've got to admit that. The message wasn't for you, but you must have known that. Hadn't thought of you in years, no offense. But you picked right up on it. Good for you, Dee. So, should we meet and talk about old times?"

"Don't play with me, Renee. I know you're no fool. You're not about to meet me and risk a trap. Tell me, Renee, why the killings? And why now?"

She *was* sharp, Shara thought, and again felt relief. She needed Deidre to understand. Not all of it. And not all at once. But, as she'd given little bits and pieces thirteen years ago, she would offer just enough now to establish a rapport; a working relationship, so to speak.

"There'll be no cutting to the chase yet, Dee. You know you'll get what you want in time, if you're patient. I want someone to talk to, okay. Someone to understand. We were pretty tight back then. We set the ground rules for the police and they agreed. Ignored the rest of the media, and there was nothing they could do about it. But, I wasn't about to give it to you all at once. You had to earn each morsel. And there were some things you never learned."

"I don't think so, Renee. Sure, it was like pulling teeth, but in the end you gave it all up. Maybe I played your little game, but you were a child, after all. I gained your trust, and you laid it all out. So, don't try getting me to second-guess myself.''

She was fishing, Shara knew, but she wouldn't take the bait. To fill in the missing piece from thirteen years ago would lead Deidre to her now, and she wasn't quite ready. She'd allow Deidre this little victory; a hollow victory because it was a lie, but she was enjoying her chat, and would most definitely call again. It had been seven years since she'd really talked to anybody, and Deidre, after all, was one of only two people she'd ever confided in.

''Do you remember, Dee, the last day in the hospital; the third day? We'd talked twice alone, and then I'd answered questions from the police. All they wanted were the facts. Why did I go with that fool Costanzo? What did he do to me? 'Did he touch you?' you asked once, and accepted what I said. But, they asked at least a dozen times. And in different ways, like I was lying and they could trap me. They seemed disappointed that he *hadn't* touched me, *hadn't* raped me. Then they left and . . . remember what you asked?''

''Why didn't he touch you?''

''Yes, YES! You and *only* you asked the important question.'' *Least you thought you did*, Shara thought to herself, but wasn't about to alienate her again. ''The fucker never touched me because he was afraid of women.''

''He'd touched your half-brother, you told me. I remember, Renee. Remember it like it was yesterday. Then I asked you if you were scared of him?''

''I liked that. I'd never said anything about ever being scared. *Everything* I told you would make that question seem ridiculous. Was I scared? Shit, yes, I was scared, and told you, too. I knew there was something wrong with Costanzo. He'd never kidnapped anyone, as far as I knew. He was so jumpy, like once he got me chained up, he didn't know what to do with me. He left me alone for long periods of time. Sometimes I wondered if he'd ever come back. *That's* what scared me.''

"The unknown, it would scare anyone," Deidre said.

"I was never afraid he'd hurt me. I was a hard-assed kid; thought I was sorta invulnerable. He couldn't hurt me, no matter how hard he'd try. But I thought he might panic. I mean, could he let me go? I knew the police were looking for me. It was all over the TV he let me have. He'd painted himself into a corner. But I didn't think he'd hurt me. No, what frightened me, *terrified* me, was that he'd abandon me. Leave me to rot in that cell. I'd never be found, least not until it was too late.''

Shara was silent, the past rushing back at her. Yes, she'd been afraid of Costanzo's abandoning her, but there was something else that terrified her even more. Something she hadn't told Deidre, and wouldn't. Not yet, and maybe never.

Deidre brought her out of her reverie.

"That's when you won me over, Renee. All these doctors on the tube were talking so much psychobabble without having spoken to you. Imagine, they said, how traumatized you must have been, feeling Costanzo might kill you at any time. They based their conclusions on studies of others. That you might not fit their profile didn't bother them at all.''

"I used to yell at them, those doctors on the tube. Until they got used to it, nurses used to run in to see if something was wrong," Shara said.

"They deserved to be yelled at." Deidre paused, as if in thought. "But, were they right after all, Renee? Did what he do so traumatize you that you've now got the urge to seek revenge on those who rape and molest innocents without getting punished?''

Shara laughed. "You *are* good. Lull me into your protective womb by talking about the past and then question your conclusions to get me to talk about the present. Sorry, though, no sale. Let me lay it out for you, Dee.

You follow certain rules, and you'll get everything. Not now. Not all at once. But I'll be an open book for you by the time we're done.''

"I'm not going to lie to you and promise not to track you down."

"I *want* you to try to track me down. I want to see how good you are. I want to see if you've changed in thirteen years. Actually, I know you haven't."

"What's that supposed to mean."

"You were always so straight with me. You always asked permission to print what I told you, even after I'd told you you were free to print *anything* I said. You weren't just being polite. It's a weakness of yours. Some might call it a strength. Compassion and all that shit. Even now, you can't lie to me. You won't betray me. You want my permission to outsmart me, to locate me. I told you this morning. Catch me if you can."

"You're no longer a ten-year-old, Renee. I'm not asking permission to hunt you down. You're a cold-blooded killer. I have an obligation to catch you before you hurt others."

"That's not what I read in the papers. I'm performing a community service. Ridding the world of scum the police and courts can't or won't."

"There's got to be more to it than that."

"There is. Want to find out?"

"You know I do."

"All right. Then it's you and me. No cops. Let them look for their killer. You find me, then you can tell the cops . . . if that's what you want. But no interlopers now."

"And if I agree, what do I get in return?"

"Answers to your questions. Why I faked my suicide. Why I let you know I wasn't dead. What kind of life I've led since. Answers to questions the cops don't give a fuck about."

"I'm still a puppet on your string."

"That's the price you pay to satisfy your curiosity. And you're free to track me down, at the same time. And, Dee, if the police do get me, it'll be you and me against the world again. I'll deal with you exclusively."

"Why do I get the feeling you're still toying with me? That I'm still coming out on the short end of the stick?"

"I guess you have your demons you have to come to grips with, just like me."

She was aware that Deidre ignored the comment. Maybe it was too close to home.

"How do I get in touch with you?"

"You don't. I contact you."

"All right, Renee. No police. Just you and me."

Shara could feel Deidre's anger building again.

"But I'm not the novice I was then," Deidre said. "Don't underestimate me. I *will* track you down. And when you've told me everything, I'll hand you over to the police. And then you'll still deal with me and only me."

"Give it your best shot, girlfriend. Catch me if you can."

She hung up.

Chapter Ten

Deidre slammed the receiver down. Renee had taken her by surprise. She hadn't been prepared, and it angered her. After Renee's visit that morning she should have foreseen the call. She was still rough around the edges. A step slow. Out of sync. Cliche after cliche came to mind, but the message was clear.

To catch Renee, she would have to be at the top of her game. No more surprises. No more lapses. She had to go on the offensive; had to rock her somehow to show she was a worthy adversary. Tomorrow, she decided, she'd track down Renee's mother, and bring it all back: the abuse, the negligence, the squalor. But from a grieving mother's eyes, not Renee's. That would piss Renee off. Get her back on the phone. And just maybe she'd say something in the heat of anger that would betray her.

For now she replayed the conversation they'd just had in her mind, writing it all down, and then going over a number of items that bothered her. She'd have to analyze them and pursue them in their next foray.

The message wasn't for you, Renee had told her. Was she referring to society as a whole? Was it a plea to herself? Or, was there someone else she was communicating with, even if the police weren't cooperating by withholding the handscrawled missives?

Renee had told her *I want someone to talk to, someone to understand*. Logan was right in thinking the killer would communicate with someone from the media, but for the wrong reasons. Renee didn't want to go public. She didn't want notoriety. She was no avenging vigilante; of this Deidre was sure. The killings were intensely personal; played out on the large screen of the entire city, to be sure, but that was purely incidental. And, she needn't worry about Renee contacting her. Now that they'd connected once again, she was sure Renee, in her own fashion, would lay bare all her secrets.

All her secrets. Deidre didn't want to dwell on it, but a thought was niggling at her memory, refusing to be locked away. *There are some things you never learned*. There, she'd said it. Had Renee told her everything thirteen years before? What disturbed her was the possibility Renee had used her then, just as she planned to use her now. Was there something significant Renee had omitted? Worse, had she lied? Had Costanzo touched her? raped her? She could understand the child's reticence to admit such atrocities. Or, had the entire incident been fabricated by a devious little girl who craved attention? Had she coaxed Costanzo to abduct her as a game? With the media explosion had it all gotten out of hand to the point she'd had Costanzo chain her up?

Costanzo hadn't shed any light on the subject. He'd appeared tongue-tied upon his arrest, uttering only garbled apologies. Then he had clammed up. Wouldn't even confide in his lawyer. His attorney wanted to plead diminished capacity; wanted a comprehensive psychological evaluation.

Costanzo had refused, and entered a guilty plea. A reticent judge had accepted the plea, but tried to pull a fast one by asking for a psych evaluation before he passed sentence.

Six weeks later several flustered psychiatrists had to admit failure. All attempts to gain Costanzo's confidence had been fruitless.

In the end the judge had little choice. Fifteen years. Costanzo had died five years later from a heart attack, having never spoken a word about his abduction of Renee Barrows. He would have been eligible for parole in another two-and-a-half years.

Deidre hadn't dwelled on it at the time. She was too involved with Renee, but why the silence? Was Renee but one of many victims, with Costanzo fearful more serious crimes might be uncovered had he not so quickly agreed to a guilty plea? If Renee had been holding back, it was something she had to probe.

No more hungry eyes. Deidre underlined this on her pad three times. Just what did Renee's cryptic message mean?

Which led to one last question that Renee had evaded. Why now? Why these killings thirteen years after her abduction? Were these the only killings? She knew the FBI had looked for similar cases, but so far had drawn a blank. If none were found, then what had triggered Renee's rampage just over a year ago?

She could see her investigation taking a totally different route than the police. Sure, she wanted to track Renee down, but solely catching her would not satisfy her hunger for closure. There were loose ends from thirteen years before that now obsessed her. And, she wanted to know what made this woman tick today.

The anniversary of Renee's release from Costanzo's "Cell of Hell" as it was dubbed, was two weeks away. She would use this when telling both the Mayor, and in all probability a more suspicious Briggs, why she wanted some time to investigate and write her retrospective.

She'd still be doing her job; it was just that she had time on her hands. All politicians kept a low profile near the end of the summer. As long as the trash was picked up on time, and no crisis, such as a teachers' strike loomed, the populace was in the throes of getting the most out of the remaining beach days. Deidre would be in daily communication with the Task Force, but she expected no hard news, especially since they were totally off base with their assumptions.

On her appointment calendar, Deidre made a note to call Royce Timmerman at a decent hour in the morning for an early-afternoon meeting. It was Saturday and unless a major story involving the Mayor broke, she had the day to herself.

She'd also call Loretta Barrows, in the hopes of convincing her to cooperate with the retrospective.

She was aware exhaustion was creeping up on her. It had been a long day. She went to sleep, but couldn't banish Renee from invading her dreams.

Chapter Eleven

Every Saturday, Robert Chattaway visited his mother for a late-morning brunch. The two-bedroom rowhouse was the only thing of substance his mother owned. The mortgage had been paid off with an out-of-court settlement; the result of a wrongful death suit filed against the city. Robert hadn't had much use for his stepfather, but his untimely death had had a definite upside. The two-bedroom house, which had once seemed to be cramped, was now spacious, as his mother was its only inhabitant.

Although he never slept there, his mother had kept one of the bedrooms solely for him, just in case he changed his mind. Robert didn't visit his mother for companionship, nor out of a sense of duty, nor for a good home-cooked meal. The brunch she cooked was little better than he could get at a greasy spoon or fast food restaurant. He visited for the pictures, hidden in an envelope beneath a floorboard he had pried loose when he was fifteen.

In his room, after a mostly silent meal, he looked at his pictures, knowing his mother would never invade his privacy. He needn't worry about his mother coming in to dust or clean either, during the week; not that she'd find anything amiss. The house, as always, was filthy. Had been so ever since his half-sister had left.

The photos were in chronological order. He'd shared the bedroom with his half-sister, and the first dozen were of her, starting from when she was eight until she was ten, the expressions on her face showing she'd been caught by surprise. He'd caught her in the shower several times, made easier by the fact they'd had no shower curtain. His half-sister would dutifully lock the bathroom door whenever she went in, but it made no difference. All the doors in the house opened by the same old-fashioned skeleton key. Robert would wait until she'd been in the shower five minutes, slip in and snap photos as she glowered at him in anger.

She had finally resorted to baths, covering herself in suds so there was nothing to see. What she didn't comprehend was he could have cared less about her body. Even at ten, she was a skinny little thing. It was the expression on her face he'd scrutinize for days after he'd developed the black and white pictures in a darkroom at school.

Surprise, embarrassment, anger, hatred. Her body had become a distraction, so eventually he'd blown up only her face with its raw emotion. He marveled at how self-conscious women, in particular, were when caught naked. With three places to cover and only two hands, there were the awkward attempts to hide everything, which often resulted in one part of their anatomy sticking out like a sore thumb. What they didn't understand was, at least as far as Robert was concerned, if they just stood there staring at him impassively, he would have turned on his heels in disappointment. For, along with the attempt to cover up, there were the many shades of emotion that quickly passed over their faces. It was these Robert craved, and with few exceptions the women he photographed obliged him with a wide range of moments to savor.

He had a second set of photos of his half-sister that he prized even more; photos he'd taken of her over a short period of time when she was ten. She was not only aware of his presence, but both her body language and facial expression challenged him. She was a captive audience, but to her credit she'd confronted him head on. These were full body shots, for in these her body spoke volumes. With these, the face alone would not do. Oddly enough, she was the only girl he'd photographed whose body had spoken as loudly as her face. There were times he wished to recreate such a scene, but—tied down—the girls he photographed now didn't communicate with their bodies.

At one time he'd visited clubs with naked dancers, but they never satisfied his need. Their bodies indeed spoke to him, but these were jaded women and the body language was fabricated. It was only the young, the inexperienced, the innocent that moved him, and he'd never found it at any strip joint.

He leafed through the next set quickly. Photos of girls he'd taken while in the army. They were full body shots of young teenage girls that had gotten him in trouble. As he'd never touched the girls, never had sex with them, it wasn't until just a year-and-a-half before that he'd gone too far and been drummed out of the service.

"Going too far" had been going after the thirteen-year-old daughter of a senior officer. While by this time he'd taken only facial shots, her father had enough pull to insure he'd no longer wear the colors of his country.

The last stack consisted of photos he'd taken since his return. Facial shots documenting innocence lost, as he threatened unimaginable sexual and physical acts of violence on young girls who wanted a taste of what adolescence had in store. He'd offered them a look at the dark side of sexuality, and their faces betrayed a naked emotion that would be dulled and muted when they actually engaged in sexual intercourse.

Robert took all of the photos home with him each Saturday, after brunch. He'd gaze upon them most of the afternoon, then hide them beneath a floorboard in his efficiency. There was the added thrill of having the photos within his grasp when he brought a girl home most Saturdays. If he miscalculated, and the police found the pictures, he was in deep shit. But life devoid of danger had no appeal for him. He almost wanted the police to demand a search. Would they find his hidden hoard of incriminating evidence? He doubted it. And, being no fool, he returned them to his mother's house Sunday morning while she was at church; with her chronic arthritis, it was one of the few times she left the house.

If shrinks ever got ahold of him, he wondered what they'd make of his perversion, for he didn't lead a normal life. He'd never been abused as a child, though a case could be made he'd been neglected. Actually, from the time he could get around he'd been left to fend for himself. That, in and of itself, though, was no reason for his desire not to have physical or emotional contact with others.

One of his earliest memories was listening to his mother and one of her innumerable boyfriends screwing. His father had long since tired of his mother, and had left for parts unknown. Afterwards a steady flow of "uncles" had visited, some staying just a night, others returning over a period of weeks or months, even one or two hanging around for a short period of time.

At eight, two years after the birth of his half-sister, his mother had ballooned into a blimp. While he didn't comprehend it at the time, the only way she could attract men was offering herself to them. At the time, she'd craved companionship. He recalled how she would cry when one of his "uncles," who'd been around for a while, tired of his mother and left. He knew it was best, at those times, to steer clear of her. While she wasn't physically abusive, she had an acid tongue and would lash him with it whenever she was alone. It was his fault, and the little "bitch" whom he shared his room with, who were the cause of her inability to keep a man around.

With his room just across from that of his mother, and the walls no thicker than cardboard, he often overheard his mother's lovemaking. There were times when he thought she was being physically abused, so loud were her cries. But he'd never considered bursting in and saving her. Hell, if he had to navigate childhood without her guidance, much less her love, he wasn't about to have his ass handed to him by some man being rough with her. She'd taught him the law of the jungle, after all, and he didn't believe in double standards.

Moreover he was often confused by her rantings, which after a few minutes changed to grunts and groans, and at times he clearly heard her asking for more. At these times he knew she wasn't protesting or in need of his help. For some reason she was actually enjoying herself.

Out of morbid curiosity, he'd borrowed a copy of *Penthouse* from another kid in school, and learned what he'd heard was commonplace. His mother's lovemaking noises, that sounded so painful, were actually utterances of joy. At what point that joy turned to pain would become *his* obsession.

He'd only been with girls a few times in his life, and had found it wholly unsatisfying. What he found most repulsive were the sounds they made as he fondled and then screwed them. Rather than hearing Jessica, Valerie, or Carla, deep into foreplay, he heard his mother's sexual bleatings. More than once he'd gone flaccid when her voice became overpowering. While some of the girls were understanding, others belittled him, as if it were his fault.

It also upset him that with their constant demands he never really got a chance to look at these girls, to differentiate what might be pain from ecstasy.

He'd gotten that chance solely by accident. At fourteen he'd gone out with a girl several years older than he was. After a few dates, she'd told him she wanted him to make love to her. At a motel she'd cajoled him to allow her to tie his hands to a bedpost. She'd then toyed with him, and had him totally under her control. She'd said vile things to him. Worst of all she'd even threatened to leave him there after she was done to be found the next morning by a cleaning woman. As she untied him, she told him it was all part of the game. Told him how much she'd enjoyed seeing him squirm at her taunts and threats. Though apologetic, she told him that was how she got off.

He'd asked if he could tie her up, and she'd acquiesced. When he was finished, he couldn't remember all he'd done, but he'd somehow terrified her. He remembered hitting her in anger over his own imprisonment earlier. He remembered the rough sex, and her pleas for him to stop because he was hurting her. Most of all he remembered being able to watch her face, and seeing the flow of emotions. At one point, when he threatened to leave her, as she had told him, she had laughed. Furious, he *had* left, though only for an hour.

When he returned the look of anguish on her face turned him on more than any lovemaking he'd ever experienced. *She'd believed him*, he thought, and all the while had been conjuring up images of being found in the morning, her parents being contacted, and the humiliation that would follow. She told him as much, as tears cascaded down her cheeks in gratitude at his return. Fascinated, he immediately left again, this time staying away for two hours. Again, upon his return he focused on the expression on her face. Now tinged with relief was fear and confusion. Would he leave again? And, if he did, would he ever return?

He'd never felt so horny, though he had no desire to relieve his needs by making love with her. He'd untied her, and again watched her face as she hastily dressed, obviously fearful he'd change his mind and tie her up again.

It was the beginning, he knew, of his lifelong obsession. Physical contact with another was unnecessary. The few times he'd had sex again were only preludes to getting his partner to acquiesce to allowing him to tie her up, so he could study her.

It was also at that time that he'd first began taking pictures of his half-sister. With a camera he was able to relive the mood swings, and naked emotion he could never hold in his mind. He soon found that he didn't even have to have sex to achieve his goals. Sex itself became a distraction.

Through deception he was able to entrap others and photograph them without having to touch them. And oddly enough, some, after the terror wore off, found the experience to be more exhilarating than sex itself. Some girls wanted—some even begged—to go out with him again. But it was never the same as the first time. Knowing he wouldn't harm them, it became a game to them, and their reactions were transparent and false.

It was also at this time that he found that there was a much more intense reaction from girls who had never actually had sex than those who were experienced. As he turned sixteen, he felt the need to date girls younger than himself. And, in fact, he found it much easier to date girls thirteen or fourteen. To be asked out by an older boy was a compliment of the highest order. "I'm too mature for boys my age," he recalled some girls telling him, when he asked them out.

The pattern established, over the years it would be fine-tuned. He'd had his brushes with near disaster in the army, but now he'd established a routine that was all but failsafe.

Now with the pictures that chronicled his secret life in an envelope under his arm, he made his way home. On the way he stopped by a playground, took out some biscuits his mother had forced upon him, and let his eyes wander.

The kids here were too young for his tastes; most with mothers and fathers hovering over them, as they played on the playground apparatus.

But a few youngsters were accompanied by their teenage sisters, and he stared at them, fantasizing their altered expressions if they were in his apartment instead of the safety the crowded playground afforded. A few even flirted with him from afar; their eyes betraying not-too-innocent thoughts.

He looked at his watch and saw an hour had passed. How he loved the weekends. With no obligations, he could have spent the day ogling at those ogling him, if he were so inclined, without feeling any guilt or remorse later.

Then he thought of the laundry. A cloud passed over his eyes. It was the *one* thing he had to do before he prepared for the evening. Then a smile replaced the frown. Tina Campanelli's daughter, Roberta, was working at the laundromat. At thirteen-and-a-half, she'd given up her jeans and overlarge Phillies t-shirts a month before, in favor of skirts that hugged her pert ass and blouses with two, sometimes three buttons undone that had neighborhood boys salivating. All of a sudden a hell of a lot of boys were volunteering to do the wash.

Roberta thought they were immature, and all but ignored them when Robert came to do his wash. He liked her; wanted more than anything to expose her to his camera, but that wouldn't be prudent.

Still, no one seemed bothered that she flirted with him shamelessly. He was a known commodity, after all. Polite, good-natured, someone who pitched in during the infrequent snowstorms that all but paralyzed the city. Someone who'd fix a minor problem with their car in the evening without charge. He even refused to take a tip. Better she come on to dependable Robert than some teeny bopper who had serious desires to get into her pants.

Robert left the playground to get his dirty laundry, a bounce to his step as he stripped Roberta bare in his mind, wiping that flirtatious smile from her face forever.

Chapter Twelve

Shara would be the first to admit she wasn't operating with a full deck. But, as she gazed at Chattaway's photo collection, she knew she was dealing with a seriously sick individual. Sicker than she could ever have imagined.

What separated the two was she knew she'd gone off the deep end. Bobby, she felt, would go to his grave fervently denying any perversion.

Shara had followed him throughout the day. She'd noted the thick manila envelope he carried as he left the rowhouse at noon and watched him fixate on young teens at the playground. She donned her blond wig to watch him fawning over the teen at the laundromat. At nine that evening, he'd driven away; Shara guessing he was out to pick up another underaged girl for some sort of recreation. She'd have plenty of time to search his flat, and plant a bug before he returned.

Chattaway's lock was of the two-bit variety, and soon Shara was searching for the envelope which she was sure documented his atrocities. It took a half-hour, but once she found the floorboard she was able to enter his world.

The full-length photos of the girl who'd been Chatt-away's first conquest intrigued her to no end. But they were ancient history. Shara wanted to know what had caused his military discharge and what he'd done to the girl the night before.

It all lay before her. She cringed at the facial expression of the girl she'd glimpsed only briefly the night before. With no full-length shots, it was impossible to tell just what he'd done, but it was clear this child had gone through a gauntlet of emotions, all of which Bobby's camera had captured.

Replacing the photos, she planted a bug behind the bed, after noticing the leather thongs she assumed he used to tie his prey down.

Outside, in her car, she waited. She was at once exhilarated that soon she'd know Bobby's secret, yet sickened at the prospect of hearing a child's spirit irreparably broken. One look at the pictures, and it was obvious that what Bobby viewed as little more than a game had devastating effects on his victims.

In time she'd tell Deidre about Chattaway, and those she'd already killed; let her into the demented world of those who tortured, humiliated and destroyed the psyche of innocents, and mocked the efforts of the police and the courts who stood idly by.

At 12:45, Chattaway arrived with a diminutive brunette Shara guessed was no more than thirteen. They walked hand in hand, and disappeared into his efficiency.

Shara's breathing quickened as the scene unfolded. Phrases stood out, and with each Shara saw one of the photos she'd imprinted on her memory.

"Take your clothes off. Now!"

—the girl's terrified pleas.

". . . your fault . . ."

Snap.

". . . off to a stranger's apartment . . ."

Snap.

—the girl's sobbing.

". . . do it for me?"

Snap.

". . . give me a blowjob?"

Snap.

". . . friends . . . do it for us all?"

Snap.

Shara had curled up in a fetal position on the front seat of her car, silent tears flowing down her face, her hands ripping at her blouse, kneading, then scratching the sightless eyes that dotted her breasts. It was as if her self-inflicted pain would absorb that of the child in the flat above.

Then silence from within. She listened intently. There were faint sounds she attempted to identify. Not the sounds of bedsprings. No, Bobby was not raping the girl. Something flowing. Her mind searched. Water! The darkroom. He was developing the pictures he'd just taken. Then he was back in the room again, talking softly to the child.

"Scared you . . ."

"Don't deny it."

". . . here in black and white . . ."

". . . could have done it all. Should have."

Then his tone became harsh and commanding.

"Get dressed, bitch. Can't stand the sight of you. Should I throw you out to be raped by the trash on the streets? Would serve you right, you know."

Sobbing from the child.

Blood dripped from Shara's breasts. Their blood; the blood of those who'd stolen the souls of others before snuffing out their lives. Better dead, she thought, than to relive the horror inflicted upon them night after night after . . . Better dead than to grow up forever scarred, as she had.

Better dead.

The slamming of the door pulled Shara from the past. Her past. Chattaway half-walked, half-carried the young girl at his side, his eyes darting right to left to assure they were alone. Then into his car. Gone.

Shara fished in the back of the car for a black sweatshirt. Her blouse was in ruins. She wasn't surprised. She'd instinctively attacked the eyes each time her prey feasted on his quarry. The first time, before the second kill, she'd looked down to find her white t-shirt covered with blood. As she often had to follow her prey or retrieve a bug, as she had to tonight, it would do no good to be seen with blood-soaked clothing. So, she kept a black sweatshirt in her car at all times. There wasn't a lot of blood; none of the scratches were deep. She'd be careful that none dripped on the floor when she went back to Bobby's apartment to retrieve the bug.

Back in his efficiency, Shara could smell the girl's fear wafting within the room. She glanced into the darkroom and saw the drying prints suspended from a clothesline. Pictures no different than those she'd seen earlier, but with a life of their own, as she'd heard the pitiful pleas and tearful sobbing that evoked them. How she wished Deidre could have witnessed what she had. Would she then be so quick to condemn? Or would she rush headlong at Chattaway upon his return, her nails groping for his eyes?

Soon she'd play the tape for Deidre. Play all the tapes, but this one in particular. Try to make Deidre understand what drove her to kill.

Later, when she had regained control, she'd plot Chattaway's death. She had her confirmation, next she'd have to learn his routine; determine when he'd be most vulnerable. Then she'd confront him.

Soon, now, his reign of terror would end. Sooner than with the others. An inner voice beckoned as never before. Bobby Chattaway had to be stopped before the following weekend or the hungry eyes would devour her, and he'd be free to plunder.

And plunder.

And plunder, again.

Chapter Thirteen

Royce Timmerman was a bookie. And a charmer. It was why Deidre sought him out mid-morning Saturday. She had called Loretta Barrows at ten, and though reluctant, Renee's mother had agreed to an interview at three in the afternoon.

Royce Timmerman had more nicknames than a porcupine had quills. To Deidre and a few select others, he was Timms. To most he did business with he was Tiny Tim, though he was anything but tiny. There wasn't a donut safe when he was around, and exercise nowadays revolved around the remote of a television. Fifty-two, he'd once been stocky, but he'd long since gone to flab. The more weight he gained, the more hair fled his scalp; an oval of thinning hair now surrounded a glowing dome.

Timms had been a successful television ad salesman, with a penchant for gambling. Unfortunately, he had a perpetual cold when it came to sniffing out winners. He'd considered joining one of those twelve-step groups after his marriage hit the skids and his bank account consisted of a few bills in his pocket. He'd been talked out of it, though, by his bookie. Lester Beaumount knew Timms hated his job, and while he was no psychologist, felt it was at the root of his addiction.

"Want to stop gambling real quick?" Lester asked him, so his version of the story went. Timms had shrugged. Another Good Samaritan with a foolproof remedy.

"You work for me. I teach you the ropes, get you connected to the right people."

Lester was sick; had been for four years. Never went to a doctor. Decided if it was his time to go, so be it, but he wasn't going to be cut open, prodded and probed only to be told he was dying anyway.

He took bets on how long he'd last, and had cleaned up to everyone's surprise. He wanted to pass his wisdom down before he keeled over, and felt Timms a prime candidate.

With nothing to lose, Timms accepted Lester's offer, and lost his appetite for gambling within a month. He saw himself in too many of the losers who frequented the bar they worked from. It easily beat getting up in front of a group of strangers and spilling his guts.

Lester died a year later, and the powers that be allowed Timms to succeed his mentor.

Deidre had researched a story on compulsive gamblers five years earlier and had been steered to Timms. By this time he'd become proficient at his craft. Anything but impartial, Deidre had come onto him with an attitude, but Timms had easily won her over.

"I'm no saint, girlie, but there's some people that got the bug. Haven't bet a dime in seven years, now, but I been there and I'm not out to screw the poor bastards. I don't look to rip the heart out of those who can't get the monkey off their back. Guy's down on his luck, I'll help him out. Guy needs a place to crash, he's only got to ask. Guy's over his head I can say no, and pass the word no one's to touch his action. But I'm not a social worker. I'm a businessman. Just like I was, man's got the fever, no way of stopping him.''

"You're a saint, Mr. Timmerman," Deidre had replied, but without as much sarcasm as she wished.

"Let me give you a tip, girlie. Make no bones about it, I drop dead tonight, someone else'd be here tomorrow morning. Maybe someone who hasn't been there before. Maybe someone who'll squeeze the last dollar out of some poor schlep, and point him to a loanshark. Sad to say, but if you're any kind of reporter you'll find there's a lot worse than me. With me here, at least there's someone looking out for them. I use, girlie, but I don't abuse. Few are so civic minded.''

And sad to say, that's what Deidre learned from the scores of anonymous interviews set up by Timmerman. And not one of them had a bad word for the man that took their money. He was a godfather to a dozen kids, and lavished them all with expensive gifts. Any man who tried to pawn one of his gifts became an outcast. They knew it, and respected his rules.

He consoled the football widows, and mediated domestic squabbles. In hushed whispers, they told how Timms had donated portions of each week's earnings to shelters for abused women. More than once he'd paid the rent for a family about to be evicted because the old man had piddled the rent money on a bum horse. Yet, he made it clear to them that he was no soft touch. He wouldn't subsidize a family forever. And more than once, he'd advised a distraught wife to move out and on with her life, as he'd no longer pay the bills.

Later, when Timms learned Deidre had a thing for kids who'd been through the wringer, she'd received whispered phone calls, which invariably led to a child with a horror story that begged to be heard. With some snooping of her own, she learned the leads came from Timms.

She hadn't seen him since she'd lost her family. At the funeral, he whispered he'd be there if she ever needed him. Now, she'd come to collect.

Deidre entered the Jockey Club, and spotted Timms where he always sat, his back to the wall in the far left corner. He liked to survey the clientele; could tell a hell of a lot about a man by how he walked or sat, what or how much he drank.

He hadn't changed much in the last two years. A little less on the top, a few more wrinkles on his face, a few more pounds on his frame.

They engaged in some small talk, and soon it was as if she'd only seen him yesterday. He made her smile. He made her laugh. Even with all on her mind, there was no escaping his charm.

"So, girlie," he finally said, a twinkle in his eye. "You didn't come down here to reminisce, sad to say. And I can't imagine what the Mayor would want with me. Possibly, a hot tip he has and a wager he'd like discreetly placed?" He laughed as Deidre was about to protest.

"Where's your sense of humor, girlie? I was just funning you. So, don't keep an old man in suspense. What can I do for you?"

Long ago, Deidre had learned the best way for her to motivate her informants was to be straight with them. They respected her confidence, and what she said never passed their lips. Some might have thought her naive, at first, but she chose her sources carefully, disdaining those with loose lips. So, now, she told Timms about her theory about a girl who'd committed suicide who was actually the Vigilante. She told him her problem, and what she needed.

"Renee ran away, but I'm betting she didn't run far. No need to. She was dead. No one was looking for her. It's no more than speculation, but I have a hunch some-one who ran a shelter back then knew who she was, and took her in. Gave her a new identity and made sure she wasn't recognized."

"And you want me to find out who took her in?"

"It's been thirteen years, Timms. All I've got are some pictures of her when she was ten." She took them out and handed them to him.

"But, if anyone can track her down, you can. A name, Timms, that's all I need. Her name. The name she took when she abandoned Renee."

He was silent for a moment. She couldn't tell if he looked thoughtful or skeptical.

"I know it's a longshot," she went on thinking he needed convincing. "I'm assuming she stayed in the area. And after thirteen years, there can't be too many people who could be of help. But I can't stand by and do nothing . . ."

He held up a fleshy hand to silence her. "Don't have to sell me, girlie." He smiled. "Good to see you doing real work again. Talking for that pansy Mayor . . ." He waved a hand in dismissal. "Your stories were your calling, and it pained me to see you give it up. But there's fire in your eyes; the same fire the first time you visited me. If they were daggers, I wouldn't have stood a chance, even if I'd had a cocked shotgun pointed at your gut."

"I'll take that as a compliment, Timms, I think," she said, laughing.

"It was meant as one. Anyway, *if* this child didn't leave the city when she up and killed herself, I'll find out." He smiled. "You can make book on that."

She planted a kiss on his forehead when he promised to get back to her in two, three days at the most.

Half an hour later, Deidre was staring into the surly, suspicious face of Loretta Barrows. Deidre really couldn't blame her for the outward hostility. The media as a whole had come down hard on her thirteen years before. And while Deidre had focused on Renee, and the media circus that surrounded the child, she'd be the first to admit she hadn't had a kind word to say about the girl's mother.

The years hadn't been kind to Loretta Barrows. Seriously overweight when Deidre had seen her after Renee's kidnapping, she was heavier now, if possible. She hid her body in a dress that could have masqueraded as a tent, but her face told the story. A triple chin had replaced the previous double version. Her skin had the pasty look of someone seriously ill. She wore her hair tied back, which only accentuated her large face and fleshy jowls. Her eyes were the color of Renee's, but where Renee hid her emotions behind her baby blues, Loretta Barrow's eyes were an open book; a mixture of anger, pain, betrayal and hostility toward the reporter who stood before her.

As if this weren't enough, her body emanated an odor of decay. As she ushered Deidre inside, she winced as she hobbled, cane in hand, to an overstuffed easy chair. As she sat down, dust billowed forth, though if she noticed it, she hid it well. Once in the chair, she didn't plan on getting up to extend hospitality.

"Don't be expecting me to offer you no coffee or tea. With what you and yours done to my family, it's a wonder I let you in." She lit a cigarette, her fingers brown from nicotine, and wheezed as she drew on the unfiltered smoke.

Deidre let the woman vent her anger; a fury which having been bottled up for thirteen years now flowed like a river through a broken dam. Deidre recalled the media had lambasted the woman after Renee's disappearance, then attacked her even more viciously after her rescue, when the Department of Human Services had put the child in a foster home. Loretta Barrows deserved the tongue-lashing she received daily, for at the least she neglected her child. At the worst she was an abusive woman who treated her only daughter like a slave.

Loretta Taglio had borne two children. Her son's father had married her when she became pregnant at sixteen, but had left after Loretta kept putting on weight after giving birth and becoming little more than a couch potato.

In the intervening five years, before she became pregnant with Renee, she'd had numerous one-night stands and short-term lovers; oddly enough, teens, for the most part, interested solely in sexual experimentation. None were in any way romantically attracted to the woman. Any one of three to five men or boys could have been the father of her only daughter.

When Renee was five, fortune smiled on the family when Anthony Barrows inexplicably fell for, and married, the ever-expanding woman. Word of mouth in the neighborhood, reporters had unearthed, was Loretta told Anthony she was preggers and old-fashioned that he was, he married her against his better judgment. He went so far as to adopt Renee, and bestow her with his surname. Loretta had conveniently had a miscarriage, but Anthony stood by his woman, nevertheless.

He'd been killed when the police had raided their home on a bad tip, having had the misfortune to be cleaning a gun he kept for protection. With the money the city eventually paid to the grieving widow, she'd paid off the mortgage on the South Philadelphia rowhouse.

She'd never worked a day in her life, and was soon on welfare, not too proud to live off a city that had so thoughtlessly taken her man and breadwinner.

Renee, eight, became the family's live-in maid. The few clothes her mother bought dwarfed the child; all the better for her to grow into. She was a frequent visitor to thrift shops, with neither her son nor daughter owning anything but underwear that had not been worn by some stranger before.

All this and more had been dutifully unearthed by the media in the course and aftermath of Renee's kidnapping. DHS, the Department of Human Services, fully aware from neighbors' complaints of neglect, had removed Renee from her mother's care upon her release from the hospital after the aborted kidnapping.

There were even intimations, which Deidre totally discounted, that Loretta had sold Renee to Edward Costanzo as a sex slave, and knew where she was the entire time she tearfully appealed for her return. She had initially not fought the DHS placement of Renee in a foster home, but reconsidered when money started rolling in; the funds put into a trust account she was denied access to. And there were, of course, lucrative book and movie offers that would benefit the grieving mother *only* if she regained custody.

Yes, the media had raked Loretta Barrows over the coals pretty savagely. Her fifteen minutes of infamy had brought her only bitterness.

She looked at Deidre now, holding up a clipping Deidre recognized as one she'd written for the *News* on the kidnapping.

"I hope you're a better reporter now than you were when you wrote this crap," she said scornfully. "This ain't my daughter you wrote about. She had you conned, didn't she? Making herself out to be some helpless little thing in need of loving. Helpless, my ass," and she balled up the article she held and threw it to the floor in anger.

Deidre knew better than to argue with this woman. To gain her trust, she'd have to confide in her; tell her some journalistic secret that the woman would be able to use as gossip with her friends.

"Let me be honest with you, Mrs. Barrows." She paused. She decided against asking the woman if she could call her Loretta. "To protect Renee, gain sympathy for her, I smoothed out the rough edges, if you know what I mean.''

"Lied! Just like all them other bloodsuckers.'' She took out more clippings from a dog-eared folder. Deidre guessed Loretta Barrows spent many a night bitterly re-reading the media's spin on her neglect.

"A LITTLE GIRL'S LOST CHILDHOOD,'' Loretta spat out, reading the headline of one article. "Fucking pansies. Never worked a day in their lives. When I was growing up *I* did my mother's bidding; did the chores like I was told, and didn't complain. Because Renee had to do some cooking and cleaning *I'm* an unfit mother.''

There was much more, of course, Deidre knew. Loretta sent her to buy cigarettes as late as one in the morning. The girl had a moth-eaten coat, too thin for the cold of winter, too heavy for spring and early fall. Renee was sent to buy groceries; told to put the bill on the family account. Even the most sympathetic store owner eventually had to send the girl away, as bills went unpaid month after month.

Nevertheless, seeing Renee shivering in the cold of winter, even those who knew better never sent her away without some morsel for herself. The food, as demanded, was duly delivered to her mother to be shared by the entire family.

Loretta went on. "Here's a good one: SHOCKED NATION RUSHES TO OFFER HELP,'' with a picture of Renee's hospital room crammed with toys and clothes. The story had captured the attention of the country. The *New York Post* sent two reporters, one to cover the Costanzo angle, another to get an exclusive interview with Renee. When Renee refused, dealing solely with Deidre, the reporter had scoured the neighborhood, printing fact and innuendo but not checking for accuracy.

According to the reporter, Christmas at the Barrows' household was just another day; no gifts, no tree, no holiday spirit. Birthdays, likewise, went unnoticed. Teachers were interviewed, and then castigated for allowing the neglect to continue. At Thanksgiving, a basket of food was routinely delivered to the Barrows. It was well known the family was in need, but that's as far as it went. Renee often had bruises on her arms and legs and teachers had their suspicions, but DHS had never been contacted. The *Post's* writer stretched the theory into three articles, and the flood of clothes, toys and money began.

"White trash, that's what they called me. Spare the rod and spoil the child. Bullshit. Them bruises, Renee got from fights she got into all the time. Dished out better than she got, too," she said proudly. "But to listen to your people, I beat her regular to keep her in line."

Here Deidre knew Loretta Barrows spoke the truth. Renee had told her of the fights she'd had in school. It was part of her kick-them-in-the-balls philosophy Deidre had kept out of her stories. And Renee had adamantly told Deidre her mother never beat her. Didn't have to. Renee knew her place at home. She did her chores, hell, kept the household running, then escaped to the streets.

Renee's friends, which the other reporters never ferreted out, consisted of hookers, street people, even numbers runners. Renee had told Deidre stories galore how they "educated" her to life on the streets.

Some neighbors had pointed reporters in the direction to those Renee hung with, but when interviewed they'd shrug their shoulders in ignorance. No one gave them shit, except when they wanted something. Seeing how Renee was raking it in without their help, they held their tongues so as not to sully the portrayal of the poor pathetic child.

Lastly, Loretta held up two articles, her face reddening as she scanned the headlines: BATTLE FOR RE-

NEE and MOTHER ASKS FOR HER DAUGHTER BACK.

"You and your kind drove my child away from me. Poisoned the minds of them do-good social workers and faggot judges till they took her away from me for good. They let me see my child one day a week, and then only with some stranger to keep an eye on me, like I'd snatch her away."

For the first time she had to choke back emotion, tears forming around her eyes. "Without her mama's love, she had nothing, and killed herself."

In point of fact, Loretta hadn't put up a fuss until talk of movie deals and books began to materialize. Big money was involved, but the focus was, of course, on Renee, and without custody Loretta was a fifth wheel. After Renee's suicide, interest waned completely. TV movies had to have an upbeat ending, and here there was none. The two reporters from the *Post* put out a quickie book, published five weeks after Renee's death. Loretta didn't get a penny. With Renee's death the cash cow was gone, and Loretta was resentful. Deidre now saw an opening.

"You have no reason to trust me, I'm fully aware. But at the same time you have nothing to lose. I want to tell your side of the story. Tell the world how you've suffered, and what you've lost. To be perfectly frank, if you help me generate enough interest, the television people might come knocking at your door. *Hard Copy, Inside Edition*, even *Donahue* pay now. MOTHER BLAMES WITCHHUNT FOR LOSS OF CHILD: SUFFERS IN SILENCE FOR THIRTEEN YEARS. That's the headline I'll suggest. As I said, you have nothing to lose, and everything to gain."

Deidre could see the woman's mind at work. Dirty laundry exposed again, the downside. But easy money, maybe even fame, could make the mud-slinging much easier to swallow. Though wary, Loretta Barrows was won over, and she and Deidre talked for another hour.

Deidre would tell Loretta Barrows' story. She would make her appear to be the aggrieved party. She'd play fast and loose with the neglect, make Loretta Barrows into a sympathetic figure, and in the process draw the wrath of her prey. An angry, out of control Renee, with her youth distorted, might well blurt out something in the heat of the passion which would lead Deidre to her. She had nothing to lose.

On her way out, Deidre was planning phase two. Her story wouldn't appear until Monday. Tomorrow, she'd interview the sister of Edward Costanzo, and generate sympathy for the kidnapper. That would drive Renee up the wall, Deidre thought. She was repulsed, but Renee had initiated this cat and mouse game, and there were literally lives at stake.

Time, too, was of the essence. Here the ends justified the means. Yet, it didn't make her feel much better. Loretta Barrows deserved no sympathy. She was self-indulgent, egotistical and took no responsibility for her actions. A sham, so transparent, she had been easily exposed within days of the kidnapping. Throughout the ordeal, she'd kept to form. And now she was bitter, not because she had lost her daughter, but because of a failed opportunity.

Deidre had seen the gleam in her eye when the possibility of turning a dollar had so unexpectedly plopped into her lap. While she loathed generating sympathy for this woman, she was comforted by the thought Loretta Barrows was so crass and devoid of humanity, the public would see right through her if she indeed received offers to appear on talk shows. No, Loretta Barrows, Deidre said to herself, you won't cash in on your daughter. They'll dig up your sorry past and crucify you. You reap what you sow.

Chapter Fourteen

Shara shed her clothes as she closed the door to her apartment, and felt her body begin to breathe again. For as long as she could remember, she'd felt confined by her clothing. Looking back, she thought the night the police had burst into their rowhouse, killing her stepfather, could have triggered her aversion.

One of the most vivid memories of that night had been standing outside in the protective arms of Mrs. Spinetti, her clothes soaked in her stepfather's blood. The blood had seeped through her clothes, and clung to her skin like a tattoo. Mrs. Spinetti had first showered her, and then let her sit in a hot bath for forty-five minutes. Still, she felt the blood like a second skin. Mrs. Spinetti had been allowed to take a suitcase of clothes, before the police had sealed the house for the night, and she went to bed in her own pajamas. The clothes felt suffocating, however, and for the first time she'd slept naked.

The kidnapping had triggered the opposite response. With only a blanket to protect her from prying eyes, she layered herself with clothes upon her release. She'd sat in class, in her new school, bundled in a coat, over a sweater, over a blouse, and no amount of cajoling could coax her out of her cocoon, no matter how hot it got.

But even then she had felt uncomfortable. The clothes were a shield, nothing else. She would come home drenched in sweat, a rancid odor permeating her body, shut her door and strip completely.

Slowly, as her psyche was brought into balance, she'd adjusted, but she had always felt most comfortable in the nude.

The claustrophobic anxiety had returned in full intensity only when the overwhelming urge to kill had taken hold of her eighteen months before. As she stalked her quarry, her body strained against the confines of her clothes. The closer she came to confronting each devil, the greater the constriction. She could feel her body release its poison in the form of perspiration, and she'd sweat so profusely she had to bring a change of clothes to work to get through the day.

Today, watching Bobby had been at once exhilarating and excruciating. Like a jigsaw puzzle, the hazy outlines of Bobby Chattaway's daily routines were coming into focus.

Sunday morning he had returned to the rowhouse he'd visited the day before, the envelope of photos under his arm. He'd let himself in with a key and was out of the house in ten minutes. At eleven-thirty, dressed in the overalls of Duvall's Sunoco, he'd sauntered off to work.

Shara had watched in her car for several hours from a *McDonald's* parking lot across the street. Bobby and an older man spent most of the day filling gas. Shara noticed how he would flirt with teenagers, seemingly taking no interest in a number of attractive women in their twenties who stopped for a fill-up.

At four, purely on impulse, Shara decided to get a closer look at the man. Her clothes by this time were drenched in sweat; her body odor pungent even to her.

She locked the door to the women's room at *Mc-Donald's*, stripped and washed herself with water from the sink. She donned a tight pair of cutoff jeans, a halter top which just barely hid her tattoos, and a red wig, then drove across the street for a fill-up.

Bobby had given her a quick once over, and dismissed her. She'd gotten out off the car, bent over while he pumped gas, giving him an even better look. Still no reaction. She'd attempted to make small talk. His responses were monosyllables. When she'd paid him, she'd purposely ran her fingers over his hand; an open invitation that was rejected.

Across the street, she fought for air, the confines of the car so stifling she thought she would pass out. So close to him. It had been purely a lark, an experiment to see if *only* young teens appealed to him, but she hadn't counted on how being so close to him would affect her. She briefly made eye contact with him, and the impulse to run was so great, she had to literally fight the urge by holding on to the door handle of her car. His eyes had measured her, but in the end rejected her.

Fifteen minutes later she saw him fawning over a girl no more than fourteen; the girl's brother, Shara assumed, who drove the car, ignoring the interplay that transpired. Bobby was animated, his hands making contact with the girl's several times. His laughter, at some crack she made, was loud enough to be heard across the street.

Yes, she thought, it was young girls and only young girls who interested Bobby Chattaway.

At six, the two men closed the station, and Bobby went directly home. Shara remained outside his apartment until eleven-thirty, but he never ventured out.

Driving home, Shara was aware she was still soaked to the bone. Her breathing was labored, and her body ached fiercely. She imagined all her pores clogged, poisons within her body unable to find escape. Lightheaded, she felt herself fortunate to get back to her place without passing out or being involved in an accident.

Only when she had been naked for fifteen minutes did a semblance of normalcy return. Situps and pushups had slowly rid her body of its toxins; sweat streaming to the floor as her pores cleared. Still, she felt tense and paced the room like a caged animal, scratching the unblinking eyes on her chest.

She needed an outlet.

She thought of Deidre and instinctively picked up the phone and dialed her number.

Deidre picked the phone up on the first ring. Had she been waiting? Shara wondered, the thought bringing the first smile in hours to her face. Ever so slowly she began to relax, at one with her body that had seemed disembodied just a while before.

"It's me."

"Been busy?" Deidre replied.

Shara had to give her credit. If she'd been fazed by the call, she hid it well.

"Matter of fact I have. I've found him, Dee. The last. After him, no more hungry eyes."

"How many times have you said that to yourself, Renee? Just one more, and you'll be free. Aren't you deluding yourself? After this one, they'll be another and another until you're caught."

"No. This is the last. This one's special. How many days was I held captive?"

"Six. Why?"

"One for each day. Five down, one to go."

"Are you so sure? Can you turn it off like a faucet or have you lost control?"

"Six, Dee. I've saved this one for last. He's special. Different from the others."

"One of the cryptic clues you promised?" She sounded put off.

"A piece to the puzzle," she said. She was feeling so much better. The eyes no longer itched, no longer demanded attention. She was giving Deidre too much, she knew. Careful, she thought. You want her in the game, but there can be no sparing Bobby.

"I talked to your mother today," Deidre said.

It was like a slap in the face to Shara. She hadn't called to hear about her mother.

"And I thought my day was tough," Shara replied, masking the feeling of unease she felt. "How was the old cow?"

"Was she that bad to you?"

"Worse."

"Were the news accounts all true? We never talked about her much, but I recall you read and reread every article written about you."

"Some of the speculation stretched the truth a bit, but for the most part it was accurate, and there was more. How would you like asking who your father was, when you were seven or eight, and being told it could have been any one of three or four men, maybe more? Even then, she wouldn't give me names. I don't even look like her. Both she and my half-brother have real light complexions, but mine is tawny. You don't know what it is not to know who your father was." She paused for a moment, deep in thought.

"You know, she didn't start to get real fat until after I was born. Blamed that on me, too. Told me time and time again her pigging out was my fault. I did something to throw her metabolism out of whack. She called it her plumbing. Gained a ton during the pregnancy, and kept going after I was born. She didn't have enough sense to go to a doctor to find out the cause. Figured I was to blame, and she made me pay, soon as I was old enough to sweep and cook and clean."

"I found her charming," Deidre said. "Your loss had a profound impact on her."

"Bullshit." She knew she was being baited. "Why did you speak to her anyway?"

"Didn't I tell you? I'm writing a series for the *News*. A retrospective to coincide with the anniversary of your release. The first part will be in Monday's paper."

"What kind of game are you playing?" Shara didn't like the feeling of losing control. This series had something to do with tracking her down. But how? "Talking to my mother won't help you find me. The clock's running out and you're spinning your wheels in sand."

"On the contrary, Renee. I'm gaining a whole new perspective on you. I also spoke with Costanzo's sister today. *That* will make for a fascinating story."

"What did she tell you? That *I* kidnapped *him?* You don't know what you're doing," she rushed on without waiting for an answer. She felt panic well within her, and had to fight to keep her composure.

"But I do, Renee. Remember *you* set the ground rules. Tell me where you are, I'll stop my probing right now."

Shara was silent. She didn't want to say anything that might betray her churning emotions at the mention of Costanzo.

"I thought as much," Deidre finally said. "So we each continue on our way. But enough about my day. Tell me about the man you're tracking. What makes him so special?"

Shara told Deidre about Bobby, grudgingly at first. She was still angry. But once she began, the words flowed. She had always kept everything bottled up inside of her. Now here was someone she could talk to who would understand the man she hunted. She was tempted to play the tape she'd made, but didn't want to risk having her hear his voice. Instead, she painted a vivid picture of Bobby Chattaway that she knew could only make Deidre cringe.

"He's the worst scum, Dee. He rapes without touching. Ravages the soul. Destroys from within. Young girls, Dee. Lures them into his web, and scars them for life. And chances are if he's ever caught, all he'd get would be a slap on the wrist. He terrorizes them, but doesn't touch them. If rape can get you six months, and you know some can, what will he get? A first-time offender to boot.''

"How did you locate him, if he's never been arrested?"

"Did I say that?"

"He's been arrested, then, but never convicted?"

"Didn't say that either."

"Playing your little game again."

"C'mon, Dee. You expect me to give you his name and address? I've already told you too much about him. Just know this. We're talking about the worst kind of rapist. These girls, little more than children, will never lead normal lives. What he's done to them will be the focus of their existence; will tarnish all future relationships.''

"Like what happened to you? Is that why he's so special? He's so much like Costanzo. Doing to young girls what Costanzo did to you?"

"Draw your own conclusions, Dee. But he's going down."

"You're a fraud, Renee."

This came out of the blue, and got Shara's attention. Deidre was clearly angry about something.

"This isn't about your ridding society of perverts. Cut the Vigilante bullshit. This is about you. You told me so. Six days held captive. Six victims in revenge. You can justify and rationalize who you kill all you want, but it's for you. The children whose lives he'll destroy are purely incidental.''

"Can you blame me, after what I've been through? I never said I was this Vigilante the media created. You people come up with these convenient labels to hype the news. Well, you have to live with what your kind has created. Of course, what I'm doing is for *me*. And for me alone. I never said I was playing with a full deck.

I'm no better than a junkie in need of his next fix, but I'll tell you, Dee, after this one I'm through.''

"Why? I don't buy the one-for-each-day-you-were-held-captive crap. If the sixth were Costanzo, I could see closure, but he's long dead. Your sixth may be reprehensible, but like the junkie you say you are, can you stop at six?''

"I've already told you too much." She knew she sounded petulant, but if Deidre knew how close she was to the truth, she'd know why Chattaway would be her last.

"You're sounding like a broken record, Renee. You call me when you want to vent your spleen, and I get nothing in return. Sure, when you're caught I've got a great story, but it's not enough. You challenged me to track you down, but you offer no clues. Give me something, Renee. Or are you afraid I'm more than a match for you?''

Shara could have called her bluff, because she was fairly certain that's all it was. But, she decided to give her a morsel. It wouldn't be much, and it might keep her from getting too close.

"You want to interview someone who can give you a lead? Try my foster parents. I'm not jerking your chain. In an oblique way they can lead you to me. We'll talk soon, Dee. I'll be looking for your article.''

With that she hung up.

Shara felt deflated. Though she hated to admit it, she had begun to think of Deidre as a friend. Their conversations, though, were becoming confrontations. She had gone seven years without companionship, and instead of communicating with Dee, they sparred with one another.

She had never had a man; knew she never would, though she didn't particularly regret it. As a dancer she'd come close, but no matter how much they offered she had never gone all the way. Any desire she might have had died when she was kidnapped.

The other Shara had been her only lover, but sex had played just a small part in their relationship. She'd learned only *she* could satisfy herself, and any pleasure she derived was only fleeting. Just another reason why Bobby couldn't be allowed his pillaging.

Her conversation with Deidre should have satisfied her, but instead she was disturbed. Deidre had put her on the defensive, had controlled the course of the discussion. Deidre was turning out to be a worthy adversary. Under normal circumstances she would have been pleased, but her obsession with Bobby clouded all else. She had to be vigilant. She was too close to her objective to be denied. Yet, she still wanted Deidre to be able to put it all together, *after* she had finished her work. She wanted to tell her everything so she would understand.

Drained, she drifted into a fitful sleep; the night filled with Bobby's eyes feeling her up, coursing through her body at will with no way for her to rid herself of him.

Chapter Fifteen

Deidre replayed the conversation with Renee in her mind. She sensed the woman had revealed more than she'd intended, but the significance was just outside her grasp. And now gnawing at her was the possible relevance of her foster parents. Was it a real clue or was she just being sent on a fool's errand? Should she allow Renee to set her agenda? She sensed Renee was truly upset by the digging into her past. But why? Regardless, she would be even angrier the next day after she read her revisionist history of her mother.

Finally, instinct told her speaking with Renee's foster parents was worth the time. She'd met them on only two occasions, yet had instinctively took to them, and knew they'd been devastated by Renee's apparent suicide. But she had never really talked to them about Renee. To understand the woman, she had to know all she could about the child. She had to learn what had driven her to disappear. So, yes, she'd speak to Anna and Paul Sheffield. Somehow she would parlay it to further bait Renee to give more.

Before Renee had called, Deidre had just completed compiling notes on her interview with Angela Mendino, Edward Costanzo's sister. A number of things had troubled her, and now she went back over them trying to gain some insight that had so far evaded her.

Angela Mendino had looked on Deidre's visit with trepidation and suspicion. She had told Deidre as much when she entered her South Philadelphia rowhouse, just three blocks away from her brother's and the Barrows'.

Even with crime, escalating taxes, and decreased city services, as well as changing family mores and white flight to the suburbs, many South Philadelphia Italians defied convention and grew up, lived, worked, married and died within blocks of where they'd been born.

Angela Mendino was nine years younger than her 36-year-old brother when Renee Barrows was kidnapped. The incident had put the entire family under intense media scrutiny. Edward's sister had every reason to be bitter. A mother of six, pregnant with twins at the time, she had seen her children teased unmercifully as the glare of the media left no stone unturned in its search to learn why her brother had become a pervert.

Beneath the surface, there was the innuendo Angela, too, must harbor some secret fetish or clandestine second life. Her husband wanted the family to pack it in and flee, but Angela and her parents had been firm. She had nothing to hide, and the family would ride out the storm. She had repeated this to the media until she was sick of her own voice. She had cooperated fully with the media, even when her statements were distorted and taken out of context, in the attempt to confirm their preconceived suspicions about her brother.

With her brother's guilty plea, life eventually returned to normal. Four of her kids were now married, all living in the neighborhood. One was at college, and the twins, now thirteen, and her fourteen-year-old remained at home.

Angela told Deidre right off she didn't appreciate the past being dredged up, and had only agreed to meet with Deidre to politely tell her she wouldn't be a part of dragging her brother through the mud as a cheap publicity stunt.

Deidre had persisted, and finally won the woman over. She had shown the woman articles she had written then, and others after; setting forth her credentials, and distancing herself from those who had twisted the facts to bolster their already formed opinions.

Recalling her statements to the media at the time of the kidnapping, Deidre had been struck by the differing demeanor of brother and sister. Despite microphone after microphone being stuck in her face, Angela Mendino had never been cowered by the media. With no family skeletons in her closet, she calmly, but firmly, answered all questions, adding just enough sarcasm to convince them she was one tough cookie and wouldn't crumble under pressure.

Angela, today, was an older version of the woman who had stood proud to defend her brother. There were touches of gray in her raven black hair, but, unlike Loretta Barrows she had not let herself go to hell. And, whereas Loretta Barrows' eyes burned with bitterness, Angela's brown eyes while suspicious displayed no spite.

Now, hopefully having dispelled any misgivings that her piece would only further cheapen her brother's memory, she made her pitch.

"Mrs. Mendino, I think it's time—long past time, actually—for a reevaluation of the Barrows' kidnapping. I'd be the first to agree that thirteen years ago there was a media circus akin to a witchhunt. Your brother confessed to the crime and then went silent. The media went out of its way to furnish proof of his guilt, and delve into his background to find a motive. They harassed you, and while they listened to your words, didn't hear what you said. I'd like to clear the air, put things into perspective. I'm writing a series with or without your cooperation, but I'd like your impressions to find out what your brother was really like."

"What my brother was really like?" She paused and suddenly smiled. "My son's principal calls me Mrs. Mendino when he asks me to come in for a conference about his behavior. He's got my husband's hot temper. All three of my sons do, so I've been to a lot of conferences with the principal. One's married with two kids of his own, and another's at college, so this too shall pass. Anyways, if you're gonna talk to me, I'm Angela or Angie, but please not Mrs. Mendino. Okay Miss . . ."

"Deidre. Or Dee."

"Fair enough."

She rose to get Deidre and herself some coffee, and Deidre scrutinized her.

Angela Mendino physically resembled her brother. Short and pudgy, though pictures that Deidre had noted scattered throughout a cluttered living room showed she was once thin and definitely a girl in demand when younger. Deidre thought eight children could have nothing but an adverse effect on one's figure. The woman who sat across from her in the kitchen looked comfortable with herself. She spoke with her hands and eyes. Angela Mendino would have a tough time lying; her eyes refused to mask her emotions.

"Let me be frank, Miss . . . Deidre. I made some calls before I agreed to talk with you. I'm told you're fair. I'm told if I open up you won't stab me in the back. So, while I'm not thrilled about your series, maybe some good will come of it."

"I hope so, too, Angela."

"I haven't thought about my brother in a long time," Angela went on. "When Edward was born, the doctors said my mother would never have another child. Obviously, everyone was more than a little surprised nine

years later when my mother found she had another bun
in the oven.''

''Did you and your brother get along? Were you
close?''

''We didn't *not* get along. We hardly knew one another. Actually, truth be told, he virtually ignored me
until I had my first child when I was sixteen. I think he
resented me at first. I was the baby, a 'blessing from
heaven,' my mother called me more than I'd like to admit. I was constantly doted on and spoiled. Edward was
virtually ignored. That he didn't pick on me, or treat me
like dirt is a tribute to him.''

''Did he resent the attention you received?''

''Yes, in his own way. I only have vague recollections
when I was young, but he spent a lot of time by himself,
often alone in his room. He wasn't athletic, nor particularly bright.

''I remember other kids calling him a nerd or a geek.
He didn't go to the senior prom; seldom went on dates,
and I can't recall his going out with the same girl twice.
It was like once I was born his social development
ended. He had no social skills as far as his peers were
concerned.

''When he was arrested, I blamed myself. If it weren't
for me, he might have led a more normal childhood.''

Once Angela got started, all Deidre had to do was ask
a question or two, and a flood of memories were un-
leashed, possibly for the first time.

''You said you became closer after your first child
was born?''

''It wasn't planned, and my parents were more than
a little pissed. Al lived next door, and my parents and
the Mendinos were tight. It almost brought them to
blows, but somehow they worked it out. Al and I would
marry; there were no two ways about it, but not right
away. We both finished high school and married at eighteen.

"Anyway, when Christina was born Edward seemed to come out of his shell. It was like he wanted to be the brother to her he refused to be to me. And he *never* abused her or any of my other children."

"He saw a lot of them?" Deidre asked.

"Almost everyday, at times. I'm not proud of it, but once he volunteered to watch the kids, we more than took him up on his offer. We were young, you gotta understand, and wanted to live life to the fullest. I was getting pregnant all the time, but between births we led a pretty active social life.

"Edward was always babysitting and constantly had the kids over to his place. You've heard of his rec room and backyard? A child's paradise."

Deidre nodded, and Angela went on.

"He was a carpenter, you know, so he built swings, a sliding board, this amazing jungle gym, and a maze you could get lost in for hours. Pretty soon it just wasn't my kids he had over, but neighbors' as well. To be honest, I don't think he ever learned to relate to his peers, so he was drawn to children he could impress. They worshiped him."

"He never made any . . . uh, sexual advances toward your children?"

"Never, and I'm not saying that to protect him. After his arrest, and the disclosures he'd had sex with some of the boys, I was terrified. My God, he had been alone with my children so often. What if it were true? My sons all had sessions with our priest. I'm not saying those other boys lied, but he did nothing to my sons."

"Did you visit Edward in prison?"

"Often . . . after the first year. At first, I tried to distance myself from him, what with reporters lurking about. But, like I said, I felt partially responsible. I began visiting regular-like after that first year. Even brought the kids with me. He got a real kick out of seeing them."

A cloud passed over her face, and it was clear she was making an important decision.

Deidre knew not to press. She took a sip of her coffee and waited. Angela bent closer as she began to speak.

"I wasn't going to say anything about this, but you said you wanted the truth. I don't deny my brother kidnapped the Barrows' child, but I never believed he did all they said. He wouldn't put *any* child in a cage, strip her of her clothes, and come leering at her like she said.

"I know what you're thinking," she continued, shaking her head, as if she could read Deidre's skepticism. "I'm his sister, and the truth is hard to swallow. But I got to know him pretty well when he opened up to my children. And we talked an awful lot when he was in jail. He couldn't con me even if he tried."

She took a sip of coffee. "You know this isn't easy for me."

"Whatever you have to say, just say it. I can tell it's been eating at you," Deidre said.

Angela smiled weakly.

"Okay. Like I told you, he wasn't real bright. I said he was normal, you know, average, but truthfully he was a little slow upstairs. Once and only once, when I came up to visit him alone, we were talking, and all of a sudden he looked around to make sure no one could overhear him. His eyes came to life. 'Ang,' he says to me, 'I never did all they said. Promised I'd never tell, never tell, never tell no one, but you're my sister. I took that girl, that I did, and I ain't proud of it, but I didn't treat her like she said. Didn't. Couldn't look at her like they said.'

"Then his eyes lost their luster, and he looked like a little boy who said something he shouldn't have. 'Sorry, Ang, have to go now,' and he got up and left. He *never* did that. He always stayed until they came to get him, even if we had nothing to say to one another. He'd look at me, and I knew he forgave me for denying him his childhood. But, that one time, when he told me something that he thought he shouldn't he just up and left.''

There were tears in her eyes, and she slapped at the air as if to apologize.

"Did he ever talk to you about it again?"

"No. I tried to get him to talk. Part of me wanted to believe that little girl lied. But there was all that evidence. For a while, I asked him about it each time I visited, but he looked blank, like he didn't know what I was talking about. After awhile I stopped asking.

"It wasn't until after you called that I remembered it again. It had become like something you weren't sure really happened. But it did. He was my brother, and I loved him. I wanted it to be true . . .''

They talked a bit more, but the disclosure had taken a lot out of her, and soon Deidre had nothing left to ask, and Angela nothing to recount. Leaving, she could tell Angela almost wanted her to stay, wanted to reminisce about her brother.

It wouldn't be hard for Deidre to paint a sympathetic portrait of Edward Costanzo. He'd never really been understood by the police, prosecutors or media that was intent on portraying him as some sort of animal with few redeeming qualities.

Deidre herself had trouble accepting his recanting his confession to his sister. There *was* too much evidence. And she had spoken to Renee at length about the kidnapping. No, after five years in prison, maybe Edward Costanzo wanted to believe he couldn't have done what he was accused of.

Deidre put her notes away. Looking at her watch, Deidre saw it was nearly three in the morning. Briggs had left a message for her earlier that he wanted to see her at eight to fill her in on the Task Force's progress. She'd worked more these past two-and-a-half days than the previous six months, and hoped it wouldn't catch up with her until she located Renee. Over the years, she'd learned to function on three to four hours of sleep during a breaking story, taking a catnap here, forty winks there. But it seemed a lifetime ago.

She went to bed dreading the alarm clock that would beckon too soon.

Chapter Sixteen

Deidre was in her office at five minutes to eight, working on her third cup of coffee, when Briggs walked in. He had a haggard look, as if he hadn't slept the entire weekend. He had a cup of coffee in one hand, a Milky Way candy bar in the other. He studied her a moment before speaking, looking slightly bewildered.

"You look like shit," he said, foregoing any small talk. "I've got an excuse, what's yours?"

She smiled. Another sign he'd accepted her as part of his team. He wasn't watching his tongue around her, and for this she was grateful. A part of her regretted not confiding in him, but she already knew he'd dismiss her out of hand. She ignored his question.

"You're looking pretty good yourself. You'll make a fine impression on the Mayor when he pops in at ten."

He choked on his coffee. "What the fuck . . ."

"Kidding, Briggs. You won't catch his holiness down here until you've got your suspect in custody. He wants to draw as little attention to the Vigilante as possible. So, any progress?"

Now he ignored her question and opened up the newspaper to her article: THIRTEENTH ANNIVERSARY OF INFAMOUS KIDNAPPING APPROACHES. He tapped the article with his finger, as if she hadn't seen it.

"A great time for you to be moonlighting. What does this have to do with our case?" he asked accusingly.

"Coincidence, Briggs," she lied. "I'd been planning the series for a while. My job with the Mayor is not exactly taxing. Nor stimulating. Kind of like if you were put behind a desk. With nothing to do with most of my day, I thought researching a retrospective would help fill the empty hours."

"You couldn't delay it? Or better yet, drop it all together. I need you living this case; using your perspective to ask questions we as cops wouldn't think of. Everyone has dropped cases they were deeply involved in. I expected the same of you," he said with an edge to his voice.

"You flatter me, Briggs, but say what you want, I'm little more than window dressing here. Don't get me wrong. I'm not complaining, but I'm totally out of the loop. Hell, you didn't even ask me to write the story to bait the Vigilante to confide in me. Anyway, most of my research was already completed. I could write this series in my sleep."

He didn't look mollified. "Sorry, but I don't have time to massage egos. I've stepped on more than a few toes the past few days. I'll just add you to the list." The bluster was gone. Briggs took another swig of coffee. "You couldn't have written the piece to get him to contact you. You're too closely tied to the case. The Vigilante would know it was a plant. But, you're right, I should have consulted you. It's your field of expertise, and . . ." He paused. "I'm learning I'm not great at delegating authority. I'm an investigator, and heading up the Task Force calls for administrative skills I may not possess.''

"Briggs, you knew this case was going to be a ball-buster when you took it on. Chievous or McCauley could have led the Task Force, but no, you wanted to run the show. You know catching a serial killer is as much luck as it is police work. And you know things will probably get worse before they get better. The article's water under the bridge, okay? And, you're right, I'm not the one who should have written the article, if it makes you feel any better. So, tell me, any progress?''

"Precious little. Phil Wakefield's story ran yesterday. We tried to push all the right buttons. Question his manliness, say he was no better than those he hunted. Went on about his playing God.'' He paused. "Why am I telling you this? You read the story, right?''

"Yeah, but if I'm such an integral part of your team, you should have run it by me before you ran it. Wakefield's good, but he's not privy to all I am. As you said, this is my area of expertise, and you bypassed me.'' Now it was her turn to sound irritated.

"Point taken. You have every right to be pissed. Next time, I'll think with my brain, not my ass.''

"Apology accepted. So, any response?''

"Plenty, though not what we hoped for. The article hit a nerve. Wakefield's phone's been ringing off the hook. You wouldn't want to be in his shoes, believe me. Most are just cranks calling him an asshole for missing the bigger picture: judicial system gone awry, criminals back on the street with a license to rape, pillage and burn with no consequences.

"We had three crackpots call saying they were the Vigilante, but none knew enough about the crimes. Two stayed on the phone long enough for us to run a trace. The third wanted to meet with Wakefield to give him proof he was the killer. We brought him in, as well as the other two. Crackpots, like I said.

"We'll run another story tomorrow. Really lay the guy out. Matter of fact, I'd like you to provide a rough outline, including phrases that might provoke him. I'll take them to Wakefield, and make sure he incorporates them in his story."

"You're good, Briggs. Tired as you are, you were about to exclude me again. Not purposely. You just don't have a niche for me yet. I'm an afterthought. Look, I'm not pissed, just laying it on the line. I'm on to you, big man, so you best be on the top of your game when you deal with me."

"Yeah, well catch me when I've had a few hours of sleep and see if you can put anything past me," he said gruffly, but his eyes betrayed him. He'd been caught with his pants down, and wasn't really upset that she had noticed.

"So, what about the decoys?"

"We can't rush it. We ran one story in the *Inquirer* yesterday. The *News* has the second today. The third will be in tomorrow. No bullshitting, now, you take a look at them and tell me if you can spot the decoy. I don't expect anything to happen right away. This guy's too smart. Personally, if Logan's right, and we have less time than between the last two killings, I think our boy already has his target.

"Between you and me, the best we can hope for is one of these three will go to the top of his list for a future hit, which means there's got to be at least one killing before he gets to these."

"A real comforting thought," Deidre said.

"If we're lucky, on the other hand, maybe he'll check out one of these three while he's stalking his next victim. Kind of doing some advance work. If so, we can pick up his scent before he strikes. But I'm not holding my breath."

"What are the others doing?"

"Starting from scratch. Reinterviewing the neighbors,

and anyone who might have seen our boy. Checking out relatives of victims of recent sexual attacks. It's grunge work, but with the FBI's profile we're asking different questions, hoping to get lucky. And we're checking the military angle; someone with expertise in surveillance.''

"I don't envy you," Deidre said. "You're in a no-win situation. The public and the Mayor are clamoring for answers, and it looks like you could be in for the long haul; weeks and weeks and still come up dry.''

"That's where you come in. You have to be the buffer between us and the Mayor and the media. Tomorrow, Wednesday at the latest, you'll have to brief the press. Obviously Wakefield and the three plants are off limits. Try to come up with some angle that will make it look like we're making progress.''

"What if we bring Logan back for the briefing? Kind of have him give his stamp of approval on your approach, reassure the public everything's being done by the book, but these things can't be rushed.''

Briggs smiled. "I like that. We got diddly, but we're going by the book. A pat on the back from Logan will buy us time. I'll get on it.''

"Anything else?''

"There will be a briefing at nine. I'd like you there, but don't expect much. You'll see a bunch of tired men and women, waiting to be told to keep on keeping on, impatient to be on their way.''

"How are the cops from the 'burbs?" Deidre asked.

"Capable. Better than I expected, actually. They're fitting right in.''

"And Chievous and McCauley?''

"As much as I hate to say it, they're team players. Maybe they feel their asses are as much on the line as mine. I can tell you this. They no longer covet my job. I'm sure they're giving the Chief an earful, but they're pulling their weight. If I fall, one of them is next in line, and I'm not sure either one wants the grief.''

Briggs rose. At the door he turned, as if not too sure if he wanted to say what was on his mind.

"Tell me to kiss off, if you want, but in my opinion I thought you were a little soft on the mother in your story today. I feel sorry for the lady, losing her daughter and all, but if she was any kind of mother her daughter would probably be alive today."

"Then I guess you won't be thrilled with tomorrow's piece on the kidnapper."

He looked puzzled. "Not going soft on me, Dee, are you?"

"Just putting things in their proper place. Everything seemed so cut and dried then, but a lot was just a knee-jerk reaction to a kid being kidnapped. Some of the stories printed were full of inaccuracies. And with Costanzo's confession there was precious little follow-up by the police. It's all hindsight, but looking back, I've got a lot of questions that need answering. Unfortunately, the victim and the prime suspect are both dead. I'm just trying to set the record straight. Good to know you read the story, though," she said with a smile.

He waved and left, his mind back on the case.

Deidre felt good. If Briggs noticed her sympathetic portrayal of Loretta Barrows, Renee surely would seethe. No doubt she'd be getting a phone call tonight. She was looking forward to it. She'd be prepared.

Her phone rang. It was Jonas.

"Called in some favors," he said in response to her asking how he was. "Got six possibilities fitting your description. I can have photos on your desk in an hour. Just give me the word."

"Sounds good, Jonas," she said, trying to remain calm, as anticipation welled within her. "I may be in a Task Force meeting. I'll leave word to let you into my office. Maybe we'll get lucky."

"Don't get your hopes up too high. The fall's worse."

"Love your optimism, but thanks anyway. Let's have a look at your six, and decide what to do then."

157

Chapter Seventeen

Shara was angry with herself. She had promised herself she'd maintain her daily morning routine and not hurry out to get the *News* to read Deidre's story about her mother. But curiosity gnawed at her. She threw a half-eaten bagel in the trash, and decided to splurge at *McDonald's* while she read the paper.

She lost her appetite for the second time that morning over an Egg McMuffin as she read, then re-read Deidre's distortion of her past.

". . . Loretta Barrows believed in tough love, but love was the operative word here," Deidre had written.

—*love*, Shara thought. Her mother didn't know the meaning of the word.

". . . cooperative to a fault with the media, Loretta Barrows became embittered as she saw her words twisted."

—*became* embittered. Hell, Shara thought, her mother was *born* bitter, and just got worse with age.

". . . while the papers pounced on big money to be gained from movie and book deals as the motive behind

Loretta Barrows' attempt to regain custody of her daughter, it was conveniently ignored she had agreed to a court-appointed trustee to oversee dispersal of any forthcoming monies.''

—That was a good one, Shara thought. Her mother would agree to *anything*, because if she regained custody she would figure a way to turn a profit.

''. . . at their last supervised visitation, Loretta Barrows claimed Renee was eager to be reunited with her family.''

—A *lie*. A bald-faced lie, and Deidre knew it.

Shara's hand shook as she picked up a cup of coffee, spilling the now-cold liquid on the article she had just concluded.

Anger welled within her, and she had to fight for control. She had thought Deidre was pulling her chain the night before to throw her off balance. Surely her mother hadn't conned Deidre into believing she had been misrepresented by the media. Deidre was too smart; her mother too transparent. Lies. Vile lies. Lies that made her *mother* appear to be the victim.

Deidre had gone too far, Shara thought. And what else had she said?—her interview with Costanzo's sister would make for a fascinating story.

She wouldn't allow it. Deidre was rewriting *her* childhood. She must pay. Would pay. Pay dearly. Today.

Shara's body was no happier with the story than her mind. At work, despite having drank nothing but a half a cup of coffee, she felt the urge to pee every half-hour. She felt claustrophobic, and waves of nausea attacked her on three occasions. Her body demanded action, and she acquiesced. Her fingers on auto pilot as she entered records into the computer, she formulated a plan. Ever so slowly her body relaxed.

Yes, Deidre would pay, Shara thought, smiling at the computer screen.

Chapter Eighteen

At ten-fifteen, with the Task Force ready to go digging for that elusive needle in a haystack, Deidre went back to her office. She wanted to check in with Timms and call the Sheffields to set up an interview. She wasn't surprised to see Jonas behind her desk, reading her story on Loretta Barrows.

"Makes for good fiction," he said with a wink. "Pull up a chair and give these a look," he said holding up a handful of photos.

Deidre's heart skipped a beat, and she felt her pulse quicken.

"Narrowed down to six," Jonas continued. "Started with a long list. Cut out minorities, those too tall, those too heavy, those too old."

He laid them down one at a time, and Deidre's heart sank. They could all be Renee, or it could be none of them. She looked at them quickly to see if any registered instinctively, as was her habit, then gave each a careful inspection.

Jonas had done his job well, she thought. All six could

be peas from the same pod. She cursed herself. Had she given the messenger more than a cursory glance and not focused on the mole and scar, she could at least eliminate a few of the faces that stared blankly at her.

"Try this," Jonas said, when Deidre shrugged in resignation. He now laid out the same women, but with blond wigs, a scar and mole. "Friend of mine added the hair and features."

Still nothing. She sighed.

"Don't give up yet." Next he produced six sheets of sketchy biographical data; one on each of the six. He shrugged as she looked at him in disbelief. "Got lots of friends. Maybe there's a clue only you could sniff out."

Deidre read each cursorily, then a second time, highlighting an item here and there.

"Roberta Bracken. Renee Barrows," Deidre said, out loud, as much to herself as to Jonas. "The initials are the same. Coincidence? Probably, but worth a second look. Three are still on the police force. Hmmm, Sheila Jeffries. The name rings a bell. Just can't place it."

"Big narcotics bust last year," Jonas supplied the answer. "An up-and-comer. Not in narcotics, per se. Warned off a case she'd stumbled onto. On her own time found a connection with new suppliers in town. A lot of initiative. High profile."

"And probably not Renee," Deidre added. "She couldn't risk a high profile. There'd be digging into her past as she rose through the ranks. Let's not eliminate her, but she's not at the top of my list."

Deidre scanned another of the bios. "This Shara Farris. She's too old. Renee's twenty-three. This girl's twenty-nine."

"*Says* twenty-nine," Jonas said, "but in the photo looks no older than the others."

Deidre looked at the photo carefully. "You're right. Renee assumed someone else's identity. She might not have had much choice. Well, we can't eliminate her solely on age." She smiled at Jonas. "You're not making things any easier."

He smiled back, shrugged and let her go on.

Of the remaining three, one worked in security at the Board of Education, one had married and no longer worked, and the last had dropped out of the Academy, gone back to college and now worked for a computer company.

Deidre had her doubts about the married woman, especially one with an infant to care for, but still couldn't eliminate her on those grounds alone.

Deidre shook her head in bewilderment. It would have been too easy to just be able to pick her out of a stack of photos. "Assuming one of these is Renee, do you have any suggestions how to proceed?"

She saw the gleam in his eye. A beat reporter thirty years' removed, he hadn't lost his touch, nor his desire.

"Mulled over some thoughts this morning."

Deidre laughed. "I bet you did. Shoot."

"First, tail them. We both have people on the streets; good as any cop. Second, call each one with a solicitation offer. Tape the voices. You've spoken to her. Can either identify or eliminate. Last, search their homes when they're at work for evidence."

Deidre shook her head in awe. "Mulled over some thoughts this morning, my ass. You've got everything planned. All right. I like the phone solicitation the best. No risk involved. Let's try that first. And, if you want, you can start planning the tails. We'll wait, though, until we get the results from the phone calls. I don't want to spook her. I don't know what she'll do if she gets onto us. A tail can be spotted. Remember, she's either on the police force, or has had surveillance training. As good as our people are, she might spot a tail in a minute." She held up a hand to stop Jonas from protesting.

"I'm not ruling it out. Let's just not be hasty. She

could vanish. Hell, she's done it before. But I want to be ready.

"For now a search is out. Much too risky. Let's try to eliminate some of the possibilities first. If we narrow it down to one or two, a search might be in order. Agreed?"

"Agreed," Jonas said, but without much enthusiasm. He gathered the files and photos without a word. Deidre knew he didn't want to discard the search, but knew better than to argue with her when she'd made up her mind. He'd come back to it, she knew, depending on the outcome of the calls and tails. He was always so much more gung-ho than she. She was the cautious one. Both got results, but she knew if they'd ever been partners for an extended period working on a story, they'd have crossed swords.

He'd taught her to be aggressive, and she *had* become much more so due in great part to his urgings. She felt, though, at times being overly assertive was both reckless and needless. This time it was her call, and as the consequences involved lives she'd go with her instincts.

"Got lots to do," he said. "Got a friend . . ." he started and smiled, "actually does phone solicitations. We'll start tonight around dinnertime. I'll line up tails, too. I'll drop by a little before midnight, and you can see what I've got."

He gave her a peck on the cheek and was at the door.

"Jonas," she called.

He turned to look at her.

"Thanks."

He gave her a wave of dismissal. "More fun than I've had in years." And he was gone.

If only it was one of these women, she thought to herself. A voice on the phone might be all she would need. She'd have her then. It was still a longshot. She would have to go ahead with her series; anger Renee into tipping her hand.

With a sigh, she got down to work for Briggs. She had a two o'clock appointment with the Sheffields, and wanted everything out of the way before she left.

Deidre had finally gotten in touch with Timms just as she was ready to leave the office.

"I'm hard at work on it, girlie," he'd said brightly. "The word's out. I should have something by tomorrow, if there's anything to be had."

Deidre hadn't expected any miracles, and unfortunately hadn't been disappointed.

She was at the Sheffields half an hour later.

The Sheffields owned a two-story corner house with a decent-sized front lawn off one of the many winding side streets of Springfield.

After several miscarriages, Anna Sheffield had been told she'd never bear children of her own. She and her husband had become foster parents, eventually adopting two of their charges. A township cop in his mid-forties when Renee was kidnapped, he'd immediately requested the child join his brood of four upon her release. With the media in a feeding frenzy and the potential for an ugly confrontation with Loretta Barrows, it was decided having Renee in the home of a cop might buffer her from both. Having friends on the Philadelphia force hadn't hurt either.

Paul Sheffield, now fifty-five, had recently retired, yet the first sight Deidre saw, as she pulled into their driveway, was the man chasing an obviously happy six-or seven-year-old across the lawn in a game of tag. Lifting the boy over his head, with the youth urging him on, he gave Deidre a big smile, and told her to go around to the backyard.

The Sheffield's backyard was filled with playground equipment; from the looks of it much of it built from scratch by Paul Sheffield.

A petite woman of twenty-four or twenty-five was

watching Anna feeding an infant when Deidre entered the yard.

"Ms. Caffrey?" the older woman asked, and when Deidre nodded affirmatively, she gave the child to the younger woman.

"This is my daughter, Heather, and my grandson, Sean," she said with obvious pride. "Pardon me for not getting up. I fell and broke my hip a few years back, and don't get around as well as I used to."

At that moment Paul Sheffield, sweat glistening from his marine-styled crew cut burst into the backyard. A large man, he did nothing quietly. Deidre could picture him a stern taskmaster, yet there was a cuddly monster quality about him. It was apparent he commanded not only obedience, but adulation.

He was also not one for idle small talk. He took out a copy of the *Daily News* from his back pocket, and his expression hardened.

"A crock of shit, this story about Loretta Barrows. She conned you, Ms. Caffrey. Fortunately, she had less success with the authorities thirteen years ago."

There would be no bullshitting Paul Sheffield. Deidre had to show equal toughness to hopefully gain his respect and cooperation. She had seldom resorted to duplicity, and now knew why. *She* didn't believe a word of the story she had written, but she'd had no choice. Yet this was the second time today she had been called to task for it. It was not something she could dwell on at the moment, however.

"I'm not going to apologize for allowing Loretta Barrows to tell her story. Actually, that's why I'm here. I'll be more than happy to run your rebuttal. At the same time, there's still the nagging question of Renee's suicide."

"Ms. Caffrey . . . ," Paul began, but Deidre put up a hand to stop him.

"I don't mean to be rude, but please let me finish."

"It's I who was rude," Paul said. "Go on."

Deidre smiled, but she felt like she was being circled by a hungry shark. "I spent a lot of time with Renee before she was placed in your care. I decided against seeing her once she was placed permanently, primarily to keep the media off your back. As long as I had access to Renee, there were those who felt I'd go on milking her for stories. You know, Renee's adjustment to a family where she wasn't the mother; Renee's progress at her new school, and so on. It was a painful decision, and I don't know if Renee understood I wasn't abandoning her.

"I even blamed myself in part for her suicide. Would it have made a difference if I'd continued to see her, as a friend and confidante, and allowed you to deal with the media fallout? In researching this series I realized I knew next to nothing of Renee's adjustment. I'd hoped you could fill in some of the missing pieces, but if you'd rather I leave . . ."

"Don't be so sensitive," Anna Sheffield interrupted. "My husband's never been too high on reporters. Don't know a cop myself who has much good to say about those in your profession. But Renee trusted you like a sister, and she was a damn fine judge of character. We both decided as a friend of hers we'll tell you anything we can. Paul just wants you to have to work for your story." She winked at her husband, who answered back with a sheepish grin.

"There goes my advantage," he said with good humor.

"You won't need any advantage with me, Mr. Sheffield. So, tell me, just how difficult was Renee's adjustment?"

"You realize, of course," Paul began, "that Renee came from a household of no rules. She knew her place, and what was expected of her, but she set her own hours, and as long as she did her chores she had no one to answer to.

"Here, for the first time there were rules to follow and consequences for violations. We set a daily routine, something Renee had never experienced. A part of her responded well to someone taking responsibility for her care. Another part tested the limits we set. She was always pushing the envelope, but we only had to tell her once when she crossed the line."

"Can you give me an example?"

"She was foul-mouthed, from her life on the streets. Expletives were part of her everyday vocabulary, but we had three other children with us at the time, and we weren't about to expose them to gutter language.

"We told Renee her language wouldn't be tolerated, and she responded. There was an occasional slip, maybe intentional to test us, but she knew the consequences, and accepted punishment when she let loose."

"And what was the punishment?" Deidre asked, showing more hostility than she wished.

"You really were fond of her," Paul said, before answering, obviously surprised at the revelation. "A part of us thought you'd used her to advance your career. Tough and street smart though she was, Renee was still a child. Forgive me for saying, more than once I thought you'd pulled the wool over her eyes. But, maybe I was wrong. You cared for her. Still do."

He paused, as if this shed new light on how he perceived Deidre and what he'd divulge.

"As to punishing her," he finally went on, "we didn't believe in the spare the rod, spoil the child philosophy. I never raised a hand to any of our children. If I had, Anna would have laid me out. Renee's punishment for cursing was a time-out period in her room. Usually an hour. We had one television in our den, so time out meant coming to grips with yourself or reading a book. Then either Anna or I would come in and we'd discuss

167

the infraction. It usually ended in a hug. Renee didn't pout or hold grudges.''

"Then the adjustment went well, generally?''

"At home, yes. There was some give and take. Her room for example. She didn't take to it at all. We'd tuck her into bed at night, only to find her on the floor with only a blanket covering her the next morning. We put up posters of popular rock groups before she arrived, and she tore them down. We offered to let her choose posters herself, but she wanted her walls bare. She didn't want to be looked at by the eyes from the posters. What with the trauma she'd been through, this was perfectly understandable. We let her know her room was hers to decorate anyway she chose.''

"What about all the dolls and toys she received at the hospital?''

"Didn't want anything to do with them. Again, the dolls had eyes. 'Hungry eyes,' she said. She gave them to our other children. There were so many a lot went back to the children's ward at the hospital.''

"Did she ever talk about the kidnapping?''

"No. We told her we were here if she wanted a shoulder to lean on, but we wouldn't put her through any third degree. We, of course, took her for therapy, but she was uncommunicative. In the end we stopped. Decided to give her time and space to make the adjustment.'' He paused.

"But as a cop I observed her. She read voraciously all the accounts of her captivity, her family background, and disclosures about Costanzo. She did so, though, as if from the outside looking in. Never made a comment. She watched reports on the news, too. What got me was her emotional detachment whenever she saw Costanzo. The psychologist who knew her best said it was shock, possibly denial, but I never bought it. It was almost like she felt sorry for the guy.''

"How could she feel sorry for someone who, well . . ."

"Raped her with his eyes, at the very least," Paul finished for Deidre. "It's a puzzle. I've dealt with more psychologists in my line of work than I'd care to admit. Get a dozen psychologists in a room and you get a dozen different opinions. Renee held no grudge against Edward Costanzo. I'll believe that to my dying day. There was something she kept hidden. Maybe that's what led to her suicide. I wish I could be more definitive. I'm just giving you my observations."

"And that's what I want. Like you said, it's a puzzle. Did she bond with your family?"

Here, Anna spoke up. "She never got close to any of the other children, but they got along. She was like someone who'd been in an accident, and had to learn everything from scratch. She had no social skills, and was afraid she might do something to alienate the other children, or worse, us. I guess she thought we'd throw her out. Abandon her. So she kept a distance emotionally."

Now it was Deidre's turn to be impressed. "You two have remarkable insight. In my line of work, I hear too many horror stories about foster parents. Those who don't give a damn."

"It's just like with reporters, isn't it?" Anna said. "There are the good and the bad. Now where was I? Oh yes, when she saw the other kids all had chores, she wanted to do her part. We were aware she'd had more than her share of housework, but we decided to treat her no differently than the others." She paused, as if in thought.

"She did seem to bond, or at least identify, with Paul to some extent. She told me one day she wanted to be a cop. That was her word, not a policeman, a *cop*, so she could protect others from going through what she did."

"I'm a bit confused," Deidre said. "The picture I get is a child who knew she was loved. Obviously things weren't nice and perfect, but . . ."

"Why the suicide?" asked Paul. "We've asked ourselves that question since the day it happened with no satisfactory answer."

"School?" Deidre asked, clutching at straws.

"School didn't go so well," Paul said, "but I can't believe that's a significant factor. There were a lot of mood swings at school. Kids being, well, kids, some naturally teased her, but you'd never know what set her off. She would come home some days and tell us the kids were taunting her, and just shrug it off. Other times when they bothered her, she'd fly off the handle."

"You mean fight?"

"Remember, she spent a lot of time on the streets," Paul said in her defense. "The few times she fought, the other kids got by far the worst of it. Anna and I would be called in. The school's policy was to suspend all offenders regardless of circumstances when it came to fighting. But, she took it in stride. She broke the rules and had to suffer the consequences. But, you see, there was no pattern to what would set her off. I guess it was to be expected. There must have been days when she felt herself back in that cage of Costanzo's and at those times the smallest incident would be magnified in her mind."

"What about visits from her mother? I understand Loretta Barrows petitioned the courts, and she was allowed supervised visitation."

"They weren't traumatizing, if that's what you're getting at," Anna said. "There was a social worker present, but I kind of eavesdropped," she said with a conspiratorial look in her eyes.

"I would have done the same," Deidre said with a smile.

"I was curious as to how Renee would react to seeing

her mother," Anna continued. "I think she genuinely loved her, although I get the feeling her mother's desire to visit had more to do with possible financial gain, if you know what I mean.

"Anyway, I don't know if Renee loved her mother as a person, but she was her mother. There were never arguments or recriminations. She never asked that the visits be terminated."

"Did she say she wanted to go back? I know Loretta Barrows was seeking to regain custody."

"She wanted to remain with us," Paul said forcefully. "Renee was a smart kid. She may have loved her mother, but she knew what awaited her at the Barrows' household. She took to the structure we provided, and told us she didn't want to have to become the mother again. Those were her exact words—*the mother again.*"

"One or two more questions, if you don't mind. Something's just not right. We're both in agreement Renee was not suicidal, yet she killed herself. Did *anything* traumatic, even something a bit unusual, occur just before she took her life?"

Paul and Anna stared at one another; a married couple's silent communication at work. Finally Paul cleared his voice.

"Nothing traumatic occurred. But, on the last visit, Loretta brought Renee's half-brother. It was a bit eerie." He smiled a bit guiltily, then looked at Anna.

"Oh Paul, nothing to hide. I was eavesdropping again. I'd gotten into the habit, and well . . . Anyway, Renee hadn't seen her half-brother in six months. She was surprised when her mother brought him. Oddly enough, they never said a word to one another. They sat on opposite sides of the room. I could see the boy scrutinizing her. You know, trying to silently penetrate this shield she'd erected. Have you spoken to him yet?"

"Not yet, but I plan to," Deidre said. "Go on, please."

"Well, for the first time Loretta talked about the kidnapping. She didn't seem comfortable. Kept looking at her son. Maybe she felt it was something he shouldn't have been there to hear and felt guilty. It didn't matter. Renee clammed up. Slowly the boy began to relax, and then sat there the rest of the afternoon with a smirk on his face."

"Did she say anything to him?"

"Nothing," Anna said. "But she was fidgety."

"Is that it?" Deidre asked, disappointed.

"Not quite. Renee was fine until bedtime. A bit quiet, but we'd come to expect that after visits from her mother. It was her mother, after all, and for all intents and purposes Renee had rejected her. She must have been torn; felt guilty on the one hand, but knew what would happen if she let her guard down and agreed to go back to her.

"At bedtime she insisted on having her light on. She'd done that the first few nights here, and we'd indulged her. As we thought, pretty soon she dimmed the lights, and within a week turned them off completely. Now, all of a sudden, she wanted them on for no good reason."

"Did you deny her request?"

"Oh my God, no," said Anna. "We were quite flexible with Renee. We knew there would be some rough times. You know, two steps forward, one step back. We'd had plenty of experience with our other children. *All* had faced traumas, so this wasn't anything new. We weren't pushovers, but providing *love* was our overriding concern."

Now Paul took over. "As a matter of fact, we had reason to believe she might be upset around that time. It was then that Edward Costanzo was sentenced. There was the psychiatric review after his guilty plea, then the five- to fifteen-year sentence. We thought it was a delayed reaction on Renee's part, her wanting the lights on. She also started talking about hungry eyes again. Irrational ravings. So, yes, we allowed her to keep her light on, but she didn't sleep much at all that night. She had circles under her eyes the next morning. The same the next two nights. The school called and told us she'd fallen asleep in class, and woke up screaming.

"We decided to put our foot down. Lights were off that night. We were determined she get a good night's sleep. The next morning, we found her cowered in the corner, her nightgown discarded. She was covered only by a blanket. And it seemed she hadn't slept a wink. We kept her at home the next day. Maybe with Costanzo in the news again, kids were taunting and it was preying on her mind."

"The Renee I knew was such a tough kid, it's hard to think of her reacting as you say," Deidre said.

"Obviously, we were both sick with worry," Paul continued. "We allowed her in our room the next night; something we'd never done with Renee. She seemed to respond to our presence. At least she slept, if only fitfully.

"Without her knowledge we made an appointment with the child psychologist she'd seen earlier. She was furious; like we'd betrayed her. Said she had nothing to say to any damn stranger. Told us she just needed time, and it would go away. Again, her words, *it would go away*. Two days later she was dead."

They were all silent for a few moments, each lost in thoughts of Renee.

Deidre had one more thing she had to do before leaving. She'd thought it out on the way over, and while it sounded lame, she hoped she could pull it off.

She took out the six pictures of the women Jonas had shown her. He'd made a number of sets. She fingered them in her hand now.

"I'm going to ask one more favor. If it in any way upsets you, just tell me, and I'll forget it. We had an artist do some renderings of what Renee might look like if she were alive today. Something that might go with the articles. I wonder if you might look at them, and tell me which you think looks most like her?''

Paul eyed her suspiciously, but shrugged. "It's up to Anna. I don't want to upset . . ."

"What's the harm, Paul?" she interrupted. "I mean, I'm curious how she would have looked if she had lived. With today's computer enhancements, maybe I can see what she would have become.''

Deidre laid the six photos on a table in front of Anna. Paul came around and looked at them, then fixed his eyes on Deidre. "Damn realistic enhancements, if you ask me." Then he deferred to his wife. "Anna, what do you think?''

Anna was clearly captivated. "Any one of them could be her, I guess." Her eyes had misted up. "I mean a ten-year-old fills out. Not just the body, but the face. I was a teacher, and some kids would visit years after they'd had me. Some I'd recognize immediately. Others had changed so much they appeared total strangers. Any of these could be her. Now if I saw them in person, then I'd know. My goodness, what a foolish thought," she said, looking guiltily at her husband.

"I'm sorry to have upset you," Deidre said, quickly gathering up the photos.

"Please dear, you haven't," Anna said. "It's just that I hadn't thought so much about Renee in a long time. Such a waste. She was such a special child. I didn't see the pain she was going through . . ." She began to weep silently, and Paul led Deidre out to the front.

As Deidre was about to get into her car, Paul put a restraining hand on her arm. She looked at him. The smile was gone from his face.

"What the hell was that about?" he asked.

"What do you mean?"

"Those weren't computer-enhanced photos. There'd

only be one. Each of those women had distinguishing features, some totally different bone structures. They were six different women. And dead or alive, they were photos of real women.'' He put up a hand, as Deidre began to shake her head that he was mistaken.

''I was a cop remember. Still spend a lot of time at headquarters. I've seen enhancements. You're not dealing with a hick, young lady. Now what gives?''

Deidre bit her lip. Could she . . . *should she* confide in him? Would he think her mad or be so angry he'd contact Briggs, and make her look more the fool. But she saw he would not be placated, nor fooled with anything but the truth, so she threw caution to the wind.

''What if I told you Renee hadn't committed suicide?''

She was surprised he wasn't taken aback.

''Why would you think that?''

She wasn't yet ready to take the plunge with this man. She couldn't read him like most she'd interviewed. He was an enigma, yet she didn't know why.

''Her body was never found,'' she said lamely.

''Bullshit,'' he parried. ''You're not out here showing us Renee at twenty-three because her body was never found. Be straight with me. I'm not going to chew off your head, no matter how daft you sound.''

He'd tried to sound friendly, Deidre thought, but she had the distinct feeling if she didn't tell all she knew, she wouldn't leave unscathed.

''I received a postcard from Renee postmarked two days after her death. I know what you're going—''

''We did, too,'' he interrupted. ''*Six months* after her disappearance.'' He took out a worn wallet, extracted a postcard folded once, and handed it to her.

''It's not your fault,'' it started. ''I wanted to stay, but he wouldn't let me alone.''

It was unsigned, but printed in the same style as the card etched in Deidre's mind. And with a Philadelphia postmark, she noted. Maybe Timms wasn't on a fool's errand, after all, she thought to herself.

"What does it mean?" Deidre asked. "Who was she so afraid of, she had to make her disappearance look so final?"

"I'd assumed it was Costanzo," Paul said. "He'd been sentenced shortly before. Been all over the tube, and the whole episode had been replayed, rehashed, and like dirty laundry hung out to dry in public view. It had to be humiliating for her. She had trouble enough at school, as it was. Now her classmates were hearing on television that this beast kept her chained naked, *naked* except for a blanket; probably fondled her, possibly raped her. It was the first time the full details had come out."

"Renee didn't liked to be embarrassed," Deidre agreed.

"Kids being what they are, there would be snickering, teasing and taunting. When Renee disappeared, neither Anna nor I believed she'd committed suicide. It wasn't in her nature. She'd tough it out. We were devastated because it was so unlike her. But when I received the postcard, it made sense. She wouldn't kill herself, but she might run away. She wanted a fresh start, totally out of the limelight. If everyone thought she'd killed herself, there would be no new media onslaught. You know, a retrospective on the first anniversary of her kidnapping," he said with a wry smile. "No 'Where is she now' pieces five years later. Costanzo haunted her even behind bars. The media was in full fury for a few days after the staged suicide, but after that, until now, not a word. In a perverse way, I admired her logic."

"Why didn't you go looking for her? You were a cop, and it was mailed from Philadelphia. How hard would it have been to locate a ten-year-old with all your connections?"

"Believe me, Anna and I agonized over it. In the end

we grudgingly decided it was in Renee's best interests to let her remain dead. Imagine the media circus if it got out she hadn't died? Think of the stories if she'd been found. And just as important, there was always the possibility her mother would regain custody. She may have fooled you, though somehow I doubt it, but that woman was pure evil. Better Renee begin a new life no matter how hard than to go back and live with that woman."

"Did she ever contact you again?"

Deidre could see a tear forming at the corner of the man's eye. He brushed it away.

"No. That's why we were so certain she was dead. Living on the streets is no easy task. Too many runaways end up in the morgue or worse. And, we were certain she would contact us again to let us know she was all right if she were alive . . ."

He shrugged, unable to go on. A moment passed. "Why do you think she's alive?"

"I've spoken to her. By phone," she added. "Twice since Friday."

Deidre could see the hurt in Paul's eyes. He and his wife had taken her in as one of their own, and she had contacted a virtual stranger instead of them.

"She only called me because she sensed I was a threat."

Paul turned away for a moment, snapping his fingers. He'd done it once before in the backyard. A look from his wife made him stop. Then talking, as much to himself as to Deidre, he spoke his thoughts.

"You're the Mayor's Liaison to the Task Force investigating the Vigilante. They think it's Renee?" he asked incredulously.

"No. I *know* it's Renee. She's told me, herself. But, I haven't told the Task Force. They'd never believe Renee could be alive. They're certain it's a man.

"I knew it was Renee when I saw the message she'd scrawled on the mirror of her last victim. NO MORE

HUNGRY EYES. She knew I knew it was her, after she saw a statement I gave on television. Renee's the Vigilante.''

Paul, she could tell, was quick to put two and two together. ''Then your story about Loretta Barrows as a victim is an attempt to flush her out.'' It was a statement, not a question.

''Yes.''

''And the photos?''

''I used the FBI profile, with the knowledge I had, and honed in on someone who'd been at one time at the Police Academy; the most logical place a woman could learn the skills, and gain access to information on the victims. You know as well as I do that the media is only privy to what the police want them to be in such a case. There is no way the Vigilante could choose some of his, or in this case, her victims without a certain background. The six women I showed you all were at the Police Academy at some time in the past few years.''

''But why these six women? How did you narrow it down?''

''Mr. Sheffield, Renee visited me shortly after I arrived at the Task Force headquarters. She was disguised, and I was preoccupied. She left a note, 'Catch me if you can.' While I didn't get a good look at her, it was plain she was short and definitely not on the heavy side. The women I showed you most closely resemble the woman I saw.''

''Let me see the photos again,'' he said curtly; all cop now. He leafed through them once quickly, then a second time, giving each a thorough examination. He shook his head several times and handed four back.

''Unless she's had plastic surgery, these two can't be her. The bone structure doesn't match. Of the other four, I can't conclusively rule any of them out.''

''What's your instinct?''

He looked at her admiringly. ''You'd make a good

cop. Why should I help you catch Renee?''

''Because what she's doing is wrong. Because she's sick and needs help. Because, if I find her, maybe I can work out a deal to get her the help she needs. If the Task Force gets her first, she's just one more serial killer.''

''And what if they never catch her?''

''You can't be serious,'' she said. ''They will, although it will be by chance, not design. Meanwhile, she may kill another two or three people; maybe some innocent who sees something he shouldn't or gets in her way.''

''Maybe you.''

''I don't think so, but I won't tell you I haven't considered the possibility. She wants someone to chronicle her story, just as I did thirteen years ago.''

She paused a moment to let it all sink in. ''Mr. Sheffield, I didn't plan on interviewing you for the series I was writing. Renee sent me to you. Told me it was a clue to her identity. I don't know if she really wants me to find her, but she wants to give me the chance. Do you know why she'd send me to you?''

''Does she know about the photos?''

''No. The way I see it, the clue you'd provide was her desire to become a cop; to help protect those like herself. She didn't know I was already looking for someone who'd been at the Police Academy.''

''You sure she wasn't sending you on a fool's errand?''

''That's crossed my mind too. Renee is a great one for games. But she didn't know about the photos, so her sending me to you may have backfired on her. You want to tell me which you think is Renee?''

''One condition. If you do find Renee, you tell her Anna and I want to talk to her. You don't tell the police until she's had a chance to contact us. We want to speak to her *before* the media crush.''

''All right.''

Paul took the four photos back, and handed her two of them.

"If any of these women are Renee, it's one of these two, assuming she hasn't had plastic surgery. Shape of the eyes, fullness of lips, and any number of other little things only someone who'd spent a lot of time with Renee would know disqualified the other two. That, and as a cop, I was trained to observe. You spent a lot of time with her, but you didn't commit certain features to memory like I did. It could be one of those two, if Renee doesn't have you running in circles chasing your tail."

"You've been more help than you know," she said as she got in her car. "I'm really trying to help Renee."

Deidre started the car, but Paul wasn't finished.

"Miss Caffrey, be careful. The Renee we knew thirteen years ago may not be the same Renee you encounter now. God only knows what she's been through *since* she disappeared. Cornered, she may lash out, even if it's not her intention. She's obviously emotionally scarred and unstable. If you want, I'll back up your story that Renee is alive. Then the Task Force will have to take you seriously."

"I appreciate your offer, but I promised Renee I wouldn't involve the police. I've operated on trust my entire career, and I can't betray my principles now."

"Principles are fine when you're dealing with a rational human being. But I've got the feeling Renee has counted on you following the rules of the game, and it's a very dangerous game you're playing."

"I share your concern, but Renee won't harm me. You've got your instincts, and I've got my own sixth sense."

"I hope you're right. You will keep in touch. You will keep *your* promise to me."

"You've got my word, Mr. Sheffield, I'll give Renee a chance to contact you before I take any action."

Driving off, Deidre felt a huge weight lifted from her

shoulders. The postcard proved Renee had not strayed from Philadelphia. Timms might yet get a lead. And if Paul Sheffield was right, her quarry was either Roberta Bracken or Shara Farris.

Bracken, she recalled, was a beat cop with an undistinguished career to date, her three years on the police force. Shara Farris worked in records; had daily access to police computers and the files they held. With any luck, Jonas' voice tapes of the two would eliminate one.

Paul Sheffield had made a keen observation she had to consider. With his confirmation, she could march into Briggs' office, lay her hand on the table and have a bunch of professionals track Renee down. Was her word to Renee more important than the life of the next victim? Deidre shook her head. No, that wasn't it. She wanted Renee for herself. She wanted to confront Renee face to face before deciding what to do. It had nothing to do with principles. To the police Renee was a serial killer plain and simple. They couldn't understand—didn't care to understand—what demons drove her to kill. She had come this far on her own. She wasn't about to cut bait and turn everything over to the police.

She knew she was being selfish, but she wanted to be the one to bring Renee to ground. Let Briggs dismiss her then.

"I'm close, Renee," Deidre said out loud, "and you haven't got a clue."

As Deidre entered her apartment at 6:30, she instantly knew something was amiss. A creature of habit, she had turned off all the lights before she had left for work, yet now her apartment was lit up like a Christmas tree. As her eyes grew accustomed to the light, a chill ran down her spine. If she didn't know better she'd swear this wasn't her apartment. It certainly *wasn't* the apartment she had left that morning. What little furniture she had in the living room had been rearranged. The television, a recliner and couch were all on opposite sides of the room than they'd been when she had left.

A burglar was her first thought. Was he still here? She backed up instinctively, banging into the door.

Get a grip on yourself, she thought. This was no burglar. Burglars *take*, they don't rearrange.

Renee. It had to be Renee. With the thought her terror was even more palpable. If Renee had gotten in once, she could do so anytime. This time she had been at work, but what if she came at night, when she was asleep? She had never felt physically threatened by Renee, but the woman was sick, and as she had been warned more than once, was it healthy to operate under the assumption Renee wouldn't harm her?

Then Deidre spotted her fishbowl. Beside it lay Leon, her lone goldfish—*dead*.

Before leaving for Bosnia, the day before her birthday, her husband had presented her with Leon and a small bowl. Leon was to keep her company nights when he was gone. Her son had been mesmerized for several days by the fish who swam in circles seemingly going nowhere. Soon though he'd grown bored.

But everytime Deidre watched Leon traversing the bowl always ending where he started, she knew her husband, traveling hither and yon, like Leon, would return home.

She had considered giving the fish away when she had moved, but couldn't. Unlike the inanimate furniture she had gladly rid herself of, Leon was alive. Of all his gifts, most far more expensive, she had treasured the goldfish most, and would never part with him.

Now he lay dead; an abject lesson of how little Renee valued life of any sort.

She knew it was her story about Loretta Barrows that had driven Renee to this. Was it a warning, she wondered, of what might happen to *her* if she got too close, or followed up with her stories on Angela Mendino or the Sheffields?

Shaken as she was, she wasn't about to back down. She would have to be more cautious, but at least she knew she had struck a nerve.

She dwelled on that last thought as she put her furniture back in place, and disposed of Leon, flushing him down the toilet.

She'd just made herself some instant coffee and settled in the recliner when the phone rang. Jonas? Timms? No way. As she picked up the receiver, she knew it was Renee, calling to gloat, and this only angered her more.

"What do you want?" she asked before Renee could speak.

"Expecting me, were you?"

Deidre thought Renee would sound smug, but she could feel the woman's fury reach across the phone line, and she instinctively moved the receiver a few inches from her ear.

"What do you think you're pulling?" Shara continued. "Acting like a *real* reporter, aren't you now, Dee?"

"What's that supposed to mean?"

"Facts be damned. You wanted to provoke me, so you wrote all that sappy bullshit about my mother. And as people's memories are so terribly short, a lot will believe the lies you've spread. How dare you?"

"I don't know. Speaking with her put events into a new perspective. She wasn't the bitch you made her out to be. My mistake was relying so heavily on you in the past. I *wasn't* a reporter then. I was your mouthpiece. Maybe it's time to correct the injustice."

"New perspective, my ass."

"Have you seen her lately?"

"I don't have to," Shara said. "I lived with the woman for ten years. I was constantly reminded I was a mistake; that my father could have been any of a number of men, and I was lucky she didn't abort me. But, none of that appeared in your puff-piece, did it?''

"Is that why you trashed my apartment? To get back at me for the story?''

"I didn't trash your apartment," Shara said. "I just—''

"You killed my goldfish," Deidre interrupted. "You son of a bitch, to get back at me you killed a defenseless animal.''

"It's only a goldfish, for God's sake," Shara said, but Deidre could tell she sounded flustered.

"Leon may have only been a goldfish to you—''

"You gave it a name?" Shara interrupted this time. Deidre could tell she sounded amused. "What kind of name is Leon for a goldfish, anyway?''

"It was a gift from my husband. My son named it," Deidre said, trying to keep her memories at bay.

Shara was silent for a moment. "I didn't know. I'm sorry," she said finally.

Her pity further fueled Deidre's anger. "Sorry! You're a fraud, Renee. You talk of exorcising your demons by killing those who prey on innocents, but you have disdain for *all* life. You're out of control. Am I next on your list?''

"No. Never! Your story. I was angry. It won't . . .''

". . . happen again," Deidre finished for her. "I wonder, Renee. I really wonder.''

Deidre hung up, afraid if she stayed on the line she would say something in the heat of the moment that might drive Renee away for good.

Chapter Nineteen

The anger Shara had felt when she had called Deidre had dissipated. She didn't regret for a moment breaking into Deidre's apartment. She *was* in control, and had wanted Deidre to know how vulnerable she was. Not that she planned on harming Deidre. The reporter was her window to the world, after all. Her spokeswoman. Her mouthpiece. She had only wanted her to think twice about running those bogus stories about her abduction.

But Deidre was right. There had been no reason to kill the fish . . . Leon. It was totally out of character. She wasn't one of those wackos who in their youth burned cats or tossed dogs onto highways.

She'd been rearranging the furniture, and the damned fish kept watching her. Its eyes. Hungry eyes. So she had removed the fish from its bowl—to rid herself of its piercing eyes. Then she had forgotten about it, finished her work and left.

Well, she had wanted to scare Deidre, and she had— more than she'd planned, though not by design. Still, why did she feel like such a shit?

*   *   *

She was dancing to her music, the episode slowly receding into her memory, when the phone rang. On the fourth ring, the answering machine kicked in. She seldom got phone calls; a wrong number here and there. With an unlisted number there were no nuisance phone solicitations. There were the occasional calls from work, though. Someone calling in sick, Shara being called to see if she could work an extra shift.

The previous tenant of her flat, a college student, had left an answering machine, and Shara kept the generic message. "Sorry, I'm not in right now. Leave your name, number and time of your call at the beep and I'll get back to you."

The call must have been a wrong number, as the party hung up without leaving a message.

She set her alarm for three in the morning. The fish forgotten, she was still furious with Deidre, and she would pay with a rude wakeup call. She not only wanted to keep Deidre off guard, she wanted to dull her senses. Random calls, in the middle of the night, not only jolted her from a comfortable sleep, but once completed, Deidre would chew on its contents for another hour. Sapped of energy, at some crucial time, it would all catch up with her. Later, she would wonder how she had missed the obvious, but then it would be too late. And, having already called earlier, she'd be taken completely by surprise by a second call.

Twelve-thirty. *Silence of the Lambs* was on HBO. Delicious, she thought. She'd seen it a dozen times. It was now like background music. She'd exercise, rid her body of the tension of the evening, and possibly drift off, not quite falling asleep before it was time to wake Deidre.

Chapter Twenty

Jonas came by at one. He had called at eleven-thirty, told Deidre the day had flown by, and he still had lots to do. Could he come by at twelve-thirty? He'd again called at twelve-fifteen saying he'd be leaving shortly, but he hadn't arrived until one.

Deidre told Jonas of her meeting with the Sheffields. How Paul Sheffield had eliminated four of their suspects.

For his part, Jonas told how the phone calls had gone. He'd reached all but Sheila Jeffries and Roberta Bracken. He'd taken a chance, one of several Deidre was to learn, and called Jeffries' precinct, saying he had an important message for her. He'd been told she was on a stakeout. Would he leave a number where he could be reached?

Shara Farris hadn't been reached in person, but he had a taped message from her answering machine; as good as the real thing. Sheepishly, he told Deidre he'd called back several times; the last at twelve-thirty, just before he'd left for Deidre's house.

"We talked about needless chances," she told him, with a hint of anger. "I don't want to raise any suspicions."

"What's the harm? If she answered, I'd say wrong number and hang up." "You got her on tape."

"Yes, but . . ."

"But nothing, Jonas," she interrupted. "We're this close," she said, her fingers half an inch apart. "I don't want to blow it now."

"A bit overzealous, perhaps," and he shrugged. "No harm, no foul, though."

It was as close to an apology as she'd get. She was tired, and knew she was overreacting. It wasn't like Renee knew Deidre was zeroing in. It wasn't as if Renee knew how important her clue had been. As long as Renee hadn't been approached directly, Jonas couldn't be faulted for what he had done. Deidre knew she needed rest. Unfortunately, when she had tried to take a nap earlier that evening, she'd had so much on her mind she lay awake tossing and turning. A hot bath and good dinner had helped, but her testiness with Jonas was a clear sign she was on edge due to fatigue.

Her mind was drifting, some part of her subconscious told her, and she pushed everything away and focused again on Jonas.

"So, you got the tapes, or you just here to schmooze?" she said, with a smile to break the tension.

He took out a tape, and she put it in the tape deck.

None of the voices sounded remotely like Renee's. She replayed Shara Farris' voice three times, but shook her head.

"No. Not even close."

"Bracken, you think?" Jonas asked.

"*If* one of the six is Renee, and *if* Paul Sheffield is right and we can eliminate the Jeffries woman, it's got to be Roberta Bracken. Damn, wish we had a sample of her voice."

"She's stalking," Jonas said. "Told you as much."

"It all points to her. Still . . ."

"Tail or break-in?" Jonas asked.

"No break-in, Jonas. You've got to promise you won't go off half-cocked and do something rash. I know your adrenalin's flowing. Mine's been since I first saw the message at the last crime scene. But now it's time for caution. And remember what Paul Sheffield said. The woman we're hunting is not the Renee I knew thirteen years ago. I'm fairly certain she wouldn't harm me, but I can't say the same for anyone else who got in her way. Don't try to be a hero, and have me find you one of her victims.

"So no break-ins. Don't even think about one," she said with a tight smile. "A tail, however, would certainly be in order at this time. Someone discreet. Someone . . ."

Jonas held up his hand like a traffic cop signaling stop. "That's why I was so late. Thought we'd need at least four tails. If it were me, I'd still tail all six." Another shrug when Deidre gave him a scathing look.

"Want the best on Bracken?"

"Your best on Bracken. No one yet on Jeffries. From all we know she might spot a tail in minutes. For now keep trying to get a tape of her voice. She has to go home sometime. I seriously doubt it's her though. Paul Sheffield eliminated her without knowing she'd kept a high profile. Bracken's our best bet for the moment. Hell, our only bet."

"Any chance Sheffield would steer you away from Renee?" Another shrug, when Deidre shot him a warning. "Just playing Devil's advocate."

"You mean he knows . . . might have known all along Renee was the killer?" She considered the possibility and shook her head no. "My instincts say no. Much as he and his wife loved her, he's still a cop. Retired or not, once a cop, always a cop. He knows she'd be caught sooner or later, anyway. No, he's a straight arrow. It's Bracken or Farris, if it's any of them, and the tape eliminates Farris. So, who's your best?''

''Jack Bishop. Ex-marine. Ex-cop. Heads a security firm. Goes on night jobs at times. Hates desk work. Say the word, he picks Bracken up after she punches out tomorrow.''

''Do it then.''

Jonas got up to leave. ''Sorry . . .''

She waved him off. ''Your intentions were good, and no harm was done. Just be careful now. Have Bishop call the minute he learns something. Nothing else. No heroics. And, if he suspects he's been made, tell him to pack it in.''

She gave him a kiss on the cheek, and he was off.

One-forty-five. She was exhausted, and had to be up at seven. She tossed and turned for half an hour mulling over the day's events. She drifted off to an uneasy sleep, thinking she'd missed something. Why had Renee disappeared when she did? Paul Sheffield's explanation rang hollow. It was within her grasp yet still it eluded her.

Chapter Twenty-one

Shara had dozed and was in the throes of a recurring nightmare.

She was back in the basement of the house Costanzo had taken her to. The man, uttering words of apology, had placed a rag over her face and she had blacked out. She'd awakened in a cell—a cage—her clothes gone, a blanket by her side. She covered herself and waited for him to return. She had been caught by surprise, but she was confident she could handle Edward Costanzo. Twenty minutes passed before she was aware of eyes on her.

He was staring at her, then telling her to toss the blanket aside. She was surprised and confused. And a bit frightened. He made his demand again. She resisted, and he smiled. He approached the cage, a metal stick-like object in his hand.

"Know what a cattle prod is? Bought it from a mail order catalog. Tried it on a cat. Killed her. Hair flayed out in all directions, first, though. You such a little-bitty thing, it might kill you, too. Now be a good girl and toss the blanket."

She'd pulled the pea green army blanket around her tighter, ignoring its coarseness.

She saw from his eyes he was amused, even pleased that she had resisted. She didn't know what to do. If she tossed the blanket aside without a struggle, she was weak and he'd push her further. If she refused, he'd inflict pain, and enjoy that as much.

She froze, her mind unable to decide which course to follow.

He touched her with the prod and an electric current shot through her. Every nerve ending in her body seemed to respond to the touch. She was on the floor writhing uncontrollably, her body in spasms; her brain failing to respond to the overload of sensory messages it was receiving.

She must have passed out. When she awakened, she was on her back; the blanket in the corner of the cage. He was staring at her body, his eyes probing her flat chest, inching down to her genitals. She could almost feel his eyes inside of her, examining her sex. She covered herself with her hand. He lifted the prod.

"You don't want to do that."

And she didn't. One more taste of the prod might kill her, or worse, leave her a brain-damaged vegetable. She'd seen druggies on the street who'd OD'd. Not enough to kill, just enough to make them walking zombies. And she wanted to live. She would not die in this cage. She would do whatever was necessary to survive, and kill him for what he was doing to her.

So she did as she was told. Stood up with her hands behind her back, so he could take her picture. Touched herself at his command, tears of humiliation welling in her eyes.

He'd leave, only to reappear without warning half an hour later. She was his to command. He staggered his appearances. Sometimes he wouldn't return for hours. Other times he'd leave and pop back in within minutes.

She knew it was to keep her constantly on edge. But the knowledge didn't help.

Her body tensed at every sound. He'd come during the day. He'd come at night. Bring her food, then tell her to smear it on her body. So much tension brought on spasms of stomach cramps. There was a pail for her to pee and defecate in. Whenever she relieved herself, he'd return, taking pictures. If she tried to get up, he'd yell at her, tell her if she made a mess on the floor she'd have to lick it up. So, she sat on the pail while he took her picture.

On a television with the on/off button ripped off, she saw news stories about her disappearance. Her tearful mother. Bullshit. Her frail grandmother. Even Edward Costanzo, who admitted to being the last one to see her before she disappeared. She screamed at them one and all, as if they could hear her through the tube.

She would turn from the television and see him watching her, that crooked smirk on his face. He seemed to enjoy the embarrassment she felt, as her fear was exposed. He took more pictures, sometimes allowing her to keep the blanket that was her shield wrapped around her.

Finally, except for raping her or killing her, there was nothing more he could do. And oddly enough, her final surrender turned out to be her salvation. He'd come, and she would shed the blanket without his asking; her face drained of emotion. She would prance around the cell, get on all fours and growl like the caged animal she was. She ran her hands down, over and into her body without his having to ask.

He would yell obscene commands, and she'd obey immediately. But she shed no tears. She had none left. A robot, an automaton, he soon lost interest. He sometimes yelled at her to resist. He would tell her to touch herself, and yell when she did, demanding she exhibit pride. She ignored him.

Soon he became bored. His visits were less frequent, and finally stopped all together on the fifth day of her captivity.

She had unwittingly learned the most important lesson of her life. One must adapt to survive. One can *always* adapt if one's survival instinct is strong enough.

Still, the price was excruciatingly high. Even after her release his eyes refused to let her be.

And thirteen years later those same eyes sought her out.

One to go, and she'd finally be free of their voracious gaze.

Or was she merely fooling herself?

The alarm interrupted the nightmare.

Sweating profusely, she smiled.

Once again, she'd taken his best shot and survived. And survival was all that counted.

She called Deidre, her fingers caressing the unseeing eyes on her breasts that had helped ward off his hungry eyes for yet another night.

Deidre mumbled something unintelligible upon answering the phone, apparently dropped the receiver and then retrieved it.

Good, Shara thought, she'd wakened her from a deep sleep. Her anger escalated as she recalled Deidre making her feel so guilty for killing her fool goldfish.

"I can get to you whenever I want, you know," she said without preface.

"Wha . . . oh shit." There was a pause and Shara heard some fumbling in the background.

"It's three in the morning."

"So?"

"Don't *you* have to go to work tomorrow? Don't you sleep?"

"Sleep? Precious little. I can sleep all I want when my work is done. You, though, I wouldn't sleep so soundly if you continue to write that shit like you did yesterday.''

"Really bugged you, didn't it?"

Shara could tell Deidre had recovered.

"It angered me at the time, but in hindsight I could care less. And it's not going to get you anywhere."

"But you do care, Renee. You care or you wouldn't have paid your visit."

"You misunderstand. It was just to let you know how vulnerable you are."

"Believe what you want, Renee, but we both know it's infuriating you to see your childhood distorted. Makes you want to strike back at me. Maybe even kill me."

"Never kill you, Dee. I'd never kill you. You've gotta believe that."

"Wish I could, but even you don't know if you can control yourself." She paused, but Renee didn't respond. "By the way, I interviewed your foster parents today," Deidre finally said, further throwing Shara off balance.

"Don't you dare write anything that would hurt or embarrass them. If you do . . ."

"What, you'll hurt me? Control, Renee. You're losing it. Don't worry, though. They're good people. I won't hurt them, but they provided me with a lot of juicy tidbits about you."

Shara remained silent. She *did* want to hurt Deidre, and the revelation frightened her. Deidre was talking again, but Shara had trouble concentrating.

". . . you promised a clue, and you sent me on a wild goose chase. That wasn't part of our bargain."

"You got your clue," Shara said, sounding irritated, "if you're the reporter you think you are. Don't go playing me for a fool, girlfriend."

"They knew you were alive. At least, they know you didn't commit suicide. I thought I was the only one."

Another curve from out of left field, Shara thought.

Careful now. Let her do the talking. "And how's that?"

"You don't remember the postcard you sent them?"

Damn, Shara thought to herself, she *had* forgotten. Not really forgotten, but it was so long ago. But it surely couldn't lead Deidre to her. Unless. No, she thought, Paul Sheffield wouldn't help Deidre. Would he?

"I didn't want them to blame themselves for something that wasn't their fault," Shara said, finally getting a grip on herself.

"Then whose fault was it?"

No answer. Shara wanted to see where she'd go with this line of probing.

"Were you afraid your mother would get custody of you?"

Shara smiled. Not even close.

"What's with you tonight, Dee? You're jumping all over the place. Is it fatigue, or are you hoping to trip me up?"

"You're not going to give me anything, are you? Then I'll give you something. The Sheffields know you're alive. I told them everything, and they're cooperating with me. Remember, Paul was a cop, just like you wanted to be."

"That was a pretty shitty thing to do." Shara was thinking if any damage had been done. Again she wondered whether her foster-father would help Deidre. More important, *could* he help her? She had to think, but Deidre wasn't about to let her. She was talking, and again Shara had missed part of what she'd said.

". . . shouldn't have sent me out there, then. Paul Sheffield's sharp. I'm working with the Task Force. I'm doing a retrospective on you. He knows you didn't kill yourself. He put two and two together. What was I supposed to do? If you hadn't sent them the postcard . . ." Deidre stopped, as if not needing to say the obvious.

"My mistake. I never could pull the wool over their eyes. Good people. Might have made something of me . . ." Now it was Shara's turn to let the thought drop. The memories of what could have been were painful.

"So why did you leave?"

"It's not time, Dee. It'll all fall into place for you, but not yet."

"Why haven't you contacted them since? You went to the trouble of letting them know you were alive, then let them worry about what's become of you."

"I wasn't Renee any longer. Not the child they took in. I didn't contact you either, and you knew I was alive."

"But they loved you, like a mother and father. Look, why not call them now? Paul asked me to pass it on to you."

"I can't. Not now. Not yet. Maybe not ever. Soon, though, Paul will put it all together. Unless, that is, you can catch me before I strike next."

"Oh, I will Renee. You can make book on it. Look, I'm bushed. Try calling earlier tomorrow."

"Who says I'll call tomorrow?"

"Read my article. Maybe you'll want to issue a rebuttal."

With that she hung up.

Shara began pacing the room. Smug. She had been too damned overconfident. Sending Deidre to her foster parents had been a mistake. How could she have forgotten about the postcard? *If* Paul was helping her, there was no margin for error. They probably hadn't thought about her in years, but after Deidre's visit, she knew Paul would let every moment she was with them fester in his mind until he figured out what had caused her to fake her suicide. And he *was* good. He might well figure out the reason, and that could be her undoing. She didn't fear being caught. Worse than capture was not completing what she'd set out to do. She'd have to move her timetable up. There was no reason not to.

As much as she had enjoyed her parries with Deidre,

it was now becoming a nuisance. Not only had she provided a clue, but a valuable resource to the reporter. Was she slipping? Was Deidre a more worthy adversary than she had counted on? And seeing the past dredged up in the papers was grating, too. She didn't want to think of her mother, but the abuse intruded upon her thoughts. And the thought of that woman getting sympathy riled her to no end.

She'd set a fox loose in the chicken coop, and had to take responsibility. No more clues for Deidre. Soon enough she'd have all of her answers, and slap herself, for it had all been staring her in the face.

She was again sweating fiercely as she recalled watching Bobby—yesterday, it was now. She'd taken up her customary spot in the lot across from the gas station after work.

Bobby's routine was unchanged. He worked in the garage. He was no gas jockey. A mechanic. But he kept an eye on the gas pumps. He'd take a break whenever a young girl stopped by.

He was brazen. Teeny bopper would stop by with her mother, and he'd flirt with her. Parents today, she thought. None of them seemed to give a damn. But, then again, all Bobby did was look. Might have seemed innocent enough to the mother, if she even gave it a second thought.

He worked until closing—eleven o'clock—then went home, no stops on the way. This must be his weekday routine. She would confirm it again today.

She hung around until midnight. At eleven-forty-five his lights went out, but he didn't. He was staying put.

Tomorrow she'd strike.

Her breasts ached something fierce. Always did when the decision was made. She looked in the mirror. There was one space left on each breast, directly above the nipple. The tattoo artist wondered why she wouldn't allow him to work there. She'd told him it was for something special. Soon she'd be complete; whole again.

Still, she began to shiver, which only made her sweat more. What if she were wrong? What if Bobby's death didn't chase away his eyes? What if they craved more?

She went to the tape deck and played her song.

Normal. Could she *ever* live the semblance of a normal life? She danced to the music until dawn, the ache in her breasts slowly subsiding as the music took hold.

Chapter Twenty-two

Damn that woman, Deidre thought, as she plopped into bed. She needed sleep. She hadn't expected a second call from Renee that night.

And she'd muddled through their conversation without gaining any new insight. Or had she? For some reason Renee was now upset that Deidre had spoken with the Sheffields. *Paul will put it all together*. Put what together? What might Paul Sheffield know that could lead her to Renee?

Renee hadn't answered her phone earlier. Jonas had confirmed that. When she called earlier it must have been from a phone booth. And now she calls at three in the morning. Stalking. She was out stalking. Roberta Bracken? Everything pointed toward her. She'd have her confirmation soon, she was sure. A tape of her voice. Then the tail. And a final confrontation, this time face to face. "I'm close, Renee. You don't know how close," she said in a whisper, and finally drifted off to sleep.

* * *

At 6:55 her phone was ringing again, and she fumbled to reach it. Damn you, Renee, she thought, but it was Tony Hill, the Mayor's closest aide.

"Dee, sorry to wake you, but the shit's hit the fan, and we're going to need you."

Deidre tensed. Had Renee struck that night?

"... negotiations collapsed ... strike on our hands ..."

Deidre focused in. This wasn't about the Vigilante.

"Slow down, Tony. What's going on?"

"I just told you. Negotiations with the municipal unions broke down last night. City workers made good on their threat of a strike. Took us totally by surprise. Shit, we all thought their threats were just posturing for the membership. Threats, deadlines, last-minute talks, a minor breakthrough and then an extension. But, no, first sign of a stalemate, and they say fuck you, you want a strike, you've got one."

"Tony!" Deidre commanded. "Get ahold of yourself and stop talking gibberish. Give me some facts I can work with."

"No garbage collections, that's what you can work with. No collections, and it's supposed to get up past ninety degrees. Do you get my drift? Doesn't matter, by this afternoon, the smell will be wafting across the city.

"Look, I know you're working on the Vigilante killing, but we need you up here to brief the press on our contingency plans. Get down here as fast as you can, and I'll brief you. It's going to be a long day. Bring a change of clothes with you. It might be an all-nighter."

Tony Hill tended to exaggerate, but Deidre had the sinking feeling this day would be lost. The strike was totally unexpected. The Unions had been working without a contract since early in the summer, but progress had been made in negotiations. The sticking point was privatization of trash removal. With the city's fiscal crisis, the Unions could forgo a raise, but privatization meant lost jobs, and this the Unions couldn't accept. With temperature in the nineties for the past five days, now, she imagined the Unions decided to flex their muscles when the city was most vulnerable. She'd remembered other strikes where trash hadn't been collected, and things got ugly. School strikes people could deal with. A minor inconvenience. Even the blue flu by police and firemen could be tolerated. As it was, the police didn't have much of a grip on crime. But, people got their dander up when their trash wasn't collected. The smell was bad enough, but the flies, roaches and rats . . . just thinking about it made her skin crawl.

She had planned on interviewing Renee's half-brother that day. It might not be necessary, after she heard Roberta Bracken's voice, but she wasn't taking any chances. She had called his job and been told he didn't start work till noon. She would have called then and set up a late-afternoon appointment, but that would have to wait now. Whatever spare time she could find would be devoted to writing her story about the Sheffields for the next day's paper. She still didn't have a handle on it. And by the time it saw print, hopefully she'd be confronting Renee, in the person of Roberta Bracken.

Before leaving, she called Briggs to let him know she wouldn't be in.

"No problem," he said somberly. "We ain't got squat anyway. The good news is the strike will take the heat off of us. You might want to see if you can prolong it for a week or two," he said good-naturedly.

"God forbid. Imagine the stink."

"Well, just a thought. I'll give you a call if anything comes up."

She called Jonas, apologized for waking him, and filled him in. When she got the feel for the situation down at City Hall, she would get back to him. She wanted to hear the tape of Roberta Bracken as soon as

Jonas was able to reach her, and know what Frank Bishop turned up.

"One more thing. Do me a favor and call Timms. Let him know where he can reach me if he turns up anything."

She looked at her bed longingly, sighed and headed for the door.

The day was as nightmarish as she'd assumed. Actually more so.

Taken completely off guard in the midst of the summer's worst heatwave, the Unions held all the cards. The City was going to seek an injunction; dump sites previously established had to be manned and announced to the public; police had to be pulled off assignments to protect dump sites, and assure picketing was free of violence.

Deidre had to coordinate all of this with the media. The public was looking to City Hall for answers during this crisis, and she was the Mayor's spokesperson. In theory, and in fact, he was meeting with the various unions, so she had to articulate the City's message and plan of action. How the public perceived the City's response in great part was determined by how she did her job. Much as she had other things to do, she had an obligation to assure the City put on its best face during the crisis.

At noon the Mayor held a press conference to dispel fears. Deidre spent the rest of the day granting individual interviews to beat reporters from both the print and electronic media. She staggered the release of news to make it appear the city had a coordinated plan, and was making progress. First, news of the filing for an injunction, followed by the announcement that dump sites were open and police would be on hand to insure the safety of all those who brought trash to the sites. And later, she told selected sources the Mayor and representatives for the Unions had met unofficially, and progress was being made.

At eight-thirty that night she was spent. Tony Hill, all five-foot-two-inches, balding at thirty-five, with a Hitler complex to boot, told her to skedaddle. All was quiet, and the late-evening news would simply be a rehash of the day's events. An hour before, the stalled negotiations had begun anew. The Mayor was reportedly willing to compromise. He didn't have the stomach, both figuratively and literally, for a protracted strike. As he wasn't sure he had enough votes in City Council to push through privatization, he wasn't about to make it a political issue for which he could be embarrassed. And a protracted strike, with garbage piling up, was not good for any Mayor's image. Local news would become national headlines, and blame would be heaped at his doorstep. If nothing else, this Mayor was a political animal, and knew when to posture and when to be conciliatory.

The Unions, for their part, cautioned their membership against confrontation. The Unions themselves were split; their unity fragile. While none favored privatization, the concept impacted only a few, and some Unions opposed going all out on this one issue at the expense of others equally important to them.

Things were back on a relatively even keel.

"I know you want to get back to the Task Force," Tony said, looking up at Deidre. "Get a good night's sleep, and I'll call you at seven. If all hell doesn't break loose you can come here for a briefing at, say, two, issue a statement and be off.

"The worst is over for now. There'll be three or four days of give and take in negotiations, and both sides will agree to what's been leaked for the past three weeks. Now it's all about saving face."

Deidre, mesmerized by the bald spot that glistened below her, nodded sleepily and left.

*   *   *

Jonas was sipping a beer when she entered her apartment.

"Tough day, kid?"

"The worst. All I want is a shower and . . ."

The sight of the tape Jonas held up wiped the fatigue from her face. Confirmation, she hoped, that Roberta Bracken was Renee was just within her grasp.

"What are we waiting for," she said, taking the tape and heading for the deck.

"Got both Bracken and Jeffries," Jonas said. "Didn't want to take any chances."

Her crestfallen expression as she heard their voices spoke volumes.

"Struck out with all six," Jonas said, his tone echoing Deidre's disappointment.

Deidre played the tape back a dozen times, then did the same with the tapes of the other four women. None were even close.

"Bishop's still tailing Bracken," Jonas said. "Something could turn it."

"Stop the wishful thinking, Jonas. We're back to square one. You might as well call him off. We've got to go back to the master list you started with, and find other possibilities.

"One more thing. Paul Sheffield mentioned a computer enhanced photo bearing Renee's likeness. It got me thinking. One of your *friends* could take Renee at ten and give us a likeness as to what she'd look like now. If nothing else, it will eliminate some on the list.

"I'm sure there's more we could do . . . *must do*, but my mind's a ball of cotton. I need twelve uninterrupted hours of sleep to become functional again, not that Renee will give it to me."

The phone rang as Deidre was heading for the bathroom to take a shower. "Get that for me, Jonas," she said without turning. "If it's Renee tell her I'm dead on my feet and she's to blame." She began laughing bitterly, shedding all pretense of strength she'd shouldered since Friday.

"Timms," Jonas said, after he'd answered the phone. "He's got something."

There was no surge of adrenalin as Deidre turned around and wearily retraced her steps.

"Sorry to bother you, girlie. I know you've had a busy day, what with the strike and all. Saw you on the news, and you looked like death warmed over."

"I appreciate your sympathy, but right now a shower, no, a long hot bath, would do a hell of a lot more for me."

"Sorry to disappoint you, child, but I think you best get down here now. Might be I've found someone your friend stayed with."

Deidre refused to allow her hopes to rise again. She'd been so close, she thought, only to be knocked down, stepped on and spat upon. It was time to be practical. Expect the worst, and hope she'd be surprised.

"Where to, Timms?"

"The shelter for battered women at Eighth and Locust."

"Do you know what time it is? Wouldn't we be disturbing—"

"Would I call you in the middle of the night if the person I found didn't want to be disturbed," he interrupted, without the slightest trace of annoyance. "No, girlie, Sister Mary Sheridan is a night person. She'll see you now."

Twenty minutes later, Deidre and Jonas were ushered into a room on the first floor of a three-story building. This was one of several shelters for abused and battered women. This one had private rooms for the thirty women who stayed at any given time. It was a halfway house of sorts. Women could stay with their children for a maximum of ninety days. In that time an attempt would be made to get them jobs or training, and locate a more permanent residence. Some would be sent out of town altogether for fear abusive husbands would track them down. There were so many to accommodate, and not enough rooms nor funds to keep any family for more than three months.

Timms provided Deidre with some background on Sister Mary Sheridan before he ushered her into a room at the end of the hallway.

There was none of his folksy charm in the recounting. She had never seen him in this light, and imagined this was the tone he'd use with an addicted gambler who owed him money, and hoped to win it all back on a sure thing.

"Sister Mary Sheridan was a folk hero in her day. For ten years she ignored the pleas of friends and the authorities and delivered food nightly to the homeless; those on the streets and subway concourses.

"Ten years ago a recently released mental patient, who had carved out his turf, wanted not only food but her purse. She refused, but wouldn't abandon him. She would come by nightly and he'd renew his plea. One night he wouldn't accept her polite refusal and beat her severely. Her hip and leg were broken.

"She refused to prosecute, or even identify her assailant. However, justice is not totally blind on the streets. Three weeks later, he was found bludgeoned to death, and left on the very spot of his attack as a warning of sorts. Only then did Sister Mary acknowledge he had been her attacker.

"A bit ironic, wouldn't you say? The person who might help you was herself the beneficiary of the type of street justice being dispensed by the Vigilante."

"Did she fully recover?" Deidre asked.

"As a matter of fact, no, and the years since have not been particularly kind to her, but don't be taken aback by her appearance. She's as sharp as you or I upstairs."

Sister Mary was sitting in a tattered cloth easy chair

near a window. The room was sparse; a bed, bureau with a legal pad and pen. Only a bookshelf, overflowing with books of every sort, separated the room from others she'd passed in the shelter.

The woman she had come to see seemed dwarfed in the chair. She was sixty, Deidre thought, if she were a day; her pale face heavily lined, devoid of all makeup. She wore her greying black hair in a bun, and was wrapped in a bathrobe.

If Deidre didn't know she was a nun, she would have taken her for an old woman pining away the last years of her life in a dingy room. A cigarette hung from her mouth, the ash half an inch long. The woman seemed unaware as the ash dropped on her robe. A minute later, still not having acknowledged Deidre's presence, she lit a new cigarette with the remains of the old, and took several puffs. She coughed after drawing on the smoke, and when she finished, Deidre became aware of her raspy breathing.

"Emphysema," the woman said, finally looking at Deidre. "Don't look so appalled. I'm a nun, not a saint. We all have our indulgences. Sit," she said, pointing to a straight-backed chair at the writing desk. Jonas brought the chair and set it across from the woman and Deidre sat.

"I don't get around much, now, since my . . . mishap," she said with a slight smile. "I'm sure Mr. Timmerman has filled you in with all the gory details. Stubbornness was another of my many vices, and I've paid dearly for my vanity. Lately, I've had to curtail my activities even more. I used to get around with a cane, but arthritis set in on the hip."

"I'm sorry . . . ," Deidre began, not really knowing how to respond, but the woman across from her waved it off.

"Nothing to be sorry about. I've lived a full life, with few regrets. The last, what, six years I've counseled the many women who fly in and out of this place. The emphysema has made even that difficult. The Good Lord must have been mightily peeved at my insolence, and this is my cross to bear.

"Still, I think I've made a difference to some. But enough about me. Your Mr. Timmerman showed me a picture. One from thirteen years ago. I won't presume to ask why you're interested in her today. What do you want to know?"

"Are you sure you recognized the girl in the picture?" Deidre asked, holding it out to her again.

"My child," she said, a mild rebuke in her voice, but her eyes afire. "I may be a cripple, but my eyes are as good as yours, as is my mind. Emphysema is not to be confused with Alzheimers. Let's not waste both of our time. With my various conditions, I don't sleep, but take several naps during the course of the day and night. When the pain's too much, I awaken, take some medication, and go about my business until I tire again.

"Mr. Timmerman was by earlier, and I told him I'd be up around this time. Pretty soon, I'll doze again until the hip or the cough wakes me up."

"I won't take much of your time," Deidre said.

She waved her hand in dismissal. "Don't mind me. I'm told I have an acid tongue, but I don't bite. Now spit it out."

As Deidre spoke the woman sat there, her eyes closed, gently puffing on the cigarette, as if to draw strength to answer her questions.

Briefly, Deidre told her of Renee's abduction, her reporting the story, and the retrospective piece she was writing. She divulged nothing about Renee's current activities, but told of her surprise when the girl's foster parents confided in her that she hadn't committed suicide.

"She's taken another identity, and I'd like to speak with her. I'm not looking to expose her, but I think she would want to know just how important she was to her foster parents. I might be able to arrange a reunion between them.''

Minutes passed after Deidre had finished, and she wondered if the old woman had fallen asleep. She looked at Jonas and Timms, who both just shrugged. Finally, a chill seemed to pass through the woman's body, and she opened her eyes, looking deeply into Deidre's.

''The last is a crock; a reunion you say. Maybe you'd also like to set up a reunion with her mother, the vile creature you wrote about in Monday's paper.''

Deidre looked nonplussed, caught up in her lie, unaware the nun had followed her story.

Sister Mary smiled. ''Child, there's more behind this dilapidated shell of a body than meets the eye. I told you so. But why you want this woman is no concern of mine. Maybe I'll read about it in the papers,'' she said with a wry smile, ''and maybe I won't. What do you want to know?''

''Did you see her anytime after she faked her suicide?''

''I told your Mr. Timmerman I had. Once or twice, mind you, and only for a moment or so. She might have needed my handouts, but I could see she had no desire to be approached. I recognized her from the picture in the paper. She'd cut her hair, wore a cap, and bundled a coat about her, the collar covering much of her face. But I was good with faces. I knew who she was. Not that I'd any thoughts of turning her in.

''She was a jackrabbit, though. If I approached, she would have bolted. In time, if she needed help, she would have learned more about me and sought me out.''

''But she didn't?''

''No. She met someone else; another child who wanted to disappear. Only this girl was five or six years older.'' Sister Mary paused to light another cigarette before the one in her mouth was extinguished. "Anything else?"

Deidre could see a faint smile on the old woman's face. She was enjoying this, Deidre thought. She'd tell her what she wanted, but Deidre would have to ask. Deidre played her game.

"Do you know the name of the other girl?"

"Shara. Never told anyone on the street her last name.· She had a job at one of those clubs where women dance with little or no clothes, and she took your friend off the street."

Deidre could feel her heart pounding. Shara Farris? Was she still alive and living with Renee? Was it *her* voice on the machine?

"Did they remain together? I mean do you know if they're still together now?"

Sister Mary laughed, then began coughing. "Together now. Hardly. They remained together until Shara died. She was beaten by a customer at the club who thought she was a hooker."

"What happened to Renee?"

"She became Shara. Danced at the club, then I lost track of her. Died, moved on, or maybe moved up out of our world. You know, became a regular citizen."

"Anything else I should be asking?" Deidre said, and now she was smiling.

"You've milked me dry, child. Nothing more I can tell you. I'm feeling a little tired now, so I think I'll doze a bit, if you don't mind."

Deidre was about to say something, but the nun read her mind.

"Don't be thanking me, now. Words don't fill empty stomachs. When you go, you might leave a little contribution with Sister Sylvia. The children barely get enough to eat, you know."

She closed her eyes, dismissing them.

Once on the street, Deidre could hardly contain herself.

"Jonas, it's Shara Farris. I don't know how she worked the answering machine, but it's her."

"What now?"

"I want to get into her room. Be there when she gets off from work. Confront her. Can you find out her shift?"

"She's dangerous," he said, and Deidre could see the concern etched on his face.

"Jonas, she won't harm me. You don't know her like I do. She needs me. She needs someone to validate what she's been through; to help explain what she's become."

"She's not sane."

"Of course not. But I'm her window to the world. She wants her story told. She knows I'll be sympathetic, no matter what she's done. Will you help me?"

"I've got friends," he replied, his voice resigned.

"Good. Now, I've got to get some sleep. Find out her shift. I don't want to get there too early, maybe an hour before she gets home, so I can look about. I won't set my alarm. Use your discretion. If possible, don't wake me until at least ten. Then we can talk about how we'll handle it."

She turned to Timms, who had made a show of ignoring them, but she knew he was soaking in their whole conversation.

"How can I possibly thank you, Timms? I was dead in the water, and you literally rescued me."

"Not me you have to thank, girlie, but the good Sister. A contribution to the shelter every once in awhile, I think, would show your gratitude."

"You've got it." She kissed him on the cheek.

"It's good to see you on your feet again, girlie. *This* is the kind of work you were cut out for, if you don't mind me saying, rather than speaking up for that pansy at City Hall. But enough. Get your sleep. I've got a feeling you'll need it.''

He winked, and Deidre knew he'd overheard everything she'd told Jonas. In her excitement, she'd totally forgotten about him. And, as much as she knew Timms would be dying to know what transpired, he'd never broach the subject. Not only that, he wouldn't come to her someday, if he were in trouble, and ask her to intercede because she "owed him." He'd agreed to help her without asking for anything in return.

It was odd, she thought, sometimes you couldn't tell the good guys from the bad without a program. When she'd first met Timms, she had these preconceptions of his being a vulture. But, even though she might despise his choice of occupation, he was every bit as good a person—better in fact—than Briggs, Tony Hill or the Mayor.

Driving home with Jonas, she felt a rush she hadn't experienced since before her husband and son had died.

I've got you, Renee, she thought to herself.

Beat you at your own game.

Beat you.

Beat you.

Chapter Twenty-three

Shara walked up the stairs to her flat at three. Though it was hot as ever outside, she wasn't sweating. It was like this whenever she had made her decision to rid herself of the eyes. A calm enveloped her like a protective blanket. The stalking over, her body was in harmony with her mind.

There had been one errand she had run at lunch. She needed the pictures in Chattaways' mother's house, yet she knew the woman would be there. Try as she might, she couldn't think of a way to induce her out of the house without raising suspicions.

So, she donned her blond wig, scar and mole, along with a generic service uniform she had purchased over a year before.

Just before one, she knocked on Loretta Barrows' door.

"Phone company, m'am," she'd answered in response to an irritable demand to know who was intruding on her. Solicitations were common in this neighborhood: from girl scouts selling cookies to Amway salesmen peddling vitamins. Apparently Loretta Barrows discouraged such unbidden callers.

"We received a call your phone's out of order. We couldn't fix it from the office. I'd like to check it, if you don't mind."

Loretta opened the door after several moments, and Renee, despite herself, allowed the woman a long hard look at her.

"Ain't nothing wrong with my phone. You're not trying to sell me nothing, are you?"

"I'm not selling, m'am. Your line's been busy all morning, and the only way I can fix it is by checking your phones. But, if you'd rather I leave . . ." she let the rest hang.

"Won't cost me nothing, will it?"

"Not a thing. Just have to check each extension."

"Well, all right, but I'm watching one of my shows, and I don't want to be bothered."

"You just go about your business. You won't know I'm here, and I'll be done in no time."

The rest had been easy. She went upstairs, ostensibly to check out the extension in Loretta Barrows' room, but went to her son's instead. Having searched the room in his efficiency, she had a pretty good idea where he kept the pictures she needed. Sure enough, she located the loose board under a throw rug without a problem. She took less than half of the photos, putting them in an empty supply case that supposedly carried her tools.

Downstairs, she found Loretta Barrows glued to the tube.

"Found the problem," she said. "Want me to show you?"

"Hush," the woman hissed, and Shara waited three or four minutes until a commercial came on. What a waste, Shara thought as she observed the woman. She hadn't changed a bit in thirteen years; her fat ass planted in an easy chair for the greater part of the day. Then, while watching her shows, she'd bellow out orders, when her daughter had returned from school. Now she just had the screen for company.

What would happen, she thought, if she said, "Mother, it's Renee, your daughter." She'd bet the woman wouldn't even turn around. Focused on her show, it wouldn't register.

While she'd told Renee she hated the woman, strangely she had no desire to harm her. A killer of five already, she could easily kill the woman if she wished. No, she didn't hate the woman. She was just nauseated by her. This wasn't her mother. This person had borne her, and done little else. She'd been a stranger most of her childhood, and was merely a stranger now.

Finally, a commercial came on and Loretta turned her head towards Shara, without getting up. "It's all fixed then?"

"Just a minor glitch. I can show—"

"No need. I won't be getting no bill, now, will I?" she asked suspiciously.

"No charge."

"You can see yourself out, if you don't mind," she said, as her show resumed.

As Shara opened the door to her apartment, she detected a foreign odor. There was someone waiting in the room. Shara smiled.

She was particularly sensitive to smells. Always had been. Loretta Barrows that morning had smelled of decay.

She'd get a jolt, in particular, when she could detect the smell of fear when she confronted her victims. She felt a rush before they died when she smelled the collapse of their resolve.

At work, she could close her eyes and know who passed by, even if there were two or three people.

And there were her own smells, of course. Her body

excreted one odor when she was particularly susceptible to the tormenting eyes. There was a totally different odor when she stalked. And, another odor entirely when the decision was made to strike. Finally, an odor after the deed was done, and another set of eyes could no longer hound her. That last odor had stayed with her a good while at the beginning. Lately, though, it lasted just a short period of time, and when the eyes returned so did the first odor.

Hunting Bobby, she'd noticed a subtle change to the odor that normally accompanied her stalking. Tracking normally held no fear for her. But hunting Bobby had been something different altogether. Thrust it out of her mind all she wished, she was afraid. It wasn't fear of being discovered. Just the terror of being near him. The odor had been magnified when she'd driven to the service station where he worked. So close to him, she had trouble breathing, her own stench was so strong. So much like an animal of prey. Fear, and the odor with it, mounted, as she wondered if he could smell her. But he had ignored her. Not young enough. The smell, though, had clung to her the rest of the afternoon and into the evening, as she watched his movements.

Now, in her room, there was the odor of only one person. A woman with a smell she remembered from the distant past. She didn't turn on the light. With the shades drawn, she could just make out the outline of a figure seated in the only chair in the room; the one by her desk.

"So you found me, Dee. Congratulations are in order."

"How did you know it was me?"

Shara could detect a trace of disappointment in the woman's voice. She imagined Deidre thought she'd be surprised, upset or stunned that she'd been discovered. Though she was surprised, she wasn't about to show it.

"You're wearing the same perfume," Shara said, but

Barry Hoffman

even without the perfume, Shara could identify Deidre's unique scent.

"Turn on the light, Renee, and stop playing games."

Shara turned on the light and approached the reporter. "It's Shara. Renee's long gone."

"Really," Deidre said. "Is it Shara who's the Vigilante? I don't think so. Shara would have no reason to kill, but Renee would."

"Point taken," Shara said. "Renee's the killer, but I've been Shara for seven years. Indulge me, won't you?"

With the light on, Shara saw Deidre was scrutinizing her. "It's really you," she said, as if talking to herself.

"In the flesh."

"The eyes," Deidre said. "It's the eyes. I could pick you out of a room of a hundred. How could I have missed it the day you visited the police station?"

"Contacts."

Deidre laughed. "Should have guessed." She shook her head in acknowledgment. "I've played the scene over dozens of times. Even with the mole and the scar, there was something wrong. I would have picked up on the eyes. Without the contacts I would have had you then."

Shara shrugged. No use in arguing.

"So what now?" Shara asked. "Do we call the police? Reminisce about the good old days?"

"You made a promise. I catch you, and you tell me all. No more playing games, Ren . . . Shara. I want to fill in the blanks, dot the i's and cross the t's. You owe me that."

"Then what?"

"We'll cross that bridge later." Deidre looked around the room. "Let's start with this," she said, her hand sweeping the room. "No bed, precious little furniture. The mirrors."

"I slept in a cage for six days. I was never able to adjust to a bed after that."

"The mirrors?"

"For two years I danced at a strip joint. Do you know about the first Shara?"

"Enough. Older than you. Took you in. Worked at the club you danced at. Died, and you took her identity. We can fill in details on her later. The mirrors?"

"I took the first Shara's place at the club. There were eyes all about me, scrutinizing my every move." She went to the tape deck, and turned on the music. Tina Turner sang.

She unbuttoned the blue police shirt, and flung it across the room; unbuttoned her bra and let it drop to the floor, all the time dancing for the eyes that peered at her from the mirrors, yet saw nothing.

"I need to see them to make sure they can't see me," Shara said.

Deidre let out an audible gasp when she saw the tattoos on her breasts. "What's happened to you, Renee?" she asked, a hint of fear in her voice.

Shara noticed a change in her smell. Yes, Deidre was afraid of her. So be it.

"Renee died in the Schuylkill. No, that's a lie. Renee died the six days she was held captive," she hissed. "Renee had been slowly dying years before. Traces of Renee remain, but soon, very soon there will be no more Renee."

Deidre shook her head, apparently not accepting the explanation. "What you told me of those six days wouldn't have killed the girl I spoke to in the hospital. Something's happened since."

Shara sat on the floor, her back against one of the mirrors. "You don't understand at all. And why not? There are gaps you know nothing of. But even without them, can't you understand the scars I bear? I saw my stepfather shot in the head at six. I lived with a woman who spent every waking moment reminding me I was a bastard; the unwanted product of her screwing anyone with pants. And after I was born, she ballooned, and that was my fault, too.

"I had no childhood. Had no friends. And then to be kidnapped, and held captive in a cage for someone to gawk at, not knowing if each day would be my last.

"Scarred, Dee. Scarred for life. What did you think became of me when I disappeared? Thought I became a frumpy housewife who abused her own kids? It's happened to others, so I'm told by Oprah and Sally Jesse and the rest.

"I didn't take that route," Shara continued. "You've created an image of me that doesn't exist."

"But I do know you . . . Shara. You poured your heart out to me in the hospital and after, until . . ."

"Until you abandoned me, like the rest."

"I had to, to protect you," Deidre said, her voice rising.

"I never poured my heart out to you," Shara replied petulantly.

"Bullshit, Shara. Say what you want . . ."

"I told you only what I wanted you to know," Shara said, her voice full of exasperation. She was on her feet now, pacing the room.

"You don't get it. I told you anything I divulged you could print. Even then you sanitized what I told you, painted this sympathetic picture to shield me from the world. But I never told you *everything*. Why would I trust you when I'd never trusted anyone in my life? I told you as much. I know how much it upset you to hear someone so young be so cynical, but you never really accepted what I'd told you. You thought I'd finally found someone to confide in. *Bullshit*. Maybe I trusted you more than anyone I'd known till then. No, I *did* trust you more, I'll admit it. But the only one I've ever trusted completely and unequivocally was the first Shara.

And, I didn't trust *her* completely, until we'd lived together for over a year. I'm not proud of it, but it's me. A secret's only a secret if you don't confide in *anyone*. Why would I confide in you, a stranger, just because you were sincere and kind?

"So believe me when I tell you I told you what I wanted and no more. And I lied to you. I used you to convict an innocent man."

"What are you talking about?"

"Eddie . . . Edward Costanzo, he drove me out to the cabin, so you can say he abducted me. And he put me in a cage, and chained me like an animal. But that's all he did. And he didn't plan that. He did what he was told, because he was scared."

"Scared of what? Of who?"

"Eddie's world revolved around children. He couldn't relate to people his own age. He provided kids like me with toys and games so we'd have the childhood he'd been deprived. He lived through us vicariously.

"Once, and as far as I know, *only* once, did he ever do anything of a sexual nature. He was like an adolescent, experimenting with his sexuality. Even then he was maneuvered. He touched a boy, played with his genitals, like two kids playing doctor. Only the boy threatened to expose him if he didn't do his bidding.

"So, Eddie bought that cabin, and he built the cage because he was told to. He took me there because he was told to. And then he left; didn't come back for six days until he was told to. Come back, he was told, and tell the police nothing, or the boy would dime on him; say he was a pervert who had molested him, and then did the same to me."

Deidre looked stunned. "Who, then, did all those terrible things to you, or were they all a lie?"

"Everything I said happened and worse. It wasn't Eddie. It was my half-brother."

"Your half-brother? Why?"

"He was a sick son-of-a-bitch. I don't know *why*, but he'd been looking at me for a year or two, photographing me when I showered, when I took a shit."

"Did he rape you at the cabin?" Deidre asked incredulously.

"Rape me? Only with his eyes. I wish he'd tried. I would have scratched his eyes out or died trying. What he did was far worse. He forced me to do vile things to myself while he took pictures. If I refused, he would shock me with a cattle prod. Rape me? He raped me a hundred times with his fucking eyes. Eyes that have haunted me ever since. He fucked my mind, that's what he did, which is worse than anything he could have done to my body."

"Why didn't you tell the police what he did?"

"Bobby's a psychopath, or sociopath or both. I'm not up on psychobabble bullshit, but he was one or both of them. Had no conscience. Had no sense of right or wrong. Played by his own set of rules.

"He told me if I said anything, the police wouldn't believe me. The day Eddie Costanzo came back, Bobby had him tell me his confession. He was too humiliated to implicate Bobby. He didn't want the world to know he'd played with another boy's privates. He knew he was in big trouble. It was bad enough to be a kidnapper, and labeled a pervert, but a faggot to boot." Renee shook her head. "Bobby had him by the balls . . . literally and figuratively.

"Tough and street smart as I was, I was only ten. If I had to do it over again, I might have taken the chance. If I knew I wouldn't go back to my mother, I might have told the truth. Eddie would have cracked under intense police questioning. At worst, Bobby would have been separated from me until the truth was known.

"But I was ten, dammit, too young and too scared to be logical. So I let Bobby use me like he used Eddie. In exchange, he promised never to bother me again.

How was I to know I'd be separated from my mother once I was freed? I thought we'd both be under the same roof. He could have done with me what he wanted. So a promise to let me be seemed like a good deal at the time.

"I only saw him once more . . ."

"At your foster parents house," Deidre said, as if she had had a revelation. "You faked your suicide just after he visited with your mother."

Shara shook her head yes. "As long as I was alive, or he thought I was alive, I could never escape him. He had my mother grill me that day about the kidnapping, looking for a chink in my armor. He knew he still terrified me, but that my life had changed with the Sheffields. He knew that, and feared me, I could tell. Would I tell the Sheffields what really happened as I became more comfortable with them? That fear meant he wouldn't let me rest. To escape him, I had to die."

For the next twenty minutes, Shara answered Deidre's questions: life on the streets when she ran away; meeting the other Shara; assuming her identity when she died; getting her GED and enrolling in a computer training program; and finally going to the Academy and joining the police force.

"Paul had a profound impact on me the six months I lived with him. He was the only man I'd ever gotten close to. He instilled me with discipline, tinged with a healthy dose of love and self-respect. I kinda had a crush on him; idolized him. I wanted to be a cop like him; someone who got the bad guys off the street.

"But after I graduated from the Academy, I knew I couldn't go after a high-profile position. I was a fraud, a woman with an assumed identity. With any notoriety would have come scrutiny. I couldn't chance that."

"Why the killings?"

"Two reasons. First, I'd become disillusioned with the judicial system. I saw men as bad as my half-brother

223

getting off with a slap on the wrist, and no one seemed to give a shit. It ate at me. Ate at me so much, I began to dream of Bobby's eyes raping me again. I won't kid you, I snapped. I felt the only way to get rid of the eyes was to punish those like Bobby.

"And it worked . . . for a while. With each killing, I was freed from their stare." She turned toward Deidre, so she could see her breasts.

"Each tattoo symbolizes eyes that can no longer see. They comfort me when the hungry eyes attack. I dance for hours looking at the eyes in the mirror, knowing they can't see me, and the terror recedes.

"One more, Dee. One killing for each day of captivity." She pointed to the lone bare spot on each of her breasts. "One more and the puzzle will be complete. One more and his eyes will go away. One more and I'll be whole again."

"How do you know that?"

She shrugged. "Instinct, maybe. You have it as a reporter. My body, my mind is telling me what must be done to heal me."

"And if you're wrong? If the craving returns?"

"Not a craving to kill. The eyes, Dee. I *must* get rid of the eyes. I hardly sleep, fearful of their return. I have no appetite. And you know I have no real life. If they return . . ." She paused and shrugged. "If they return, when I commit suicide this time, they'll find my body."

"And I'm supposed to let you kill again to meet your sick needs?"

Again, Shara shrugged. "You do what you must. You found me. I'm in your hands."

Now Deidre was on her feet, face to face with Shara, her blouse brushing against Shara's bare breasts.

"You're so damn infuriating. You think you know me. Good old soft Deidre Caffrey. Someone victims could pour out their innermost secrets to, knowing I wouldn't humiliate them. Well, maybe I'm starting to get cynical. I've lost a husband and a son. I've been told the cornerstone of my career was a fraud. I'm a lot tougher now.''

''Then tell the world about me. I don't have to give you permission. My philosophy hasn't changed. Whatever I divulge is fair game.''

''And you wouldn't give a fuck if I did, would you? Maybe I won't write about the trauma that drove you to kill. Maybe I'll just call the police and be done with you for good. When will you learn you can't manipulate me anymore? Maybe you don't know me as well as you think.''

Shara drew even closer, her mouth within inches of Deidre's ear.

''But I do know you. *That's* what's so infuriating, isn't it? You really haven't changed. You have your code, and it guides your life. Break it, and you free fall. You're no longer on solid ground. You invalidate your entire career. Can you take the risk?

''Dee, you still don't have the balls to go for the jugular. I know it and you know it. I chose you thirteen years ago and I choose you now. You'll tell my story, maybe dispassionately, but you won't turn me in.''

''You didn't choose me, Shara. I got into that hospital. *I* befriended you. *I* earned your trust, so you'd confide in me.''

''And it made your career. Deep down you feel grateful. Without me, you'd have been nothing, just another reporter. I gave you a purpose. I gave you direction. Look at the types of stories you're most associated with. I do read the papers, you know. Victims, especially the young, gravitate to you. Why? Because of the series you did on me. Because of that fool sympathetic picture you painted that must have infuriated my mother.

''And, sorry to say, I *did* choose you. You got into my hospital room, but I didn't have to tell you squat. I decided what to tell you, and what to delete.''

Deidre was shaking her head no. "You were ten. No way you could be so conniving, especially just after you had been rescued."

"I was ten going on thirty. And I began planning what I would tell the police on the way to the hospital. The police peppered me with questions on the way, but I remained mute. Then you came in and I led you step by step. Remember when I interviewed you? It was a technique you used to get information out of me. But it also told me what I needed to know about you. We used each other, Dee, face it. I don't begrudge you your success. It's to your credit you understood how to parlay your stories with me to get close to others. At the same time you allowed me to avoid the scrutiny of the media. Insulated, I was able to feed you what I wished."

"What would you have me do, now?"

"I won't make it easy for you. You know my plans. One more and soon. Tonight, Dee. And if I'm wrong, I'll call you before I take my life. You'll have a real exclusive.

"Or you can go out that door and tell your Detective Briggs where to find me. You'll still have an exclusive; an even better story. *You* found the elusive Vigilante while the cops set up traps I ignored. Oh, I know about them. So transparent. Like I'd go after one of the those guys the newspapers all of a sudden are talking about. Or, contact that reporter who's trying to turn the public against me. We both know I don't give a fuck.

"We've both kept our end of the bargain. You didn't tell the cops about me, and I've filled in all the gaps. You do what you have to, and so will I."

Shara went to the tape deck and turned on the music again and, dismissing Deidre, began to dance to her audience of unseeing eyes.

She was unaware when Deidre got up and left.

Glancing around and seeing her gone, she merely smiled and again let the music take hold.

Chapter Twenty-four

Deidre needed time to think, but if what Shara told her was true, she'd have to make a decision soon. She left her car and walked home, oblivious to all around her, trying to make sense of all she'd been told.

There was so much to digest. Worse, she couldn't rid herself of images of Shara, herself, that dogged her as she attempted to focus on what to do. There was the incongruity of the child she had known at ten with the woman she had seen today; her bared breasts undulating, as she danced seductively to the music. A woman who could have no relationship with a man, she made love to her music.

While watching, Deidre had wanted to chastise herself for not being able to take her eyes from the tattooed eyes on Shara's breasts; eyes which seemed alive, even if unseeing.

And she had to deal with the excitement she had felt within herself as she'd watched Shara. She didn't want to admit to herself she may have been sexually aroused. With so many more pressing concerns, she wanted to bury the implications of her feelings, at least for the moment. Yet, she couldn't deny the heat that radiated through her when they'd made contact. She had approached Shara in confrontation, getting so close her body had touched Shara's breasts. And then Shara had gotten even closer, when she'd whispered in her ear. This woman was not at all what she had expected.

The whole experience had a surreal quality to Deidre. Oddly, whenever she had thought of Renee, even though she had seen her briefly at the police station, it was as the child she had met thirteen years before. The girl, though, had become an alluring woman.

Deidre recalled friends telling her of the dread they felt when their sons or daughters went off to college. A chapter in their lives had ended. A stark reality had to be faced. Their children had grown up. It seemed like yesterday, they'd say, they were taking a reluctant child to his or her first day of school.

Now Deidre could relate to them. Renee was gone, forever. The child had become a woman . . . Shara. Deidre had to come to grips with this new reality, and what she must do.

Deep within, she knew she could never turn Shara in to the police. Shara might be certifiably insane and irretrievably lost, but she had just cause.

Of equal importance, Deidre was a reporter, not a cop. She had learned the answers to her questions, though she had no doubt that, as always, Shara had held something back.

Catch me if you can, Shara had challenged, and she had. She should feel vindicated. She had gotten the better of the street-smart woman. Beaten her at her own game. But a part of her felt empty; the chase was over. And she felt no duty to betray her to the police.

By the same token, she couldn't allow Shara to kill again, if it was in her power to prevent it. No matter how vile a creature Shara pursued, his death would forever stain her conscience if she sat idly by, an interested bystander.

A classic Catch-22.

Not really, though.

There was a way to avoid betrayal, yet protect the next victim. A way, because Deidre knew who the next victim was.

She had arrived at Shara's flat an hour before Shara had gotten home. There wasn't a whole lot for her to look through. Sadly, there was no diary; something she had written for herself in which she'd let her defenses down.

But there was the bulletin board. She saw news clippings on each of the killings, and photos Shara had taken while she stalked them. But there had been six, not five.

Under the sixth was a name, business and home address, plus a terse description of the man's crimes. The name rang a bell and triggered memories. A child molester slapped on the wrist because all of the victims' parents had refused to allow their children to be further traumatized by a trial. He had accepted a plea bargain and spent six months in prison.

He must have been at it again, Deidre reasoned, and she had to admit that if this were the case she had no real desire to see him go unpunished.

She mulled it over in her mind.

She'd strike a deal with Briggs. She would tell him Shara's next target in exchange for a promise of a thorough investigation into any molestation that may have taken place since his release.

She wouldn't be betraying Shara, for Shara had repeatedly told her anything she was told she was free to use. It was a simple leap that anything she *found* in her apartment, likewise, was fair game.

She thought it ironic that Shara would be caught as a result of her own life philosophy. Shara herself, she was certain, would find it fitting. She had railed at Deidre for her half-truths and sympathetic portrayal. She'd known Deidre would keep her word and not go to Briggs *before* she confronted her. Yet, now Shara would be captured because Deidre had learned who her next victim would be.

Once captured Deidre would write her tragic story; do all in her power to portray the woman as a victim who had gone over the edge, and ask for the public to demand hospitalization and psychiatric help, rather than incarceration. Her story would also dispel any notion there was a Vigilante safeguarding the public. Shara's own demons made her kill, not any sense at balancing the scales of justice.

Her decision made, she hurried home and called Jonas, asking him to pick her up.

An hour later, she was in Briggs' office. She had told Jonas about her meeting with Shara, and knowledge of the next victim. Jonas had the look of a proud father as Deidre told him her plan. He offered a few suggestions, and she had felt reasonably comfortable when she entered Briggs' office.

Seated, however, she felt a bit like a rudderless ship making its way through a treacherous current. There were flaws in her cover story, she knew, and Briggs would badger her to reveal what she wouldn't.

Briggs, she could see, was in a foul mood, brought on by fatigue and mounting frustrations. While the municipal workers' strike had briefly taken the heat off the Task Force, there was continuing pressure to show progress. To date, there had been none. No new leads had materialized from dozens of interviews with potential witnesses, and the list of people yet to be interviewed seemed endless.

The stories Deidre had helped shape to entice the Vigilante to use Wakefield as a go-between had produced nothing. Still more cranks had contacted the reporter, but the Task Force had quickly eliminated them as suspects.

And, so far, no one seemed to show the slightest interest in the three straw victims the Task Force hoped to use as bait to lure the Vigilante out into the open.

Finally, the list of suspects from the FBI profile was equally extensive. Background checks had been made on an *A* list of prime suspects, and a few had been brought in for interrogation, but as of yet, they had nothing to show for their efforts.

As with most cases, where a family member or neighbor was not the perpetrator, most of what had been done was drudgery and non-productive. Briggs not only had to deal with pressure from above, but he had to rally the Task Force itself, as the enormity of its task became apparent.

All felt, even if they didn't articulate the frustration, their work would be for naught. As was so often the case, the killer would eventually be caught by some fluke, and very probably by someone not involved with the investigation.

All in all Briggs looked worn down. Deidre having been gone the better part of two days hadn't helped. She saw in his eyes that he no longer viewed her a member of the team; just a representative from the Mayor's office who would come and go at the Mayor's behest. In a sense, she guessed he felt betrayed.

"What can I do for you, Dee?" he said shuffling through papers, his stiffness showing his displeasure.

Deidre decided to toss out her elaborate script and force him to take her seriously.

"I know who the next victim will be, and I'm reasonably sure the attack will occur tonight."

He looked up at her open-mouthed.

"And how did you come up with this information?" he asked incredulously.

Despite herself, Deidre was angry at his reaction. She

was tired, too, and didn't want to deal with his condescending attitude.

"Look, Briggs, you forgot that as a reporter I have contacts, many just as or more reliable than your snitches. No matter what you may have said, I've been viewed as an outsider from the outset.

"You wanted me to handle the media and keep the Mayor off your back. I can understand your reluctance to make me an active member of the investigation. We come from different worlds. I'm looked on with suspicion, even hostility, by most of the Task Force members. I'm just not part of your little fraternity."

Briggs looked as if he wanted to protest, but Deidre shook her head in dismissal.

"I can understand the bunker mentality. Your asses are on the line. Regardless of your success or failure, I won't be covered with any of the shit if he kills again and it hits the fan."

This time he didn't protest, but let her continue.

"As a fifth wheel, I decided to do some investigation on my own, using *my* people, along with your FBI profile. I lucked out, plain and simple. Someone overheard someone who knew something." She passed a paper over to Briggs with the name, address and sketchy background.

"I literally found out about this less than an hour ago. The source is credible, and while I know nothing about the killer, I'm told the attack could be tonight."

Briggs scanned the paper, seemingly dwelling on each and every word.

"You won't tell me your source." It wasn't a question.

"You know I can't."

"Your instincts tell you this is the guy?" he asked skeptically.

"All I know, Briggs, is I've got a source who tells me this guy will be offed by the Vigilante. I'm not saying you can take it to the bank, but would you rather I ignored it?'' she responded testily.

''Don't go ballistic on me. Look, it's a bit of a shock. You're gone two days, and then you walk in here and hand me the next victim. If you were in my shoes you'd be skeptical too.''

''Then toss it.''

''Right. And find him dead on his bed tomorrow and with egg on our face. We obviously don't have time to adequately check this out, if the attack is tonight. So, we run with it. Just make sure the media doesn't get wind of it, if it turns out to be a crock.''

''I'll handle the media. Hopefully, you'll have a suspect which will make my job relatively easy.''

''All right. Let's get to it, then.''

There was a renewed spring to Briggs' step as he left the room. Deidre could sense his excitement. He might not show it, but this was the first tangible break in the case. Briggs, a man of action, must have felt like he was trapped in a straitjacket having to sit back waiting for the next shoe to drop. With a lead, no matter how fragile, he was back in charge; on the offensive.

Deidre hoped he wouldn't be disappointed. She knew she had Shara. Yet, the only thing predictable about Shara was her unpredictability.

Chapter Twenty-five

Shara settled in a chair in Bobby Chattaway's efficiency, a billy club in her hand. She had arrived at nine, sitting in her car, the lights off, a block away from his apartment, checking out the surrounding homes.

When she was certain there was no one looking, she made her way to the apartment, used the key she'd made from an impression and, once inside, soaked in his presence. He wouldn't be home for an hour and a half, but she didn't need him there physically to be reunited.

His smell permeated the room, just as it had her cage thirteen years before. She was aware of another smell, faint but lingering; the odor of the last girl he'd mindfucked.

She recalled the fetid odor of her body as he'd violated her with his words and camera thirteen years earlier. She'd become keenly aware, for the first time, of the differing secretions of her body as her mood changed. Her body had responded one way to fear of imprisonment, another to the unknown, and another still to the humiliation of being watched and photographed.

Each hour she had become more attuned to the subtle difference her response had on her body. Waiting for him to return each day, she wondered if he were aware of the minute but clearly perceptible changes, and if it gave him an additional rush.

By the end she decided his sensual fixation extended solely to the visual; her reaction to his intimidation and degradation.

She'd become aware, too, of changes in him. There was the odor of domination, intimidation, arousal and satisfaction. When she had snapped and given up completely, posing seductively for his camera, asking him what more she could do to please him, she had smelled boredom. Crushed, no longer a challenge and unable to be further terrified, he had tired of her, and no longer responded to her.

In the months that followed, and again over the past year-and-a-half, when his hungry eyes assaulted her at night, so did the odor that had accompanied it earlier. It was as if he were in the same room with her. An animal, if she desired, she could track him wherever he ventured. But all she had to do was wait.

The fly was coming to the spider.

While she waited she also dwelled on her meeting with Deidre. Deidre had considered it a confrontation. She'd viewed it more as a reunion. She had, of course, been startled that Deidre had found her. Rather than being afraid, there was a sense of relief, as well as pride. Relief in the fact that the game of cat and mouse had ended. She no longer had to watch every word for fear Deidre might locate her *before* she was prepared to strike. Pride, in that Deidre had proved a worthy adversary.

It had been good to tell her the truth about what had happened to her when she was kidnapped. She had never felt guilty allowing Costanzo to take the rap for what her half-brother had done. Pawn that he was, Eddie *had* kidnapped her. His sentence had been relatively light, as she never accused him of violating her.

Once she had started talking to Deidre about Bobby, she could hardly contain herself. Bottling up what he had done to her had affected her more than she thought. Maybe part of the reason he preyed on her mind so was the fact she had never confided in anyone what he'd done to her. In hindsight, it had been a mistake. Had she told Deidre then, she would have made sure Bobby couldn't get to her. But once she had started lying, there was no turning back. She hadn't lied when she'd said she had never trusted anyone except for the first Shara. But, she had gotten close to trusting Deidre. Unfortunately, by the time she had known she could have told her the truth, she was trapped by the story she had fabricated.

At that point, she cared only about survival. Dumping on Bobby after accusing Costanzo would destroy her credibility. There would always be a reasonable doubt. Which story had been the truth. And, young as she was, she had been certain Bobby would get to her if she dimed on him.

Opening up to Deidre earlier, though, had released tension pent up since the day of her release. Deidre shared this secret. She'd left nothing out, at least about the abduction and her captivity. She had let her guard down, and damn if it didn't feel good.

She hadn't told everything, of course. She still had to take care of Bobby or everything would be in vain. She hoped Deidre wouldn't hate her for the betrayal. Deep down she was certain Deidre knew she hadn't revealed *everything*. She'd never revealed all to anyone, except the first Shara, and bad habits die hard.

Maybe, just maybe, she could square things with Deidre. Deidre hadn't turned her in. A weakness on her part, to be sure, but a sign of, what . . . friendship? Could she trust Deidre to tell her everything?

Maybe, just maybe, she'd have a chance.

Maybe, just maybe . . .

Her thoughts were interrupted by the smell of his presence. 11:22. She could smell him outside the door. He entered, and she hit him once on the back of the head with the billyclub.

He came to twenty minutes later, naked on his bed, arms and legs tethered by the very binds that had held his victims.

Shara stood over him in her police uniform.

Focusing on the uniform, she could see, could smell the terror that began to envelop him. Twinged with his fear was confusion. She knew what he was thinking. Why wouldn't a cop just arrest him? Why was he bound to the bed? Why was he naked? Good, she thought, let him bathe himself in the confusion and horror his victims experienced. For once, let him be on the other side of the door.

She said nothing, allowing his fear to mount. The smell was so pungent, but so good. Better than she had ever imagined.

Finally, he couldn't contain his curiosity. "Who are you? What the fuck do you want?"

"I'm your past, Bobby, here to make you pay for your sins. Recognize me?" she said, in a teasing voice. "There were so many. Which one do you think it is?"

She could see him searching his memory and drawing a blank. It further fueled her anger.

"You little shit. You stole glances at me daily when we shared the same room. You held me captive, and made me do things to myself so vile, I wanted to die. And now you don't recognize me?"

She bent down, her face almost touching his. He smelled of death and decay, and it all but overpowered her, yet she retained eye contact with him. The curtain she had hid behind was gone. The Renee Barrows he had known so well was there for him to see.

237

He stared back at her blankly.

"Bobby, Bobby, Bobby, you really disappoint me. Faces are your life; the tortured expressions of children who expect to be raped, sodomized and killed."

She shook her head in exasperation.

"You look, Bobby, but you don't see. For all your prowess, you're a fraud. A fucking fraud."

She held a picture so he could see. A picture of her he had taken thirteen years before, in a cage in an isolated cabin.

His eyes shot from the picture to the woman before him; his look one of disbelief.

She balled her fist and gently tapped his forehead. "Knock, knock, anybody home?"

"You're dead," he said, his skin turning deathly pale.

"I'm back, big brother . . . *in the flesh*. It's you who will be dead, unless you do as I say."

She could smell self-preservation kick in. *Anything I say*. Yes, he would do anything. He was no different than the children he tormented.

She took out a microcassette tape recorder. "I'm your past, and I'm here for your confession."

He didn't need prompting. Like a river overflowing its banks, the words poured out. The infantile sex with Costanzo, which *he'd* initiated. His threats to expose him. How turned on he was by her looks of anger, exasperation and embarrassment when he'd barge in on her in the bathroom. How he hungered for more. He told her he'd considered killing her at the cabin, but knew Costanzo would crack under the grilling of a murder interrogation. He recounted how he finally decided she wouldn't tell; she could live with anything except the humiliation of the world knowing what he had put her through.

Here, she was wrong, Shara thought to herself. Fuck the humiliation, she feared what he'd do to her physically if she told. But she held her tongue. She wouldn't

238

give him the satisfaction of knowing the truth.

"I'm sorry, Renee. I truly am. I was sick. I never meant to harm you. When I thought you had killed yourself, I considered suicide too. I . . ."

"Did you ever do it again?" she said, interrupting him.

"How could I, after I saw what I had done to you; that I had driven you to suicide. What kind of beast . . ."

Shara pulled out another picture. The girl he had tormented on Saturday.

"Don't lie to me, brother. One lie, just one, and I'll cut off your balls and make you eat them." She took out a knife to emphasize the point.

"Now tell me how sorry you were?"

Tears welled in his eyes, and it took him several minutes to regain his composure. She could smell him plotting, wondering what avenue might secure his release.

"You want the truth, *bitch*. I loved every minute . . . up until the very end. You fought, you resisted. Your face was so full of emotion. I wanted it to last forever, but you cracked. Cracked, just like all the others. Gave up, and I lost interest. You're all so weak. But I'd do it again if I could. In a heartbeat." He smiled.

"Go on brother. Why did you come to the Sheffields with mother? To see if I would dime on you?"

"It was more than that. I thought about coming after you when they put you with that cop. Maybe to kill you, because without me around, you might have told them what really happened. But, I also thought of taking you again. Back to the cabin. To the cage. Starting all over again. Seeing how long you would last. I really didn't give a fuck if I was caught. And you knew, didn't you? Knew you'd never be free of me, so you faked your suicide. And look at you now. Hardened. All the emotion I captured gone. You're nothing to me now." He tried to spit in her face, but she pulled back just in time.

He looked smug and self-satisfied, possibly having forgotten his precarious position.

She brought him back to the present. "Why the others?"

"To recapture the power I had over you. And to see if any could meet the standard you had set. They couldn't, you know. All so soft and weak. Half an hour, an hour tops, and they'd melt. You. *Six days* before you succumbed." He sounded almost as if he were proud of her.

"I've been looking for you all my life. Searching for someone to challenge me as you did." A cloud passed over his face.

"So I spoiled you. *I'm* to blame for what you've become?" she asked.

"You can't imagine the disappointment when the first is the best, and no one, *no one*, can come close. I was a novice when I had you then. What I could do to you now . . . if you were young again. Yes. You spoiled me. There's times I've hated you for it. You were simply the best."

"And you're one sick fuck," Shara said, not wanting to hear anymore of his demented ramblings. She stuck one of his socks in his mouth, and from under the bed took out a stack of photos.

"How many of these children have you destroyed?" she asked, showing each to him. "You fucked with their minds, which is worse than taking their bodies. They can never trust again. Can never sleep in peace again. Can never divulge their secret, their humiliation. They'll never forget you, Bobby. And never forgive."

She bent down beside the bed and removed a bottle, unscrewing the cap and producing an eyedropper.

"You've got hungry eyes, big brother. Eyes that have tried to devour me."

She grabbed his hair, and as he stared wide-eyed at her she released the contents of the eyedropper. The acid tore through his left eye, and she felt a cloud over her begin to dissipate. The acid, like a worm, bored its way deep within his eyeball. The smell of the acid working on his eye mixed with his agonized terror was almost overpowering. She was repulsed. She was exhilarated. She was literally shutting the windows to his world, and it felt and smelled so good.

He struggled in pain, a silent scream unable to make its way past the sock.

When he finally began to relax, several minutes later, she grabbed his hair again and poured acid into his other eye and for the first time in thirteen years she was free of him; free of his searching eyes, his probing, mind-fucking eyes. She was tempted to let him live; to spend his life devoid of his most important sense. It would be hell on earth, and fitting.

In the end, however, self-preservation won out. When he relaxed a second time, she bent down to his ear. There was so much bottled up inside of her she wanted to tell him. In the end, though, while breathing, he was already dead, and she would be wasting her breath.

"See you in hell big brother," and she pinched his nose.

He struggled, coughed, and she could smell the vomit that began to choke him to death. When he was still she held his nose for several minutes more, knowing he was dead by the putrid smell of his bowels, which had released their contents.

"You always were a shit, Bobby," she whispered, as she gathered the bottle and picture of herself. With lipstick, she scrawled NO MORE HUNGRY EYES on the mirror, and this time it was true.

She left the house, got into her car, and only then did she remove the rubber gloves she had worn, and place them in a plastic bag.

At home, she burned the bag, flushed the remains down the toilet, and turned on her tape deck.

Much as she wanted to wrap herself in her music, she replayed the song only once. Looking at her breasts in the mirror, she was full of anticipation, wondering if the tattoo artist could do justice to the last set of eyes that would now see no more.

And, as much as she wanted to sleep, without the specter of those eyes haunting her, she resisted the urge.

She had other preparations. There would be plenty of time to sleep, and savor her freedom. There would be one last confrontation; one she anticipated with mixed feelings. And she had one last visit to make.

Chapter Twenty-six

Sitting a block away from Eddie Pasqual's rowhouse with Jonas, Deidre for the first time was able to relax enough to sift through her conversation with Shara.

At first she had felt strangely vulnerable, as she waited for Shara to arrive. Briggs had told her eight members of the Task Force were nearby, but the street appeared deserted. She could picture Shara knocking on her window, waving and escaping the net Briggs had weaved for her.

While the thought was unsettling, the feeling of unease that crept through her had nothing to do with a possible confrontation with Shara that night. Buried within her subconscious she knew she had missed something. Why was Shara so sure her rampage would end with Pasqual's death? The one victim for each day of her captivity was too pat; something an amateur psychiatrist would grasp at. It had to be something about Pasqual that would release the hold the eyes had on her. But on closer inspection, Pasqual was no different from the others. He wasn't the first of those she had killed to victimize children, so why was his death of such tantamount importance?

Deidre had been stunned by the revelation that Costanzo had been a mere pawn in the kidnapping. It was difficult to believe Renee's sixteen-year-old brother could have plotted such an elaborate scheme so he could have his way with his half-sister. He must have been a psychopath even then.

Deidre bolted up in her seat, almost knocking a cup of coffee Jonas held.

—a psychopath even then
—even then
—even THEN

If he had been a psychopath *then*, what had he done in the intervening thirteen years? Either Shara was pulling her chain, or she was on a wild goose chase. Could Shara have steered her to Pasqual, knowing Deidre would intervene, so she would be free to kill the one person whose eyes still haunted *her*? Free her to kill Robert Chattaway—her half-brother; a psychopath who was guilty of God knew what horrendous crimes. No, Shara had told her his crimes. Crimes against children, teenagers, *young teenage girls*. She'd laid it all out for her before. It was Chattaway she was after, not Pasqual.

She couldn't go to Briggs with her theory. How could she explain a second suspect? Her instinct, though, told her Chattaway was the last victim, and she couldn't sit still and do nothing.

"Jonas, you've got to trust me. I've been duped again, but I know Shara's next victim. Will you drive me?"

"Yours to command," he said, starting the engine. "Just don't keep me guessing."

She told him her theory as they drove, and he concurred.

"What a fool I've been, Jonas. It was staring me right in the face the whole time. I was going to interview Shara's, or Renee's . . . whatever, half-brother for my series. He had been discharged from the army and returned here a few months before Shara began her rampage.

"That's what triggered her. It's bugged me all along. Why the gap of over a decade before she felt the urge to kill? She'd been through hell and back, but survived until a year-and-a-half ago."

"Then her half-brother returned," Jonas said.

"Right. She couldn't screw up enough courage to confront him, so she went after others like him."

"It didn't work, though," Jonas added.

"No." It was all falling into place for Deidre now, hopefully not too late. "Each killing brought less . . . I don't know, satisfaction. That's not the word, but the killings didn't rid her of her half-brother's presence. In fact, each strengthened his grip on her. At some point she must have decided she could kill forever, but until she rid herself of the source of her dread, he'd still be there, just around the corner. Still there taunting her. The only way she can be certain this will be the last killing is . . ."

"If it's her half-brother," Jonas finished for her.

But how did she know to plant Pasqual? Deidre thought to herself. How did she know I'd find her? How could she know I'd break into her house, snoop around, and be waiting for her?

With each answer a dozen new questions surfaced. She sat sullenly the last three blocks, tension mounting within her. She was glad for Jonas' presence; glad, too, he knew her well enough to let her brood without making small talk or overanalyzing the situation.

When Jonas stopped outside Chattaway's apartment, Deidre bolted to the front door. Jonas caught up to her as she looked at the mailboxes, and saw he was on the second floor. Upstairs, her heart sank as she saw his front door opened a crack. The killer had done this each time, so the victim would be found quickly, by a curious neighbor.

She must be too late. Shara wouldn't leave the door ajar if she were still inside.

With Jonas behind her, she opened the door, and when she saw him on the bed she felt lightheaded and her knees almost buckled. From behind, Jonas steadied her.

On the bed lay Robert Chattaway, a sock in his mouth, his eyes and the skin around them charred from acid. On the mirror, Shara's message in lipstick. NO MORE HUNGRY EYES. This time, with a double line under the word NO. Only Deidre would understand its true meaning. This time the message *was* meant for her.

"Damn it to hell," she said, wanting to scream, yet knowing it would draw attention. "Played me like a Goddamn violin." She turned to Jonas, her face ashen, tears streaking down her face.

"Jonas, could I have subconsciously known she would go for her stepbrother, but buried it so she could? Am I an accomplice to this murder?"

Jonas shook his head no. "She manipulated you. Given more time, you would have figured it out. She didn't give you that time. Part of her plan."

He paused a moment.

"What now?"

"Now?" Deidre tried to clear the cobwebs. Did it matter? Yes, it wasn't over. She thought over her options for a few moments. She couldn't call Briggs. He'd pummel her with questions she wouldn't be able to answer. As it was her credibility with him was shot. Unless she told him all she knew, which she still refused to do, he would never trust her so-called sources again.

As it was, if the media found out the Task Force was staking out Eddie Pasqual's house the very night of the latest killing, Briggs would not only have egg on his face, he'd lose command of the Task Force.

No, she would deal with him in the morning. For now, she had to confront Shara; find out how she had been one step ahead of her, and made her look the fool. *Again.*

"I'm going to her house. Alone." Her tone left no room for argument. "I left my car there, so I'll be able to get around when I'm done. She won't hurt me. She'll want to gloat, I suppose. Want to see if I'll break my precious code of ethics and turn her in. It's all part of the game she's playing."

"Will you turn her in?"

Deidre shrugged. "To be honest, I have no idea. A part of me wants to, just to show her she can't read me like an open book. But can I live with myself if I do?"

"Can you if you don't, and she kills again?"

"I'll let you know. I just need to be alone with her."

When she got to Shara's, the door was unlocked, and Deidre was surprised to find it vacant. Not just unoccupied, totally cleared out. What few belongings Shara had were gone. Only the chair and desk remained. On the desk was a brief note with a "D" at the top.

"Sorry, but it had to be this way. Meet me at my parents' house tomorrow at noon. Come alone."

The note was unsigned. For a moment, she thought Shara meant Loretta Barrows' house, and wondered if this was another loose end Shara had decided to tidy up. But she had said *parents*, and Deidre knew she meant the Sheffields. That was, of course, unless the note was another hoax; further manipulation while she made good on her escape. Deep down she thought it the truth, and decided to find out the next day. For now, she would drive back to the stakeout. No sense, she thought, in antagonizing Briggs anymore than necessary or arousing his suspicions.

Deidre was dozing when she heard tapping on her window. She was staring at Briggs; a mixture of rage and defeat etched on his face.

"Wake up, Caffrey. Open the fucking window."

She did.

"The bastard's struck, but not here. Your source had the right night, but the wrong victim. Looks like my ass is in a sling, as soon as the word gets out."

"How . . . ?"

"Chievous or McCauley. Don't think they're not relishing my failure. Way I figure it, the price for keeping our little escapade from the media will be my removal. The Mayor doesn't need the embarrassment, so he'll hush up our little indiscretion, but replace me to placate the Chief.

"Tell you the truth, I don't give a shit. Got the feeling there'll be a lot more careers going down the tube before this joker is caught. We got squat, and our man's not cooperating in the least."

"Don't be so hard on yourself," Deidre said lamely. "You hardly had time . . ."

"Thanks, but I know when a trail's cold. You don't catch serial killers with old-fashioned police work. Leastways, not this time. This guy has no pattern. If we had a chance in hell, Logan, from the FBI, would be down here so he could claim credit. He knew better, though. Gave us a little hope, and got out of Dodge while the going was good. If our guy's found, it'll be a fluke. And, know what? It doesn't faze me too much that I won't be a part of it."

"What do you want me to do?"

"Damage control. Washington and Hodge are at the crime scene with the lab boys. Press will get wind of it soon. Give them some innocuous statement. Yes, it looks like our killer, but we won't know for sure until at least the late afternoon. MO's the same, but it could be a copycat. Feed them the information we're allowed to divulge. Call the Mayor's office. I assume he'll want to issue a statement. My replacement."

"All right. Should I follow you?"

"Yeah, sure." He began to turn, then thought better of it. "Dee, want to tell me your source? Just might save my ass."

"C'mon Briggs. You know I can't. He fucked up, anyway, didn't he?"

"Got that right. Hell of a coincidence, though, getting the night right. An off the record chat . . . ," he let the words hang.

"Briggs!"

He shrugged. "Can't blame a guy for trying. C'mon, follow me."

The morning passed quickly. The media was out in full force, and none too pleased with Deidre's evasive replies to their questions.

The Mayor called her at ten, and told her McCauley would be taking over the Task Force. He would issue a brief statement at four. He didn't mention the stakeout, but she knew he had been told. Briggs had to be sacrificed to avoid any embarrassing leaks. All unsaid, but clear as a bell.

At eleven-fifteen, Deidre was driving to the Sheffields. For the first ten minutes she thought of Briggs. While she felt bad for him, she knew McCauley was in for his share of frustrations. Briggs would land on his feet. He was a survivor, much like Shara. Meanwhile, he'd been spared weeks, possibly months, of drudgery that was to follow. If Shara's rampage was over, the Task Force would be running on empty in no time. There was still a lot of grunge work to be pursued, but in the end the Task Force would be dissolved once the killings stopped. There would be no glamour for McCauley, and in the meantime, Briggs would be back doing real policework. Maybe it had turned out for the best, after all.

She turned her attention to Shara. How that woman tormented her. Though the fog had been penetrated, there were many unanswered questions. The most significant, as far as what she would do, was whether killing her half-brother had rid her of her demons? If so, did she have any right to betray her? If not, did she have an obligation to turn Shara in before she got the urge to strike again?

Paul Sheffield was standing in his driveway as she pulled up. By the excited look etched on his face she knew Shara had probably arrived unannounced. She wondered if he could be objective.

"Are you alone, Ms. Caffrey?" he asked without greeting her, his eyes intent on her to read the truth of her response.

"Yes, Mr. Sheffield, though to be totally honest, if I perceive Shara to be a danger, I won't hesitate to call the police."

"She looks wonderful, don't you think?" Paul said, after nodding he understood. "A bit on the thin side, but all things considered . . ."

Shara had won him over, Deidre thought, whether by opening herself completely or spinning a web of half-truths. Deidre knew she wouldn't find an ally here, if she considered Shara a risk to others.

"Has she told you everything?" Deidre asked.

"All business," Paul said, taking on the familiar role of the former-cop she had met the last time they'd spoken. "Yes, Ms. Caffrey, she has told us everything. Leastwise, her perception of what happened then, and her response now."

"Do I detect some skepticism?"

"You misunderstand me. Whether Edward Costanzo was merely a pawn of her half-brother or an accomplice we'll never know. A ten-year-old went though a harrowing experience. I believe her half-brother did all she claims. It explains why she ran away, feigning suicide. But, she experienced the trauma through the eyes of a child, then hid the most gruesome aspects from the police, you as her spokesperson to the world, and us, who'd loved her as if she were our own. Are her perceptions distorted? Possibly. Probably. But not to any great extent.''

"She told you she killed her half-brother."

"And the five others. Look, the cop in me says she's gone over the edge; is clearly a danger to others and possibly herself. Turn her in and hope a judge will see she needs psychiatric help, not punishment. On the other hand, forgetting I'm a cop for a minute, what if she's finally exorcised her demons. With the hell she's gone through, isn't that punishment enough? I mean, she's been in a prison of sorts since she ran away."

He raised his hand to silence Deidre, who was about to speak.

"Hear me out. Her whole life's revolved around her half-brother's raping her mind, whether she knew it or not. I know I can't ignore she's killed five other people. But, even as a cop, a part of me applauded the Vigilante before I knew it was Shara. Rapists and child molesters getting off all but scot-free. I wonder whether a jury would convict her of murder one. My point is, what if she's cured, for want of a better word, because she has gotten rid of the source of her disease? I don't know if I'd want to turn her in."

"Sounds like you're already convinced, Mr. Sheffield, and trying to sell me."

He shrugged, a sheepish look on his face betraying his guilt.

"Say you're right," Deidre went on. "What's to become of her? Go back to work as if nothing's happened?"

"We've discussed that. She can't stay here. She's got to begin fresh. She needs someplace where she can feel free to advance without having to look over her shoulder."

"And you know just the place," Deidre said with a

tight smile, letting him know she was on to him.

"In my career, I've made a lot of contacts. Let's just say there are a lot of small towns where Shara could build a life for herself. A deputy who wouldn't have to hide behind a computer. Hasn't she earned another chance?"

"That's why I'm here, sir. I've got to be able to live with myself. If Shara's manipulating us, and understand this well, she's manipulated me from day one, I don't want to be responsible for additional deaths. Remember, she's had a free ride. What if she's not done? What if she kills again, and the sheriff where she relocates corners her? Will she give up or kill him, too? That's my only concern. I'm not here to pass judgment on what she's done. I just have to know the killing is finished."

"Talk to her, then, Ms. Caffrey. Then do what you must."

Deidre smiled. "You've got a lot of confidence in her. She'll wrap me around her finger, just as she's done before."

Deidre shook her head as Paul Sheffield stifled a smile.

"I'll say this for her. She did the right thing coming back to you. And she didn't run from me either. I'll keep an open mind, even though she's played me for a fool over and over. Now, will you take me to her?"

"The backyard. She's expecting you."

"That's what I'm afraid of," Deidre said smiling.

Paul Sheffield returned the smile.

Chapter Twenty-seven

Shara swung gently on a swing set that had captivated her as a child. There'd been swings in South Philly, where'd she'd grown up, but even then playgrounds were more for gangs and drug addicts than kids. It was heroin then, crack now. Glass usually littered the ground, graffiti decorated the walls.

But the playground set in the Sheffields backyard was something else. She had felt in another world. She had marveled how she could come out at dusk without fear, and have the swings to herself. She'd pump, her anger, humiliation and fear spurring her to new heights. She'd pump until she could nearly touch the surrounding trees; pump until her momentum all but catapulted her off the swing. She could see the Sheffields' watching from indoors, and wondered if they'd rush out to admonish her to slow down, play it safe. But even then, she knew they were aware she knew her limits, and wasn't self-destructive. Though she could see Anna cringe, grasping Paul's shoulder, they never interfered.

That was one reason she had written them the postcard after she'd run away. They had taught her so much in so little time. She had learned discipline. She had learned manners. She had found someone who loved her. At first she'd thought they'd taken her out of pity, but she had soon learned different. They loved kids. As important, while they set rules, they respected her idiosyncrasies.

She had torn down the posters they'd put up, expecting a rebuke. She didn't like them, and the eyes brought fear, but she had torn them down as much to gauge their reaction. *Her room*, they'd said, and her room they had allowed it to be.

And *a room of her own*. Liberating. Terrifying. She had always had to share one with Bobby, and as they got older, he got more curious. Now she had privacy, for the first time, and reveled in it. At the same time, fear gnawed at her every night. At first, she wondered if it was the fear of being alone, but it was more than that. It was Bobby's eyes. She couldn't escape his eyes, no matter how she tried. Slowly, though, she had adjusted, until Bobby's visit. She knew then there was no escape, unless . . .

So, she had run away. But to keep Bobby at bay, she'd made it look like a suicide. Months later, with the first Shara, she couldn't stop thinking of the Sheffields; thinking of how they watched as she pumped on the swing, knowing she wasn't self-destructive. So, she had sent them a postcard because she didn't want them thinking they might have been responsible for her death.

Now on the same swings, she felt strangely liberated, her mission accomplished. She noted changes in her body. She no longer sweat bullets; the toxins within released. She wore jeans and a tight fitting t-shirt she had bought earlier that day. Unlike her other clothes, they didn't feel constricting. She felt no need to shed them.

She had also gotten her final tattoo that morning. Both her breasts ached and itched fiercely, but it was a small price to pay. For the first time she felt complete. Bobby was now a permanent part of her, but his eyes would no longer torment her.

She had viewed the completed puzzle upon her return. The tattooist was more than an artist. He was her biographer. On her first visit she had told him there'd be six separate tattoos, a puzzle of sorts, of six men in her life. He had captured the essence of each man in his work.

With the last he had outdone himself. Though the eyes were blind, Bobby's pure evil radiated from the tattoo like a photograph of his soul. Where the colors of the others were somewhat muted, Bobby's was dominated by shades of orange, red and bright green.

Without having to tell him, the man knew this was the centerpiece of the mosaic he had begun over a year before. He'd even adorned each nipple with a single red tear, symbolizing to her the pain Bobby had inflicted upon her.

She knew deep down this man knew who she was, but just like Deidre he wasn't about to turn her in. He never asked about the men, but spent as long as twenty minutes staring into her eyes, nodding now and then, mumbling to himself, before he would begin. She also saw a copy of the *News*, its headline blaring the latest killing. It wasn't the first time she had noticed he had read an account of one of her killings before she came in for her tattoo.

She'd looked at herself in the single mirror in her room for a full half-hour when she returned. Her mission complete, she mustn't forget what she had endured. The tapestry on her breasts insured she wouldn't.

She had come unannounced to the Sheffields shortly after two-thirty in the morning. Paul had recognized her immediately; Anna had taken just a bit longer. She had felt as if she had never left. She was incredulous at the love that poured from them, like a bottomless well.

Paul had made everything easier by explaining from Deidre's visit that they knew what she had done. They were not there to pass judgment, he'd told her, only to offer shelter and a friendly ear if she felt the need to unload.

And she had told them everything: what really happened at Costanzo's cabin; why she had left; the years with the first Shara; the empty years following her death; the depravity that drove her to kill; and finally, killing her half-brother earlier that night. She omitted just one detail; something she'd tell only Deidre, if she showed up the next day.

Paul had peppered her with questions. His focus had been on exorcising the demons that had made killing necessary. Could she be sure that with her half-brother's death the urge to kill was vanquished?

"I didn't feel any sense of release or fulfillment with the others," she had answered. "Deep down, I probably knew I had to confront Bobby, but he still held me captive. I can't describe the sense of relief I felt with Bobby tied to the bed. He had become bigger than life in my mind, but there he was no different than the others. As I felt the life leaving his body, his sightless eyes no longer a threat, I felt a weight lifted. Psychiatrists would label it closure, I guess. I'm not proud of what I've become, but at the same time I'm no longer the person I was a few hours ago."

"Get some sleep," Paul had said. "Anna and I must talk."

Shara had gotten up, feeling no fear whatsoever at placing her future in their hands. It was so totally foreign to her. Trust. They had taken her in, warts and all, once before. They would not stab her in the back now. She told them she had to be up no later than eight the next morning. Deidre would probably be there by noon, she told them, and she had errands to run before she arrived.

She had fallen asleep immediately and slept dreamlessly.

At eight, Anna awakened her with a kiss, Paul by her side. They'd both agreed, Anna announced, to stand by her. For what it was worth, they felt with her half-brother's death she was "cured."

"Have you given any thought to what you'll do now?" Paul had asked.

"I hadn't given it much thought," she said drowsily. "Go someplace to start anew, I guess," she had answered without much conviction.

"Easier said than done," Paul responded, "but we agree and we can help."

After a brief discussion, she had agreed to Paul's plan. He could provide her a fresh start. He would make it work. She was both excited and relieved. She would have had to face up to her future sooner or later. Like good parents, they had outlined a course of action for her to accept or reject. What they suggested felt right.

Now there was just one piece of unfinished business. She had fucked with Deidre's mind since she had first met her as a young reporter. She owed her an explanation. She knew Deidre would have questions. She knew Deidre would have trouble resting until they were answered. It was time to repay a debt. So she waited, happily reliving the six months she'd had with the Sheffields.

She'd heard a car pull in the driveway, and assumed Paul and Deidre were discussing her future. For the first time she was glad others would make decisions for her.

She knew Paul would prevail. After all, Deidre, protest all she might, wasn't tough enough for the likes of Paul Sheffield or herself. In a perverse way she envied her. At least she had a code of ethics to guide her through the minefields of a society where your dearest friend one day was just as likely to stab you in the back the next.

Deidre entered the backyard alone; stood for a moment watching her, and finally approached. Deidre eyed her, saying nothing. Shara made the first move.

"If I was to kill again, Pasqual would be my next victim. He's a vile man, Dee, and I hope the police won't ignore him. If they do, you might want to expose him before he adds to his list of victims."

She had opened the door for Deidre. There was only one question she could ask.

"How did you know I'd break into your apartment and take your bait?"

"I *knew* someone was poking into my files. Remember, I'm a computer expert. In layman's terms, I put a flag on my personnel file. If *anyone* checked it out, I'd know. I wasn't up for promotion, had kept my nose clean, and there were no ongoing internal investigations in which my file would be randomly or routinely pulled.

"You were after me. You alone knew I was alive. And, I'd pointed you to the Sheffields. When I found someone digging in my file, it was no great leap to assume it was you. Regardless, I was too close to take any risks. If you went to the police, I was fucked. But I knew deep down you wanted me for yourself. So, I planted Pasqual just in case. Did you go to Briggs or wait for me yourself?"

"I went to Briggs. Not the best of career moves, not that you care . . ."

"But I *do* care, Dee. Maybe not yesterday, at least on the surface, but I never meant to hurt you. Yesterday I said I'd made you. I was wrong. You would have done well without me, but I do think I steered you in a certain direction. It wasn't my intention. Hell, I was ten, and I was using you as a buffer from the outside world, while I sorted out for myself what to do. Bobby's threat, his presence, was very real to me. I used you, yes, but I needed you, too.

"And look at what you've written since. So many of

your stories deal with victims. You chose a path, until the death of your family, because I chose you. Knowing what I had to do to Bobby, and with you at my heels, I was too into myself to care how sending you on a wild goose chase might impact on your future. But I care, Dee. I never intended to take you down with me.''

Shara saw Deidre looking at her strangely, as if measuring her words for duplicity.

"I don't know, Shara. You are different from the woman I met yesterday. Different from the one who sparred with me over the phone the past week. The arrogance is gone. But is it real, or just another ploy? I'll be honest with you. You've got me doubting myself; second-guessing where instinct seldom led me astray. Are you manipulating me once again, or are you finally at peace with yourself? How am I to know you won't kill again, that you can control yourself?''

"There's one last secret. Not even the Sheffields know." She lifted her t-shirt, exposing her breasts. "It's complete, now, Dee. I've got Bobby. Finally got him where he can't peer at me, can't frighten me. Bobby's been the key all along. With him out of the way, I'm whole again. Least, as whole as I'll ever be.''

Shara saw Deidre try to avert her eyes, but she was drawn to the now complete tattoo.

Shara pulled her top down. "The last secret, Dee. I was never a serial killer. Killing Bobby was premeditated murder. That's why I know I'll never kill again.''

"What are you talking about?''

"I was able to cope with Bobby while he was in the army. It was he I ran away from, you know that already, faking suicide as a child. When he returned, so did his eyes. It's not rational. It's not logical, I know, but with him around the terror returned. So, I decided to kill him.

"If I killed him outright, an investigation might somehow unearth me. I needed to cover my tracks, so I became the Vigilante. I went after the predators who'd escaped the system. With a pattern established, Bobby's death would be considered only in the context of the other killings. Only *his* past would be scrutinized: the reason for his frequent transfers in the army; the girls he mind-fucked on his return. The pictures I left on his bed were all victims of the past year. If Renee is mentioned, it will only be in passing.

"I killed five loathsome creatures, who preyed on society *after* they beat the system, to cover the killing of the source of my nightmares."

"You really are sick, Shara."

"What would you have me do?" Shara's hardened eyes met Deidre's, which had suddenly gone cold. "I was sick. I was also terrified. I told you there's no logic to it. I had to get rid of Bobby, but there was no way in hell I was going to be locked up for defending myself. Jail would be no different than the cage Bobby had me in. Instead of Bobby, there'd be others who would want to get a good look at me, strip me naked with *their* eyes. Bobby had to die, *deserved* to die, not just for what he did to me, but what he did to all the others."

"So it was all about revenge," Deidre said. "Maybe you thought his eyes were still fucking with your mind, but in fact he didn't know you were alive. You killed him to avenge what he had done to you, plain and simple. Judge, jury and executioner."

Shara balled up her fists, as if the act itself would make Deidre understand.

"He took all I had. He wouldn't even let me be when I'd been placed with the Sheffields. I was a witness he would eliminate. So I ran away to escape him, and look at the life I've had. I wanted to be a cop, but with Shara's identity all I could be was a glorified secretary. Maybe it was revenge, but the bastard deserved to die.

"I had been in a cage once. I planned his death, and covered my tracks so I'd never be caged again. That's all there is to it. It's not pretty, but it's the truth. And that's something I owe you."

"Why did you have to tell me, Shara? Add this to the equation—"

"You wanted the truth!" Shara spat out. "I've told you half truths from the day we met. I manipulated you when you realized I was the Vigilante. But all along you asked for . . . *no*, you demanded the truth. Now you have it and you don't like its smell. Well, the truth's ugly. I can't win with you, can I? I've given you proof I won't kill again. But that proof is more revolting than any new web of lies I could spin."

Deidre laughed bitterly. "The final manipulation. I told Paul, told myself, if I thought you wouldn't kill again, *I* could live with you starting a new life. That was the sole determining factor. That you're a cold-blooded killer . . . ," she stopped, shaking her head in exasperation. "You're right. It doesn't make a difference. It's not for me to judge you. You gave me what I wanted, though, you're right, I wish you hadn't. You're free of me. I hope you can find happiness."

Shara could see tears forming as Deidre turned and walked away. She thought of calling her back. She didn't want it to end this way. Under the swing was a paper bag. Inside, a plastic bag that held a goldfish. She had bought it that morning. An apology of sorts. Much as she wanted to give it to Deidre now, the timing was wrong. She would ask Paul or Anna to deliver it to Deidre.

She wanted understanding. And, dammit, she wanted forgiveness. Maybe that's why she had bought the fish. She knew, though, she wouldn't get it from Deidre. Not now at least.

The truth had set her free.

The truth had cost her a friendship.

Life was sure a bitch.

Epilogue

Four Months Later
Vigilante Task Force Disbanded

Deidre looked at the headline of the *Daily News*. The Task Force, under McCauley's lead, had sifted through every shred of evidence, interviewed and re-interviewed any and all witnesses, and had come up dry.

That they plodded on was due to the fear that when they least expected it, when they'd dropped their guard, the Vigilante would strike again.

Though Deidre was no longer on the inside, she had been told sources close to the investigation speculated the Vigilante himself may have been injured or killed. Anyone who'd died or been admitted to city or area hospitals since Robert Chattaway's death was probed. Any of a dozen cadavers *could* have been the Vigilante. But no concrete evidence was located.

There was even conjecture the Vigilante may have fallen prey to his next victim, and was decaying in a ditch or a wooded area. Some felt he had moved on, having generated too much heat for himself in Philadelphia. But, he hadn't surfaced anywhere else yet. Psychiatrists interviewed on the news didn't feel he had the power to stop the killing.

In the end, inertia alone could not sustain the investigation. The Mayor and police merely sighed in relief as each day passed uneventfully. In this case, no news was good news. The last remnants of a bad memory were all that remained, so the Task Force was disbanded.

The news was greeted with a big yawn.

Briggs, Deidre was glad to see, had already bounced back. As week after week dragged on without a single break in the case, Briggs' failure was put into proper context by his superiors. Deidre had seen his name surface, recently, in several high-profile cases.

She had called him on a whim a week earlier. They'd skirted around the case most of the conversation.

"Maybe it was a blessing you got relieved," she said finally. "At least you've been able to get on with your career."

"You wouldn't be feeling guilty, would you, Dee?"

"Guilty?"

"You know something, don't you? Your *anonymous* source. Was it you, Dee?"

"Do you really want to get dragged back into the case?" she said, avoiding his question.

"Thought so. I'm no fool, Dee. If I wanted to, *really* wanted to, I could put it all together. Focus on your activities. *Your* retrospective, to be specific. Funny how the last victim was related to the child who committed suicide. If I hadn't been relieved I would have had something to explore. You lucked out, girl. They wanted to cover their asses. Good soldier that I am, I let it rest."

He paused.

"Off the record, want to satisfy my curiosity?"

"You got some imagination, Briggs. Let's let sleeping dogs lie."

He was quiet, and she was about to hang up.

"Dee. I shouldn't have underestimated you. If I'd played my cards right, well . . .''

He didn't have to finish. Like Jonas, it was as close to an apology as she would get.

Deidre, herself, had given notice to the Mayor the day she had left Shara. Confused, disillusioned, distraught, she needed time to come to grips with what she had learned. This time, though, she didn't withdraw into herself, as she had when her family was taken from her. This time she wrote a book; albeit one that would never see the light of day.

A book about a loss of innocence, about victimization, and its consequences. A book where the media merely regurgitates facts, and slithers away when the story loses its appeal. A book that delved into the consequences of victimization. When she was done she showed it to Jonas. His reaction:

"Pity you won't publish it. Raises unsettling questions about *all* the victims that pass through our lives each day, doesn't it?''

Deidre smiled. "My thoughts exactly. The day I left Shara I hated her and loathed myself. Pitied myself. She had chartered my career, and I saw it as a sandcastle. Everything I believed in swept away by one wave. God knows, I was tempted to call Briggs and turn her in. In the end . . . ,'' she shrugged. "Who was I to judge?''

"But, could I ever trust again? Should I ever again get so caught up in stories, as I had for eleven years? Or, should I become the dispassionate reporter; spewing out facts so as not to chance being manipulated?

"The truth was staring me in the face all the time. My future lay in the past. If Shara was so warped by what had happened to her, what of the others? I remembered her asking whether I'd thought she had become a housewife who beat her kids. I hadn't given it much thought. But, the truth is too many of my stories beg for closure.''

"So what have you cooked up?"

"A series of 'What happened to. . . .' I'll start with stories I've worked on, and focus on what's happened to the children. The father who attempted to kill his entire family and then himself, yet a seven-year-old managed to survive. What the hell's happened to him? The class held hostage by a former student. Shot a teacher who gave him a failing grade, terrorized the class for two days, and then shot himself in the head. The woman who randomly shot and killed five people at a mall. Two killed were parents at the mall with their children. The kids witnessed their parents' deaths. What's become of them? Remember when I was sent to Florida in the wake of the killer hurricane?''

"You came back a wreck. It really got to you."

"Kids lost homes, schools, friends—all that was familiar. They were traumatized then. Had nightmares. What about now? Have they recovered? Some, but I'll bet not all.

"There are so many others. I covered a story of a boy teased so often he shot himself to death in front of his class. I remember the guilt they felt; both those who taunted him daily, and, worse, those who allowed it to happen without saying a word. Are they normal . . . ?''

"What is normal?" Jonas cut in. "Divorce, alcoholism, sadomasochism, cheating on your husband or wife?''

"That's part of the whole story,'' Deidre said excitedly. "I want to reexamine each story. I'll let the outcome of each speak for itself. This won't be a scientific study.

"Tell you what I think, though. There are more than a few Sharas lurking out there. Kids, who as adults, have gone off the deep end. Not just the victims of incest, like you see on *Oprah!* The kids spared at a *McDonald's* where a sicko went on a rampage, killing dozens, and then blew himself to smithereens. Can that one episode create a Shara?''

''It could be dangerous.''

''So can crossing the street. Dammit, I've hidden in my safe cocoon all my life, and what do I have to show for it? A wall of awards, and a dead family.''

''You're being too hard on yourself.''

''And what if I am? I have no death wish, Jonas. I'm not going to walk the subway concourses at night waiting to be mugged, so I can identify with victims of society. I'm going into this with my eyes open. Better than that, I'm going to look at these victims through Shara's eyes. I'm going to push buttons. I'm going to manipulate, if need be. Shara will be with me wherever I go. My barometer. My eyes.''

As she spoke she looked at the fishbowl on a small end table next to the couch. A goldfish circled the bowl. Paul Sheffield had brought it to her, saying only Shara hoped it would soothe any hard feelings.

Jonas smiled. ''Do it, then.'' He paused. ''Good to see you alive again.''

''It's good to be alive again.''

Shara lay soaking in a hot bath. Paul had been true to his word. She had been hired as a deputy, in this relatively small town, and been accepted almost immediately. While she spent more time tracking down runaway dogs and cats than kids, she wasn't stuck behind a desk, watching her life waste away.

Paul and Anna had visited twice, already. Her family.

She had worked with some troubled teens, and had even considered becoming a foster parent.

She couldn't have been happier.

She looked down at her breasts, and Bobby Chattaway's eyes stared wide-eyed back at her. Only for an instant, and then they were as unseeing as they had been since she'd had the tattoo applied.

But her breasts now ached ever so slightly. Despite the warm water, she shivered. Was it over? Could she begin anew, or had she created a monster who would now devour her?

She wondered if she would sleep that night.

She wondered if the urge would return.

She wondered if she could keep the promise she had made to herself, if it did.

Since her arrival, she had slept each night with her gun under her pillow; to protect herself *from* herself.

She wondered if she could use it if Bobby returned.

She wondered . . .

Elizabeth Massie

Sineater

According to legend, the sineater is a dark and mysterious figure of the night, condemned to live alone in the woods, who devours food from the chests of the dead to absorb their sins into his own soul. To look upon the face of the sineater is to see the face of all the evil he has eaten. But in a small Virginia town, the order is broken. With the violated taboo comes a rash of horrifying events. But does the evil emanate from the sineater...or from an even darker force?

___4407-2 $5.99 US/$6.99 CAN